SAVAGE

THE KINGWOOD DUET

S.L. SCOTT

S.L. SCOTT

Cover Design: Okay Creations

Cover Image: Adobe Stock Images, Jacob Lund, Nuzza11

Editing:

Marion Archer, Making Manuscripts

Karen Lawson, The Proof Is in the Reading

Marla Esposito, Proofing Style

Kristen Johnson, Proofreader

Amy Bosica, Proofreader

ISBN: 978-1-940071-54-1

You're the sky.
I'm the Earth.
Together we make our own universe.
To My Forever and a Day

SAVAGE

Welcome to the mysterious world of the rich and the damned in this gritty, modern day fairy tale. Two star-crossed lovers will either find their destiny or meet their fate in a world where demons come in the form of familiar faces and pawns aren't just players, but deadly.

She was my destiny.

I was her downfall.

We were a match made in hell.

But when we were together, that hell was pure heaven.

The moment I laid eyes on her, I knew she would pay the price for my sins. I wasn't much older than she was, but old enough to know better. Old enough to know she would be good for me and I was bad for her. But I pursued her anyway. Back then I had hope that maybe she could change my future.

Maybe together we could change our fate . . .

PROLOGUE

The sun shouldn't be shining
Considering the pain I'm feeling, it's too bright.
Too happy.
Too blue.

The periwinkle sky reminds me of the only blue I want to see. Brilliant blue eyes, not found in the heavens, but here on earth.

The world dims momentarily. "Where's your boyfriend?" the man asks.

How did I end up here? *Like this?*

I know. I just don't want to admit the truth. *Even now.*

Closing my eyes to block him out, I search my mind for the answer. "He'll come for us," I whisper.

Us.

A sharp slap to my face sends my head to the right. I'm too stubborn to scream, to give him any further satisfaction, even as the taste of copper coats my mouth. Curling to the side, I hold my stomach, attempting to protect the only thing that matters. I haven't told Alexander. I haven't had the chance. I was going to, but an unforeseen detour brought me here.

Grief begins to envelop me, but I try to hold on, just a little longer. Reaching out, I touch the red pooled in front of me, wondering if that's someone else's blood. *It can't be mine.* There's too much to be mine. I'm alive, but now I'm wondering for how long.

"Where's King?" is shouted, but I'm too tired to answer. Even if I could, I don't know where he is.

He didn't answer his phone. I allowed him to ride away, and the memory of his face causes my breath to stutter in my throat. As I cough, and blood splatters my present, I wish I could change the past. I wish I could go back to the beginning and relive our love from the start.

I would do so many things differently. Despite how we ended, I wouldn't change *us*. I wouldn't change our love.

His life is full of lies—the kind he tells and the ones he lives. Lies that have become mine and will haunt me as I learn to live without him. Those lies still haunt me as if they are mine to survive.

He once told me he would give me the life I dreamed about—the ending I deserved—a happy ending—but with rocks cutting into my skin and a stranger kicking the life from me, I start to wonder if all hope is lost.

Until I hear that familiar sound—the distinctive sound of a Harley's exhaust foreshadowing my knight in leather armor.

It doesn't matter how long it's been since I've seen him.

It won't matter what bad has happened between us.

Our love will never die, even if I do.

"I told you he'd come for us."

Knowing he'll be here soon, I close my eyes, and dream of the fairy tale we once had . . .

1

ALEXANDER KINGWOOD IV

This is my favorite way to wake up.

Often pretending to be asleep, I spy on her as she climbs out of bed, finding peace watching her day begin. Life is better with her around.

Simpler.

Happier.

A kiss to my face. Location varies from the tip of my nose to forehead, the occasional closed eyelid before she sneaks out of bed, tiptoeing into the bathroom and then back out. I struggle to stay still this morning, needing her in ways that aren't quiet. The night clogs my throat, my voice still gruff. "Come back to bed."

Standing at the dresser, digging through the top drawer where she keeps some of her things, Sara Jane looks back at me with a smile at play on her lips, simultaneously giving me a peek at some side tit. "I thought you were asleep."

I stretch my arms up and grab hold of the top of the headboard behind me. "I'm up." Her back is smooth. The curve from her waist to her hips defined more with each year that passes. Her ass sits high and tight above her legs.

Her body caught at the other end of transitioning from a girl's into a woman's. Giving her a solid once-over, she knows what's on my mind. "Come back to bed," I repeat the request without a plea. She'll come. She always does for me.

Sara Jane is not just good to me. She's good *for* me. She's kept me from burying myself or being buried more than a few times. My pretty firefly has seen me through my highs and lows and now stands by my side as the one constant in my life, the only person I can truly count on.

Her lace panties slide down her thighs and she returns. She knows what I want. She wants it too, so I don't have to put on a big production or sweet talk her back into bed. Settling on top of me, she slides down over my cock, ready for me, slick with desire. Slow and steady feels like a good idea this morning. I hold her hips, keeping my grip light as she fucks me.

Her hands press to my chest and she leans down to kiss me. Before she has a chance to pull back, I grab her face, making sure our eyes meet, and I hold her gaze. "You know how much I love you, right?"

Softness covers her expression as she smiles. "As much as I love you, Alexander."

Alexander. Hearing her say my name keeps me grounded to her and planted in reality. She's the only one who calls me that, the only one I *allow* to call me by my full name.

When she sits up, she begins to rock, her head dropping back, her hair long, the tips running over my thighs. Her tits are amazing, full with weight to them. For someone so small, she was blessed in all the right places. My pretty little firefly has changed a lot since we first met. If possible, she has become even more stunning.

The first time I saw her, I knew she would be mine.

Nothing would keep me from her. Something wild and untamed stirred deep inside just from the sight of her.

Cruise hadn't understood. He'd been busy talking about some cheerleader he scored with the night before, but my mind had drifted, which had been standard anytime the chicks from school were brought up. I'd lost interest in the easies by tenth grade. But after what happened two weeks before, I'd struggled to find pleasure in anything. My taste buds had dulled, and life lacked color.

Except for that damn blue polka-dot umbrella and the girl standing beneath it, who stole my world from under me. She was sunshine on a rainy day, a rainbow against gray clouds, hope in a Catholic school uniform. She was why poetry was written and art created. I could deny I became a fool for love the second I saw her, but it would be a lie. She made me want to be a better man, a better person in life. She made me think twice about the direction I was heading. But we both knew better. Our course was already set, our love a sweeping storm that would brew for years before raging.

Her hair hung down, darker because it was wet, soaked as if the umbrella hadn't protected her. Her eyes were wide with innocence as she ate a candy bar like it was the best treat she'd ever tasted. Her skirt . . . damn that short skirt. I saw the man in the car next to me staring at her and I wanted to beat the shit out of him for looking at her like she could be his next tasty treat. That fucking pervert was around my dad's age. *Fucking asshole.* She couldn't be more than seventeen.

I was tempted to go over and cover her bare legs with my jacket. The girl was oblivious to the attention she attracted, and I almost felt I should become her protective knight in shining armor. I wanted to kick my own ass for that thought.

So fucking lame. Until she looked my way. My throat went dry and my lips parted. The humid air wouldn't save me. I was lost to this girl from that moment on.

She looked away, and the sweetest of pinks colored her cheeks. *Damn.* Her purity shined like a beacon. I've never been one with a need to take a V-card to feed some locker room pride. Nah, I didn't need to prove anything to anyone, least of all some jock-asses who bragged about every girl they bagged. But when she dared to look my way again, a deep-seated desire stirred. I wanted her.

It was a carnal reaction I felt in my gut, but it had nothing to do with sex. Sure, sex crossed my mind, but its images were blurred like visions of déjà vu.

With no justifiable reason, right there at a busy intersection in the suburbs north of downtown, I became determined to be everything she would ever need. I would risk it all just to talk to her. If she'd never been kissed, I'd kiss her so she never desired to kiss another man. If she was still innocent in other ways, I would earn her trust and not just make love to her, but create it, a bond so strong she'd never need anyone else. I would be her first *and* last love. That day as the rain came down, I made sweet Sara Jane Grayson my mission. With nothing left to lose, I vowed to steal her heart and own her soul.

As I watch her moving on top of me, buried deep inside her, I hope I've changed her for the better. Three years ago, when our worlds collided, she changed me.

She collapses on my chest and I hold her tight as our bodies relax after the intense release. Fingertips tap across the tattoo that honors her, the one she hates. To be fair, she doesn't want me to have any, but she calls this one an ugly bug. There's nothing ugly about the firefly. Just like her, its strength is illuminated in the darkest of times.

Lifting up, she rests her chin on my chest, and asks, "What are you doing today?"

In any other room, in any other house, with any other couple, this question would be so easy to answer. But it's not in another place and we're not just any other couple. We're complicated and my life is twisted. I try hard to spare her from getting caught up in my tornado. My self-destructive ways have become worse, but I don't mention most of that to her anymore. Instead, I respond like we are one of those other couples, where answers are easy, and life is simple. "I'm going into the office, and have a meeting with my father. I'll pick you up on campus later."

Sitting up, she maneuvers away, but I'm quick and grab her wrist. When her sweet, soulful eyes—that melt me like butter—reach me, I add, "More."

"More?"

"I love you more."

A smile slips into place and she pokes me in the chest. "You're not so tough, Mr. Kingwood." It's a game she likes to play, to pretend that some of my bad isn't as bad as her mind imagines.

I play along because despite the light she brings into my world, I only bring darkness into hers. The smile she evokes from me comes naturally though. "Nah, I'm not so tough."

Leaning back down, she kisses my cheek and then gets up to shower. I watch that ass I'm so fond of until she disappears into the bathroom. My phone vibrates on the nightstand. It's been going off for at least an hour. We both ignored it, but I can't any longer. Reaching over, I grab it and glance at the messages.

The sigh is automatic as soon as I see the text.

Cruise: *When are you coming in? Your dad is flipping out.*

Me: *I'll be in shortly.*

Cruise: *Fucker.*

Me: *You know it, Sucker.*

I toss the phone on the bed and head into the bathroom. I open the shower door and look in, eyeing her. "Perfect timing."

Sara Jane laughs and her hands go up. "Oh no, you stay back. I can't be late again or I'll be counted absent."

Taking the soap from her hands, I step in and run the bar over the silky skin of her breasts and down farther until the bar is dropped and my fingers are between her legs. "If that's the worst that can happen . . ."

"Damn you."

"You love it, baby. So much. Just like you love me."

Her eyelids dip closed when her shoulder blades hit the white tile wall. I lean over her and kiss her breath away when my mouth covers that little O her lips are forming. Hands press against my chest then slide up to grab hold of my shoulders, pulling me closer.

Soap and sex covers her as I glide my tongue up until it's discovering every curve and alcove of her mouth. I want to fuck her. *Again.* So fucking hard that she forgets she has classes altogether. She forgets the outside world. She forgets everything else, everything but me. Pressing my cock against her hip, I push as my fingers fuck her pussy. I'm trying to be good, trying to make it about her. Only about her, but she makes it damn hard when she grabs my cock with both hands and starts to get me off.

"I want to fuck you." My words are minced under the water's spray as I lean my head against the wall and take the shell of her ear between my teeth.

"God, Alexander." Her body folds against mine, her orgasm close enough to feel her tightening around me.

"Why do you do this to me?" Her question is loaded, and I'm not sure it only concerns our sexual deviancy.

"It's what you do to me. Turn around." I take her by the ribs and spin her toward the wall. Her hands go against the wall in front of her and she parts for me. Such a good girl.

My dick is big and she's small, so I bend down until I feel her wet heat with my tip. I bite her shoulder lightly then thrust hard. Her cry echoes off the walls with her hands braced higher up. I take her hips and fuck, lost in her, lost in the sensations of her sweet little pussy.

My fingers dig deeper as our bodies gyrate together, slicker by the second. I close my eyes and let the water rain down over me as movements become erratic, compromised by the slipperiness. Close. So close. I will never have enough of her, never satisfy the heavier urges my heart craves. So I stake claims for her, but more for me. "You're mine. You know that?"

"I always have been." Her words are strained and then sucked back in as she takes another deep breath.

"Mine. Fucking mine. Always. Say it."

"Always yours, Alexander."

"King," I demand, fucking her harder. She knows what I want. It's something she only gives me when I'm at my best, in my opinion, *worst* in hers.

She won't say it. I know her too well to know she won't play into that game. And I'm coming too fast. "Fuck," I shout and pull out, my cum covering her lower back and dripping lower. Backing away to the corner, my breathing is harsh as I stare at my painting with pride. I shrug. "What can I say? You feel too good." She rinses her body and steps out of the shower without a word.

She's pissed off.

I won't make apologies just yet. She felt too good to be

sorry. Lazily, I clean up and shut the water off. I step out and grab a towel from the rack. "Come on. Don't be mad."

"Easy for you to say. You came."

Her feistiness is a turn-on. If I didn't just fuck her, I'd try again. This time I'd fuck that damn sexy mouth of hers. "I'll make it up to you."

"I think you've done enough. Now I'm late for class and wound up."

I take the ends of the towel wrapped around her and tug her to me. "Don't be mad." I kiss her on the head, and then give her the smirk that will win her over, easing her irritation. "I'll make it up to you tonight. I promise."

"I have a group project to work on tonight. I'm going to stay on campus." She backs away, not looking at me while running the towel over her hair.

My brow cinches as I watch her. "Hey, are you really upset?"

"I'm not happy."

When she still doesn't look at me, I nudge her. "Don't be like that."

That gets her attention. She stands straight up, throws her hand on her hip, and narrows her eyes. "Like what, Alexander? What am I being like?"

"I know where this is going, and I'm not doing it. Don't start a fight where there is none."

"I learned from the best. It's what you do every day."

"Not with you." When she turns her back on me, I lose it. "I'm warning yo—"

Spinning on her heels, she points at me. "You're warning me? I'm not one of your lackeys, Alexander. Stop trying to make King happen. I don't call you King, and I never will. So don't you dare warn me about anything."

If she were one of my *so-called* lackeys, she'd be knocked

right the fuck out for that. Seeing her with wet, messed-up hair, a towel wrapped around her, and her finger poking my chest, I stand down, deciding to give her the respect she demands. "Fuck, you're scary, Firefly."

Her hand falls to her side, and she rolls her eyes, but the smile I wanted to see is there and brings one to my mouth. When the tension in her muscles loses its momentum, she says, "You're ridiculous. Get dressed. We're both late."

Thirty minutes later, I kiss her before we open the door. I straighten the backpack on her shoulder and wrap my other arm around her. She whispers, "Be civil with your father."

"It will be a struggle, but I'll try. For you, I'll try." Stepping back, I hold a few fingers up pledge style, not sure if it's supposed to be two or three. "Scout's honor."

"You were never a scout," she corrects and laughs, stepping into the hall. "But try. Okay?"

After slapping her ass, I wink. "I always do."

2

ALEXANDER

The elevator doors open wide and the gleaming gold Kingwood Enterprises logo greets me. I flip it off and take a left, pushing through the spotless glass doors. Kimberly, the receptionist, smiles before tapping her watch. "Good morning, Alex."

"If it's still morning, I'm ahead of schedule."

One eyebrow is raised. "Your father is in a mood."

She's pretty. A hot redhead with her hair in its typical tidy bun, and her librarian fuck-me glasses blocking her real beauty. My father's fucked her. A couple times. What she sees in him is beyond me. The egotistical asshole has slept his way through a bevy of beautiful women since my mom's death. Kimberly's the only one I wish he hadn't. She's nice and talks to me as if I matter. The rest are just after his money. She deserves someone better. He treats her like shit, and I know it's never going to be anything more than side action for him. Leaning against the counter, I ask, "You got a boyfriend these days?"

"Why? You asking me out?" she smarts back.

"Eh, I'm no good. Hasn't my father told you?"

Her smile comes gently, sympathy built into the creases at the corners. "What does he know anyway?" She hands me a message, and asks, "How's that pretty girl of yours?"

"Mad at me." I chuckle remembering how tough Sara Jane tries to act when all I see is a cute little snuggler if scary movies are on.

"You probably deserve it."

"I definitely deserve it. She deserves better." I pat the counter twice. "So do you by the way."

She shrugs and fidgets with a pen. "Things happen for a reason. I guess I'm willing to stick it out a little longer to find out what that reason is."

Nodding. She'll find out the hard way. *Sadly.* "Take care and thanks for the message." I head toward the bullpen and open the door.

"Good luck."

"Thanks," I reply, entering the chaos of cubicle city. Phones are ringing, conversations are whispered, and the sound of typing can be heard. I head to my desk before paying the inevitable visit to my father.

I pat Cruise on the back when I pass. "Any news?" I ask the same question every day, for reasons I don't talk about anymore. My friend knows, and he's proven he's here to help me. It's a mission that never seems to end, an emptiness that fills my gut waiting for answers.

"No. Sorry, King."

Breathing out a sigh of relief, I realize that besides Sara Jane, that answer is the only constant in my life. "Okay." I sit down and turn on my computer.

From the other side of the cubicle wall, Cruise says, "Your dad came looking for you about twenty minutes ago. He's in with some suits now."

"Alex?"

Speaking of . . . I look toward his office and see him leaning in the doorway. Waving me over. "Come."

Treated like a dog in front of everyone, I only go because I can't make a scene without risking everything. I enter his office and two men in suits stand and straighten their jackets. I take it as a sign of respect for me. My father takes it as a sign for him and clears his throat for the introduction.

Whatever. I'm not here to quibble. I'm actually in a fairly decent mood despite having been summoned to the office today. I put on my best Kingwood smile, the one my father's one-night stands compliment me on, the one my mom told me I inherited from him. Under my father's disapproving once-over, he says, "This is my son, Alex Kingwood. Alex, these gentlemen are here to help with the restructuring."

Walking toward them, I raise my eyebrows and begin to say, "What res—" Over their shoulders my father warns me with a shake of his head, and I fall in line. *For now.* "My father has mentioned he was bringing in the experts."

While shaking their hands, they smile too enthusiastically to be trusted. "We like to think so. We've helped many businesses make their transitions smoother. We have complete confidence we'll be able to do the same for Kingwood Enterprises."

They talk too fast and I still don't know their names. They're nervous about meeting me. A bead of sweat forms at the top of the left guy's hairline and the other one has shifty eyes. There's nothing to trust about them, especially in the cheap suits they're wearing. "And you are?" I ask.

"Nastas O'Hare," the guy with the sweat responds, then adjusts his green wool suit.

Tightening my handshake, I ensure my grip is more solid than his, which isn't hard. Weak handshakes are for meek men.

Shifty eyes speaks. "I'm Connor Johnson. Your father has told us you have a bright future in the business."

I trust him less, if that is possible, for having two last names and no real first. "Future?" I ask, shaking his hand. At least his handshake is more solid.

"Your college credentials are quite impressive. Tough university to get into in the first place, and building your résumé at Kingwood Enterprises adds credibility not easily attained these days."

"Thanks," I reply with ease, not impressed with these jerkoffs. I'm shocked they even scored a meeting with Kingwood Enterprises, much less that my father is entertaining this idea.

My father sits and tells them to take their seats. With no chair for me, I walk around the back of the desk and lean against the bureau. After crossing my arms over my chest, my father looks back, but says nothing. He likes to intimidate as much as I do. As a team, we're menacing as fuck. It's times like these that I forget my father is actually my number-one enemy.

At the end of the day, the end of our lives, for good, for bad, for evil, for reward, we're Kingwoods, and that means allies. Sharing a last name secured that and my future, even if we're the worst of allies.

As my father goes over some plan that's been in the works for months, but is just now bothering to tell me about, I stare at him. There's a reason Alexander Kingwood III gets pussy on command. He's younger than most fathers with twenty-two-year-old sons. My mother called me a joyful surprise.

At forty-seven, Alexander Kingwood III has minimal gray hair, reserving it for his sideburns that are trimmed to perfection, and he's as physically fit as someone my age. He knows how to talk women right out of their clothes and into his bed. They're gone by morning because there's something that keeps him from letting them stick around. Despite their pleas to stay, he sends them on their freshly fucked way. He claims he's trying to be a good example for me by keeping women who don't matter at bay. I say it's the ghost of my mother haunting him, reminding me of years ago, the summer after Sara Jane graduated from high school

. . .

"There are so many stars out tonight."

My sweet girl leans over and rests her head in the nook of my arm, which I wrap around her. When Sara Jane shivers, I pull the blanket over us and hold her closer. She likes to be held after we make love and I'd do anything for her. So I'll lie here as long as she wants.

"What do you dream about, Alexander?" she asks, her hand running over my chest.

"I don't dream."

"You must sometime." She lifts her head up enough to look at me when I don't answer. "Never?"

I like seeing her face. A lot. She's fallen in love. I can see it in the inner blue coloring of her eyes and in the concern she has for me over little things like dreaming. She doesn't realize how far I've fallen for her though. "I used to when I was younger, when my mom was alive."

Resting her chin on my chest, she looks sad and I hate that I've caused her to feel that way. "You never talk about her."

"There's not much to say."

"I'm sure there's a lot to say, like what did she look like? Were you close? Was she strict or easy going?" With each question my heart starts beating faster, my mind racing, and my anger fueled. "Did she cook dinner? Like movies? Hands-on or off parenting? Part of the PTA?"

"Enough, Sara Jane," I demand. "I don't want to talk about my mother."

That silences her, and she leans her head back down. Fuck, now I feel bad. I've never allowed her into my head, or my world where my mother lived . . . still might live.

I can tell she is closing off to me when Sara Jane closes her eyes. I don't want that, so I give her what I can, starting slow. "My mother was an angel on earth. Now she's one in heaven."

She looks back up at me, her warmth shining again. "I'm sorry."

"So am I." We sit all the way up, and I wrap my arms around my legs. The cool night feels good while hot emotions course through my body. "I never believed in heaven growing up. Madeline Kingwood tried her best to keep me good inside. It was an uphill battle in the Kingwood home, and she knew it. She protected me from my father the best she could. She protected me from the evil she knew was leaching into our home. Dirty dealings brought unsavory sorts around, but there was no one to protect her."

"I want to ask you about it, but I'm afraid."

Looking at her, her frame so delicate even at eighteen. "What are you afraid of?"

"You."

"Why are you afraid of me?"

"Because you don't let me in." Her honesty comes easily because unlike me, she remains good.

"I'm letting you in now."

She nods, knowing my emotional confessional is not going to last long. "What do you remember?"

"I was a kid. I didn't see behind the curtain. The truth. The inner workings that extended beyond Kingwood Enterprises and lurked behind closed doors of Kingwood Manor."

A stabbing pain shudders across my chest. I hate it. I

remember it too well. I always feel it when the memories haunt me.

"When she was murdered, I started to believe in heaven because I needed to know she was someplace better than this hell on earth. Souls like hers deserve the fable of the golden gates and the peace that comes with it."

"What about yours?"

I laugh. "I'm the devil himself and hell has a special place reserved for my soul."

"Don't say that, Alexander."

"If you haven't figured that out yet, Sara Jane, it's already too late for yours."

. . . Nastas O'Hare is halfway through his report when he asks, "What do you think, Alex?"

When my eyes land on him, I swear a smarmy grin peaks the right corner of his thin lips.

Fucker.

I look down at the notes in front of me, quickly skimming over them. My gaze darts to my dad. "You're selling the company?"

"Not yet," he replies coldly. "We'll be restructuring as we already said. During the transition, I'll be talking to potential buyers."

This company has been his baby, even when I was one. He always chose business over family. Over me, and over my mother. Money. He loves money. "Why are you selling?"

"We'll talk about this later. How do you feel about this strategy?"

I look down at the paper again. "It's rough and not well-thought-out. We can't just throw ideas on a piece of paper and expect that to be the plan. I want to see the whys and hows. Why is this the best plan for Kingwood Enterprises? Why do you think breaking it up into smaller divisions will help to eventually sell it? How do you plan to make it more attractive to buyers? How do we go about implementing your ideas so it's not disruptive to day-to-day business?"

With pride and a wry grin on his face, my father sits back and crosses his arms. "I warned you about my son."

3

ALEXANDER

The song and dance in my father's office is over and I'm left fuming at my desk. How can he sell? How can he betray my mother like this? How can he betray me? Our relationship is a rocky shoreline at best, but every once in a while it would be nice to have some smooth sailing.

Why does it always have to be about what's best for him? I'm his only fucking son. What about the Kingwood legacy? What about my future? What about his? What does he have up his sleeve?

I watch those assholes leave his office, their conversation light as a feather in the breeze. It's almost like they don't realize how this changes my entire future, as if it doesn't alter my life. I'm walking before they reach the elevators. My dad has shut his door, but I walk in anyway.

He looks up, his expression souring. "I'll call you back, Reg." He sets the phone down and I shut the door. "What do you want?"

"Restructuring?"

"Business is business. Go back to your desk and get to work."

His gaze lowers, and he starts sifting through papers covering his desk. I stare. When he realizes I'm not leaving, he looks back up. "What, Alex? Say it so we can both get back to work."

"Mom would not approve of what you're doing?"

"Your mother isn't here to have a say."

That's like a slap to the face, and I shudder. His blows have always been low, but this is even beneath him . . . or so I thought. He's right. She's not here. My grip is firm on the arm of the chair, but my legs are unsteady. My mother isn't here to reason with him, to fight for me, or to discuss the future of the company. "She should be." I turn my back to him and walk to the door.

"Alex?" When I don't stop, he repeats, "Alex? Stop."

With my hand on the knob, I reply, "What?"

"I miss her too."

My glare moves from the wood grain of the door and settles on him. "Do you?"

"Don't be ridiculous. Of course, I do."

"And what about me?"

"What about you?"

"How do you feel about me?"

A *pfft* accompanies an eye-roll, and he returns to tending the papers in front of him. "I don't have time for your childish games, Alex. You have work to do and courses to study for."

"I used to love you. When Mom was alive."

His busy hands stop, but he doesn't look up. "Close the door behind you."

I don't. I leave it wide open and walk through the bullpen. I nod to Cruise to join me. He falls in line as we head for the elevators. When my eyes meet Kimberly's, I say, "You were right."

She replies, "I'm sorry."

Cruise punches the button for the elevator ahead of me, but I stop at the front desk. "No need to be sorry. You warned me."

I've seen that sympathetic smile too many times to count. "Take care of yourself, Alex."

"I always do."

Cruise and I ride down to the basement in silence. He knows the boiled tension that exists between my father and me. Sometimes I talk about it. Most times I don't. I hate where my head goes when I let myself dwell on it too long. It wasn't always like this though it's all I remember now.

We get in the car and head out of the garage. "Hungry?" I ask.

"Starved. Pizza?"

"Yep."

I turn on the music, and turn it up, hoping to wash away my anger so I can enjoy my pizza with a clear head. *The asshole told me to get back to work. Fuck that.* Cruise will cover his own ass later. A clear conscience isn't possible, so I try to temper my thoughts instead.

Only one piece of pizza is left when Cruise slurps the last of his soda, then says, "You have class in fifteen."

"Drop me off, okay?"

I push back from the table, stuffed, and drop some money to cover the tab and some extra for the service. Speaking of service, the waitress is cute. Cruise was all over her, though she seemed to want to be all over me. He gets plenty of pussy, so I never feel sorry for the dude. He also scored her number, not one bit upset to come in second best. Maybe he's used to it with me. Not in looks. I'm not judging one way or the other on how the world sees him, but he's my second-in-command, my right-hand man, and my best friend. I guess I'm his wingman in life too.

The door swings open and we step out onto the sidewalk. The sun is bright and I pull my shades from the front of my shirt and slip them over my eyes. The trunk of the car is popped at the curb and I grab my backpack and set it down. I pull the tie from my shirt and roll up my sleeves. I hate going to school in dress pants but my dad insists on a suit while at work. He also insists I stay and work, but fuck him and this whole mess. How can I be expected to treat today like it's just another normal day when my inheritance is suddenly being broken into pieces.

Once I'm dropped off on campus, I'm tempted to sneak over to the psych building. If I could have gotten here earlier, I would have, just to steal a glance at Sara Jane. I like spying on her. There's an innocence to her eyes when she's in class staring off into space or taking notes. I can still see her in that Catholic school girl uniform—wet hair, bare legs, eyes that always saw the good in me. She pretends she still does, but I see the darkness clouding her eyes, the despair she's better at hiding. It's not all bad. I see the hope in the blue skies of her eyes as well. If I could spread it with a brush, I'd paint over the darker corners, and let the sunshine back in.

I drop into my seat, my backpack landing loudly on the desk. The professor always likes when I'm dressed up. He takes it as a sign of respect. Fuck him.

Resting my chin in the palm of my hand, I turn to look out the window. She'll be leaving the building too far for me to see and heading to . . . Where does she go after her psychology class? I should ask her one day. Or meet up with her and walk her to her next class. It's been a long time since I did that. It's been a long time since we just existed. Our lives have been running full speed in two different directions, and I'm not sure how to slow it down. She has the whole world ahead of her—opportunity, job options, potential. I have Kingwood Enterprises and a heart that's almost black. Correction, I may not have Kingwood Enterprises anymore. What will I do?

"Mr. Kingwood. You with us today or taking a mental leave by staring out the window?"

Among bored laughter, my gaze lands on the professor up front. "Carry on."

"Thanks for the permission, Mr. Kingwood," he replies sarcastically. "As I was saying . . ."

Fifty minutes later, I grab my backpack and get out the door before he can call on me. I'm long gone, cutting off other students, and down the hall before I hear the faint call of my name. I ignore it and push through the double doors that lead to the quad.

"Hey, Alex?"

I turn to the sound of a girl's voice. Blonde. Big tits. California tan from her spring break to the Golden State that she bragged about last week, spoken loud enough for me to hear. Or she wanted me to hear. "Hey," I reply because I can't remember her name. I'm not sure I ever knew it. *Or cared to.*

"You done for the day?"

"No."

"Oh, bummer. A few of us," she says, then glances behind her to a group of girls all watching like this is their entertainment for the day, "are going to get margaritas and wanted to know if you'd join us."

"I have class." And a girlfriend.

"Skip it."

"I don't drink margaritas."

"I'll buy you a beer, or even better, your own pitcher."

"Alexander."

Shit.

The voice I love. The tone not so much. Turning, I see the prettiest girl I've ever laid eyes on. "Hey, babe."

"Really?"

"Don't be jealous. It was nothing."

"How would you feel if the roles were reversed?"

"I'd kick his ass without a second thought," I reply, smiling and taking her by the waist. Pulling her close, I kiss her neck since she turns away from me. "Don't be jealous over nothing."

She sighs and the tension in her rigid body softens under my touch. When her arms wrap around my neck, she looks up at me, and I know I have my girl back. "Why do you have to be so damn handsome?"

"Just born this way."

Sara Jane rolls her eyes and steps back. "I see you went to class. Your professor must have been thrilled by your presence."

"I got my paper back. My A still stands so he doesn't say shit to me about my lack of attendance."

We start walking and like so often lately, silence intervenes. I try to muffle it with stupid conversation just to hear her talk, to bring the happiness back into her life. "You have more classes, right?"

"Yeah. And the group project."

"I'll still pick you up."

"Thanks."

Silence.

Fuck. I hate silence when it comes to her. Normally, I crave it. Not with her.

"I should get going," she says, stopping and looking up

at me.

Taking her hand in mine, I kiss it. "Everything okay?"

She looks away and then shrugs. "I don't know."

"Hey, look at me." When she does there's a slump to her shoulders and not a smile in sight. I lift her chin and step closer, smothering the silence between us. "What's going on?"

"I just have a lot to deal with. School stuff. This project and a paper." She looks away again.

"Look at me, Sara Jane." She does. *Such a good girl.* "Tell me what you're thinking about."

"What do you see in me, Alexander?"

Whoa. I didn't see that coming. It's the easiest thing I've had to answer all day. "Everything. Anything good in my life is because you're a part of it. If it weren't for you, I wouldn't be standing here."

"Don't say that."

"It's true. You know the truth deep down even if you don't like to talk about it."

Her patience is worn today and she looks across the aggregate quad toward the English building. "I need to go or I'll be late." Her hand, so small in mine, slips away.

I won't lose her. She's my sanity in the storm I've created. "I'll pick you up, okay?"

"Outside the library."

"I'll remember." I give a wave before feeling stupid and shoving my hands in my pockets.

I start walking in the other direction but look back. *She never does.* How can she ask me what I see in her? Surely she can't look at girls like California spring break and think she is less? *She's less than no one.* With all this shit at work happening, am I missing something? I refuse to lose my Firefly. I refuse to lose.

4

SARA JANE GRAYSON

Alexander Kingwood IV.

He is so easy to spot. When every other guy on campus is dressed in slouchy jeans that hang too low or tattered cargo shorts, university T-shirts, and Abercrombie & Fitch, Alexander strides onto campus in fit-to-a-T jeans that highlight his great ass, and a shirt too expensive to be called a simple T-shirt, pullover, or button-down. It's like he walked off a runway. I stopped shopping with him years ago because he spends money without a care in the world. I don't have such freedom. He's more than generous, and would pay for everything, but I like to feel I own something from earning it or working for it.

I'm no martyr. I have no problem accepting gifts. I just don't believe in spending hundreds of dollars on a cotton shirt that looks the same as a five-dollar tee right out of the pack.

When I see him through the library windows, I'm quickly reminded of the difference. The white shirt accentuates his biceps, fits his shoulders—that might be broader now than when I left this morning—and the hem hits at just the right length, exposing a brown leather belt. If he reaches up, I bet I'd get a glimpse of his amazing abs too. I might have to test this out. He takes my breath away like the first time I saw him. It's funny that, at that moment in time one week before my eighteenth birthday, I had no clue how much my life would change forever. Deep down, it's like he did. Alexander was sent to steal my heart and corrupt my mind. But I love him. I love him so much that it aches to be without him.

What's not to love? The man looks at me like I'm an angel on earth and *his* savior. I wish I could save him. Whatever he's gotten into, he's dug himself in pretty deep. Maybe too deep for me to save him any longer. *To reach him.* It used to be exhilarating—an exciting adventure—when I was with him. The thrill is still there, but I worry about the future now—mine with his specifically.

He once called me naïve.

I didn't believe him. *Now I do.* Now I *know* I was.

Never would I have predicted I'd be with him years later. My love for him has kept me by his side. His looks—*lady-killer looks*—but that's not enough. I wouldn't be here three years later because he has a face I love to look at. I stay because our souls have melded together over time. I ache from his absence when he's away too long. The hours are weights that drag me down. The heavy chains are broken the moment I see him. Time flies when we're together. He's an addiction I can't break, and one I don't want to. But for my innocence he stole, he's given me life and love that far exceeds the loss. *My heart soars with him.*

There have been times over the years I've questioned whether I should stay. There was no question to my love because the answer was unyielding. It almost didn't matter what Alexander Kingwood IV did *or* hid from me, because my soul was sold to him the day we met. It was in that moment that I knew I was meant to love him and harbor his sins in my safe haven.

It was a job I took seriously. So yes, maybe I was naïve when we met, but now I know what I've gotten myself into and I refuse to get myself out because my life wouldn't exist without him being a part of it.

Hidden behind exorbitantly expensive designer clothes, his secrets have multiplied, layering the burdens he carries in his eyes and the tension in his shoulders. I believe there are lies that will destroy him, and most likely me.

Yet, here I am.

Loyal to his misguided labors, protecting myself is a skill I've honed. Alexander would never hurt me, but I feel pain is the only byproduct of a future with him.

Yet, here I am.

Feeling like the little girl once again, I've fallen for blue-sky eyes and a smile so bright I swear the stars' shine was stolen in the night. To the outside world, he's King. To me, he's Alexander. *Everything.*

I had plans. Big plans, like finishing my junior year, then my senior year as unscathed as possible. Freedom would be found in attending a university far from here. I'd start fresh. I'd become who I wanted, who I was meant to be before my heart took over my head. I knew what was next, but I never saw *him* coming, and then it was too late . . .

The rain is so thick I can't see beyond it. I grab my umbrella from my locker, swing my backpack onto my shoulder, and head out to go home.

I pop the button that sends my umbrella up but one step outside the building and my socks and shoes are instantly soaked. It's not a long walk home, but in the rain it feels like miles more. Needing a quick reprieve, I stop inside the grocery store, grab a

Payday candy bar, then head to checkout. I've seen the cashier a million times. Gray hair tangled into a low bun in the back. She smiles, and says, "Awful day to be outside."

"I like the rain." Have I ever been convinced by my own words?

She's definitely not. Her glasses slide down her nose as she studies me. My white cotton shirt is sticking to me, my plaid skirt drenched and dripping on the store floor. "You need to borrow a raincoat?"

I shrug. "Doesn't matter now."

"Seventy-five cents. Head straight home. I'm sure your parents won't want you sick."

My parents. I sigh louder than I intend. At seventeen, I still dream of a car one day, but my dad reminds me that being born is the only privilege I've deserved. I roll my eyes and set my dollar down. "Thanks."

Waiting at the corner of a busy intersection to cross the street, I take a bite. The rain lets up and the pedestrian crossing sign beeps, but I don't move. Not one step. Not to chew. Not even to breathe.

My heart balloons in my chest and despite the rain and humidity, my throat goes dry. Across the intersection rumbles a Harley-Davidson. I recognize the style of bike from watching TV, but it's not the bike that holds my attention. It's the man who rides it. His hair is darkened from the rain, but light enough for me to guess it's probably medium brown when dry. A section has fallen over his forehead, resting on the tips of his eyelashes, probably to his dismay. Light, but angry eyes are directed at me, a hard stare that makes my heart race, fear coursing through my veins. The intensity invades my body in ways I've never felt before, confusing my thoughts and causing me to look away. I'm not scared of him, but I am frightened by the emotion welling inside me.

The signal to cross the street stops beeping, and I'm stuck on the corner under a thieving glare. Parts of my soul I didn't know existed are exposed, and I drag my hand down the front pleats of my skirt. My breath comes short when our eyes meet again, and the candy falls from my hand. I summon every ounce of bravery and give as good as I'm getting, glaring right back. But I can't hold it. He's not a boy. He's the guy my parents warned me about.

Turning away quickly, embarrassment comes as fast. I must look like a drowned rat and even worse, I'm stuck in my school uniform under the microscope of the most handsome man I've ever seen. Even though I'm not looking at him, I just know that nothing breaks his stare. I feel his gaze penetrating my body, touching me deep down in ways I barely know how to reach. My face heats as my body blooms, the petals of my innocence unfolding for him. "Hold on. Don't lose yourself." Licking my lips, I know I could. For him I would.

A loud horn sounds, startling me. The toes of my shoes are off the edge, much like the thoughts of him possessing me in ways that would send me to confessional.

Thank God for small miracles. The light turns green, and his bike is revved before he takes off, leaving a trail of rain water behind him.

How is it possible that every last warning of what to heed embodies that man? I've never so desperately wanted to break every rule in the book until now. I could swear his middle name is Danger, and I'm intrigued enough to need to know his first.

I don't look back over my shoulder. I don't follow the sound of his bike as it drives into the distance. I don't allow myself to fall any further than I have already. I cross the street, not noticing the clouds have cleared or that the sun is peeking out. I walk like the last few minutes haven't changed my whole life, the makeup of my thoughts, and twisted my chemistry to match a man's I'll never meet.

At the next street, I turn the corner and stop. The motorcycle is there, but I barely notice it behind the man standing in front. His smile makes my knees weak and his eyes make my heart speed up again.

Fear.

Fear of what I already know I'm willing to do for him.

Fear of what lies ahead when I find out that first name.

Fear of the trouble that's wrapped as tightly as the leather across his shoulders.

Fear of everything he possesses.

Fear of never getting this chance again.

Without fear, I walk right into his life, hands shaking and starting to sweat. When I get closer, the other guy rolls his eyes and jumps, starting his bike. As he drives away, I'm left alone. The air is sucked from around us and filled with his presence. He's cocky and powerful, owning every muscle in his body as he stands tall before me. "Hey." Husky, deep, and confident.

"Hey." I stop, keeping five or so feet between us.

"I saw you back there."

I nod, but don't add to the conversation.

"What's your name?"

"Sara Jane," I confess before I have a chance to think otherwise.

His smirk turns into a genuine smile as he holds eye contact. That was the first time I saw the smile that would make me reject all others. "Hi, Sara Jane. Pretty name for a pretty girl." He steps closer and I step back, making him chuckle. His feet stay planted when he says, "I'm Alexander."

Alexander. The name becomes a melody as it plays over in my mind. I didn't expect that name, but I love it all the same. Alexander. Alexander. Alexander.

He reaches out for me, his hand an open palm in front of me.

Knowing I should go, that I should have never stopped in the first place, I shift.

"I can see the fight in your eyes. The decision to stay or leave wages a war. I won't hurt you, Sara Jane." When I don't take his hand, something in his eyes—a kindness, sincerity—fills the grayish blue coloring, making me believe he'll keep that promise.

With the compliment given, I reach out and our hands touch. A silent deal is struck, my heart now his, our fates sealed. Is it his smile or confidence, the attention, or touch? In the moment it's everything.

I wonder if I'll regret this handshake later. If I'll regret stopping and talking to him, giving him my real name. I could have lied, but I didn't.

The noise of his friend's bike rounding the corner is heard in the distance before I see him. He pulls up and parks next to Alexander. Losing patience, he whines, "C'mon, man. Let's go."

Alexander remains, our eyes locked in a silent standoff as our hands remained joined together. I may be young, inexperienced, but I know I don't stand a chance against his wicked ways. I'm smart, but he's clever. "How old are you, Sara Jane?"

I like the way my name rolls off his tongue, and savor it before answering, "Eighteen next week."

A smile crosses his lips, one that causes me to bite my lower one. "Seventeen, huh?"

"She's jailbait, King," his friend calls from atop his bike, looking bored. "Let's move on."

With his gaze still firmly attached to me, he calls over his shoulder, "I can wait a week. She sure is pretty." As if he's speaking to himself, I hear him add, "And so very tempting."

I've never been called tempting before and the word itself evokes illicit thoughts. His leather jacket is worn, scuffed at the cuffs, the T-shirt underneath is some brand I've never heard of, and his jeans are faded, nicely worn in. He needs to shave and his hair is close to violating school code, but I have a feeling it's not the first time he's broken a rule. He's a bad boy in the flesh, a devil in disguise of a fractured soul that's almost too handsome to look at.

"Guess I should go," he says, nodding toward his dark-haired friend. "You want a ride home?"

I may only be seventeen but cable TV has taught me a few things about accepting rides from strangers, even good-looking ones. "I'm fine walking."

"You sure are." He glances up to the sky. "Dark clouds are rolling back in."

"They won't do me any harm, but I'm not so sure about you."

The right side of his mouth rises, almost meeting the dimple in his cheek. "Smart girl. So you turn eighteen next week?"

"Yeah. Saturday."

Swinging his leg over the bike, he settles on the leather and grips the handles. "What about a boyfriend?"

"I've got no priors," *I reply, making a really bad joke, so dumb that my face feels hot from embarrassment.*

He laughs, but I'm sure it's out of politeness, although he doesn't seem the type to humor anyone. "Let's hope not." *Shifting, he looks ready to go.* "What's a girl like you talking about priors anyway?"

With mustered courage, I reply like I've found some confidence lying on the ground. "I'm not so little, and you're not so bad."

"What do you know about being bad?"

"I've seen some."

His smile disappears, replaced by the stormy clouds he spoke of earlier. Anger. Curiosity. Respect. A fury of emotion brews inside his captivating eyes. "I said I wouldn't hurt you."

My hands tighten around the strap of my backpack. "I'm not sure I believe you."

"I don't need you to believe me. I don't need anything at all."
Kicking his stand up, he jumps, his bike roaring to life. I miss the
silence. I miss the clarity of his dulcet tone, but I hear him over
the loud rumble, "You should get home, little girl."

My eyes trail across his lips and then over his shoulder. I pass
him without further conversation, but I don't get far.

"Sara Jane?"

I do what I know I shouldn't. I stop walking and turn back.
"Yes, Alexander?"

A grin appears in response to hearing his name, or maybe
something else I'm too inexperienced to know by the deviousness
that's revealed. "Don't talk to strangers."

I laugh and it feels good, like too much pent-up energy finally
being released, the balloon of my heart being popped. "Then I
wouldn't have met you." When I turn away this time, I'm left
with the image of his smile and that dark hunger in his eyes. I
don't look back, loving this memory too much to ruin it.

My steps are slow enough to hear his friend ask him, "Why
are you messing around with some girl?"

The question doesn't bother me because Alexander's answer
comes quick.

. . . I can still hear him as if he said the words to me
himself, as if that afternoon was just today.

"She's not some girl. She's my girl."

5

SARA JANE

The library is bustling with people tonight. Our midterm projects are due in two weeks, so everyone's scrambling to finish them before final exams. I think I've reread the same page in this reference book five times and still not absorbed a word. Alexander seems to own my thoughts even when he's not around.

As if summoned from the depths of my mind, I hear, "King is here." His preferred name these days drifts across the large table, bringing me back to the present. I look up at Shelly when I hear his name. She signals to the side before returning her eyes to the book in front of her. When I see him, I smile. It's an automatic response to the man I've loved for the last three years, maybe my whole life. I excuse myself from the table. The weight of my project partners' stares traverse along with me as I head to meet him.

It's not unusual to see other college girls wanting him. Propositioning him. Even when I doubt why he wants me, he greets me with a grin that can get me to do anything. "Hey, Firefly." His deep voice hums with sexual implications for later.

A profound satisfaction is awakened, filling my veins. Our attraction to each other never falters. "Hi—"

My greeting is inhaled by a kiss. With his arms still around my waist, holding me tight, he leans back and asks, "Still mad?" *Yes. No.*

Two answers. Each with a different outcome.

If I say yes, we'll drag this morning's incident into a bigger deal than it is. If I say no, he wins. Although it's not about winning or losing, but understanding what I'm feeling, I don't like to fight with him, so I stay neutral. "Sort of."

He always did like a challenge. "Come with me." Taking my hand, he leads me to the human anatomy aisle and down to where it dead-ends. The aisle is empty, and I'm starting to get the feeling that I hope it remains that way. My back is pressed against the wall and he leans in, his hand above my head. Looking down on me, the creases around his eyes soften. A hand goes to my cheek, his palm warm. "Do you trust me?"

"You know I do."

"I want to hear you say it, Sara Jane."

The lightness of his mood moments earlier is gone. Time spent with his father tends to do that to him. I tend to do that to him, a deep-seated fear of losing me makes him edgy. It does the same to me, but I'm better at hiding it. "What's wrong?"

His body is tense, his answer defensive, "Nothing's wrong."

"Then why are you asking me if I trust you?"

"I just want to hear you say it. Indulge me."

I give him what he wants like I always do. "I trust you, Alexander."

His smile reappears and he kisses me in reward. "I trust you, too."

"I hope so," I tease.

He doesn't laugh. "I trust you with my life."

I shift under the weight of his gaze. "What's going on?"

"Nothing. I just want you to know that I've shared more of me with you than anyone else."

This time, I reach up, and touch his cheek. "I know, and that means a lot to me."

A whisper works its way through the books. "Sara Jane, the group is getting antsy waiting on you." *Shelly.*

"I'll be right there." My eyes never leave Alexander's— partly due to how mesmerizing his always are. His need for me right now is the other reason. He's right. I know him better than myself these days. "What happened today?"

"Nothing. They're waiting on you."

"Since when did you care if we keep anyone waiting?"

"I don't, but I know you do. Go. We'll talk later."

"You sure?"

"I'm sure." The charming smile that wins everyone over comes out to play. "You'll always be my girl."

Lifting up on my toes, I kiss him, but before I drop back down, I say, "I'll always be your girl." I slip out from under his arm and head backward, down the aisle. When he turns to watch me, I raise an eyebrow, and point at him. "And *you'll* always be *my* guy." I blow him a kiss, turn, and hurry around the bookcases back to the group.

When I sit down, I apologize and we start discussing our assignment. Every few moments, I glance toward where I left Alexander, waiting for him to walk by. I miss the possible wave or smile, though. It's unsettling how easily he disappears, at times.

Maya leans over, and whispers, "That guy is really cute."

My eyes meet Shelly's, but she looks down quickly. I

smile, but my shoulders move back defensively. I know how girls work. "Yeah, he is."

My clipped tone doesn't deter her, and since our other project partners—Cal and Ryan—aren't paying attention, she continues. "How long have you been dating?"

While looking back at me, Shelly rests her chin on her palm, leans forward on her elbow, and cuts in, "King was her first boyfriend. Her first kiss. Her first everything." Her tone is dreamy, wistful. She's always been supportive of my relationship with Alexander, even when she probably shouldn't have been . . .

"Hole. E. Crap. Who. Is. That?" Shelly surprises me when she sounds out the words so dramatically.

"What?"

"That."

Looking across the school parking lot, Alexander leans against his bike. Waiting. I dreamed about him last night, and every night since I met him last week. "I know him," I reply, and I have questions. I start in his direction, but my best friend Shelly tugs me back by the shirtsleeve. "What do you mean, you know him?" Her wide eyes dart between Alexander and me. "How do you know him?"

"If you promise not to say anything, I'll tell you later."

"I need to know now, SJ."

"Later. Okay?"

"Fine." She zips her lips and tosses the imaginary key over her shoulder. Alexander's friend is with him again, looking as annoyed as ever. Maybe Shelly will interest him long enough to give Alexander and me enough time to talk. I stop, keeping some distance between us. Our eyes steady on each other. My heartbeats sound in my ears as I center my thoughts on being strong in front of him, even if it's just a front.

"Hi, again." His gaze slides over to Shelly. "Who's this, Sara Jane?"

"This is my friend Shelly." The girl is so boy crazy she's almost drooling. Me, on the other hand, I gather enough bravery to keep my voice steady. His being is bigger than the whole of us. Turning to Shelly, I say, "And this is Alexander."

"Hi." She giggles while speaking.

Alexander's eyes are locked on mine, never deviating. "Can I speak to you in private?"

My breath wobbles like my knees when I'm around him. With Shelly here, I try my best to play it cool. "Sure." I walk toward the bushes that line the parking lot, putting space between our curious friends and us. Alexander follows behind. When I turn back, he's close. Lifting up just a bit on my tiptoes to get a good look at his face at this proximity, I let my eyes travel his expression and linger on his features. His skin is smooth, clean-shaven, and tempting me to touch him. His eyes are clearer than the other day. Taking him in this close, his shoulders are broader than I realized, his biceps straining the leather to fit. He licks his lips, pulling my attention to his mouth, and he asks, "What are you doing, Sara Jane?"

"Looking at you. I want something to remember you by."

A crooked smile lifts higher on one side, but is quickly joined by the other. "It's only been four days. Am I a thing of the past? You've already moved on?"

My heart may be thundering in my chest, but I find comfort just being here with him. "I don't know when I'll see you next and the memories from the other day are starting to fade."

His grin falls as he looks me over. One step closer and I can smell the cinnamon gum he's chewing. "I've been thinking about you."

"What have you been thinking?" The butterflies in my stomach have turned into raging hormones.

Reaching out, he dares to touch the ends of my hair, the strands manipulated between his fingers. "You're brave for only being what, five three?"

"Five four. Anyway, what does bravery have to do with my height?" *I brush my hair behind my shoulder and watch his hand fall back to his side.*

He chuckles. "I think you've proven it makes absolutely no difference when it comes to courage."

"Speaking of courage, why are you here?"

"Does it upset you?"

"No, just curious."

"Like I said, I've been thinking about you."

"How'd you know where to find—?" *I don't finish. I just shake my head.* "My uniform."

"What are you doing for your birthday?" *He's direct.*

"I'm not sure." *Glancing to Shelly, I say,* "I think she's concocting a big plan."

Looking at her, his brow furrows. When his gaze returns, he replies, "I want to see you again."

"Maybe next time we can attempt to get to know each other."

"Yeah, maybe." *The tips of his fingers brush under my jaw.* "You're very pretty." *The words don't come out light like the rest of our conversation. His eyes have darkened, his pupils widening as he stares at me.*

"How old are you?"

The warmth of his hand falls away. His laughter filters around me and then swallows me whole. "Are you really worried about my age?"

"I am. You could be seventeen or you could be twenty-five."

"And if I were twenty-five?"

"I'd be sad."

"Why?"

"Because I couldn't see you anymore."

"I'm nineteen."

My smile is quick. If I don't leave now, I might stick around long enough for him to touch me again. I already miss the goosebumps that cover my skin. The bell rings and I look back at the school that will save my heart the trouble. "Lunch is over. I need to go."

When I turn to leave, he catches my wrist, his hand encircling it. "I'll see you Saturday."

In that final four-word exchange, I'm not sure if I should be happy or scared, my feelings straddling the emotions. I'm tempted to ask how, but don't. I already know if he wants to find me, he will.

. . . "He's also my last," I add, flipping the page of the reference book.

Maya asks, "It's that serious, huh?"

When I look up at her, I see through her, her eyes giving her away too easily. Just like all the others, she's attracted to him. I sigh, disappointed she was so easy to see through, but it doesn't matter. We'll never love anyone as much as we love each other. *Alexander is it for me.* "Very."

6

SARA JANE

Two hours later, I'm walking out of the library. The fresh fall air hits my face as the sun starts to duck behind the psychology building. I don't get far before I see him. Alexander pushes off a wall and walks to me. My backpack is swung over his shoulder and his arm swung over mine. A kiss is placed on my cheek and sweet whispers in my ear. "I missed you."

"I missed you too."

"You did?" he asks, straightening to his full height.

"I did." Patting his chest, I add, "Don't act so surprised. Just because you owe me a good time doesn't mean I don't love you."

He stops, his arm slipping from my shoulder while I keep walking. When I stop and look back, my heart dances wildly in my chest. Just like the first time I ever saw him, he takes my breath away. Alexander's eyes are locked on me, seriousness overtaking his features and darkening his expression. "I would do anything for you. Anything to take care of you. Anything to protect you."

Like how easily his arm slipped around me, his mind slips into the darkness he can't seem to shake years after the death of his mother. I've been told he used to be the center of everyone's attention—friends, mothers, his school—happy, always the charmer. Some things never change, but others, like the burden of the rain clouds that hover over him, I wish would. "I know you would," I reply with certainty. "You've never let me down."

Coming closer, he stops in front of me, taking my hands in his. "I mean it. I'm not just saying it. Nothing matters to me more than you. We'll always be together."

When he says such things I sometimes wonder if he's saying it for my benefit or his. For such a brave man, seemingly unafraid of anything, he's afraid to lose me. "Always." I reach up and touch his cheek. "You're not going to lose me." A large hand warms my waist and pulls me closer. I find comfort in his physical strength and his beautiful eyes; eyes that hold a million secrets and buried pain. As much as I wish I could ease that pain or erase it altogether, they represent the Alexander I know. I do know something that will make him laugh, even if I don't. "Maya said you were cute."

A smirk pops into place. "Only cute?" he asks. I push him in the chest and turn to walk away, but I'm quickly swung around and right into his arms, our bodies flush. "Hey."

I dare to look into his eyes, knowing he'll own me the second I do. "What?" My arms go around him, my cheek to his chest. I love listening to his heart, each beat the tick of my life's clock. I am only because of this man.

And he knows it . . .

"You don't like me looking at you, do you?" I hate that he can hear my nerves even through a hard swallow. I cross my arms

over my chest and tuck my shaking hands. When I don't say anything, he touches my cheek, the back of his fingers warm against my cold skin. He lifts my chin and turns me so I look in his direction. He doesn't speak until my eyes finally meet his. "Don't be shy. Be brave. Be strong. Show the world who's in control. Show them they won't beat you. Don't let the world win."

His confidence in me is tempting to believe. "How?"

"Hold your chin up even when you're scared, or shy, or embarrassed."

"Why?"

"Because you're meant to be queen."

Then it clicks—King.

I hold my chin up on my own accord when his hand goes down to my lap. I uncross my arms and sit straight. With the slightest nod of his approval, I find my own courage in the moment. "Because every king needs a queen." Lifting up with my hands against the park bench on my eighteenth birthday, I kiss him.

I. Kiss. Alexander.

I. Kiss. My king.

. . . What he doesn't know is that he is who he is today because of me. His edges were dull, numbed by the death of his mother when I met him. I gave him someone to believe in again. *Someone to love.*

Like a knife, his senses, his intelligence in life and business, his softer side sharpened over the years. Before me is a man, a leader, a legend in the making. I fell for his mysteries, his smile, and his piercing blue eyes. He's the catalyst to something greater for both of us. It wasn't planned. I was too innocent to ever devise such schemes that he plots. I never knew life could teeter between good and evil so easily until I met Alexander Kingwood IV.

Shelly saw him for who he is now, even then. She knew he was a force to be reckoned with. And I thought he was captivating . . .

"Are you going to wear that?" she asks, doodling on a random page in my physics textbook.

Looking down, I grimace. "Well, I was going to. It's all I have.

"I have something cuter."

I cross my arms and roll my eyes. "I don't need cuter. I need warmth."

"I think Alexander will warm you up just fine."

"Shelly," I reprimand while staring at her in shock.

"He's hot. You do realize that, right? And he'll be more than happy to keep you warm. I see how he looks at you."

I turn back to the window, embarrassment replacing the chill. Curious, I ask, "How is it?"

"The look?"

"Yeah."

"Like you're everything."

Our eyes hold steady as the words drift between us. Feeling the heaviness of her tone, I pull the sweater tighter around me, the buttons folding in on themselves. "Don't say that."

"Why not? It's the truth. But I have a feeling you haven't told me everything."

"I have."

"A boy doesn't look at a girl he barely knows like that."

"How do you know?" I meet her eyes again.

"Because I'm not dumb, Sara Jane. What's really going on?"

"Nothing."

"You sure about that?"

Love floats around my head, but I sweep it away. "I want to say I like him, but I don't know him."

"He seems to know you." She turns and picks up her jacket before putting it on. "Look, if you really don't know him, be care-

ful. He seems to have intentions for you even though you've only just learned his last name."

Kingwood—His last name.

King—His preferred name.

"I'll be careful." I smile, the mood lightening between us. "But you do the same. Chad seems nice, but don't get yourself in trouble."

"What's the fun in that?" She smiles, her bubbly self back intact as we sneak out of the house. Down the street, two unlikely people have become friends. Alexander and Chad are waiting for us on Chad's tailgate.

Chad is in our grade and finally made the move to talk to Shelly instead of staring at her another year. Shelly may be boy crazy, but more than that, she's Chad crazy. He's cute with curly dark blond hair, trendy dark-framed glasses, and his body finally caught up to his age. I think every girl noticed him this year, but he still only had eyes for one. His dream girl became his girlfriend and they've been an item ever since.

Alexander hops off and walks to meet us halfway when we round the corner, making my heart flutter from the thrill. It may be cool out tonight but looking at him, watching his swagger and confidence in full effect walking straight toward me, heats me on the inside.

"Hey," he says, taking my hand in his and kissing me on the cheek.

"Hi."

Shelly wraps her arms around Chad's neck, and they kiss like they've dated longer than a few weeks. But what do I know about couples and how they kiss? I had a terrible kiss at fifteen and never tongue deep. Looking into the elusive Mr. Kingwood's eyes as they shine from the streetlight above, I'm hoping to change that.

Shelly turns to us with a big grin, and asks, "Where should we go?"

And the kissing moment passes just like that, the bubble popped.

Everyone turns to Alexander, his presence naturally commanding attention and authority. A rush of pride runs through me, my heart reacting by thudding louder in my chest.

Alexander says, "Here's good. Just in case her parents come out looking, we'll be close."

Shelly's disappointment is heard in her huff. "I was hoping we'd go somewhere."

Chad adds, "I think King is right." His use of King weighs the final decision as if there's not a discussion to be had. "We can listen to some music in the cab, if you want?"

Listening to music means making out, but it's a good effort on their part to play it off. Nodding, Shelly says, "I'd like that."

Alexander shoves his hands in his pockets, and eyes me. "Want to go for a walk?"

"Sure." My response must show my disappointment as well. I know I shouldn't want to, but he's got my stomach tied up in knots. It's like the slowest burn ever. My insides hot like an inferno for him. Why does he torture me so?

"Stop torturing that lip." He angles down in front of me and grins. "We have time, Sara Jane."

"Time for what?"

"Everything that you're so disappointed we're not doing." Lifting my chin so we're looking into each other's eyes, he whispers, "We have time: hours, days, and years. I promise you."

"You're making me a promise of years?"

"I made that promise long before now. We have all the time in the world to sin together."

He makes me strong, his strength bleeding into my veins. "Is that what you are, Alexander? Are you a sin waiting to happen?"

"I'm a sin waiting to be confessed."

"Then take me to church because I want to kiss you."

Nothing less than what can be called a smirk shapes his lips. The cup of his palms flatten to my cheeks. "I've been told you're bad for me, but you're so damn good for my ego." In a sudden rush of passion, his mouth crashes over mine, and I'm lost to the bliss of his lips. When his tongue pushes into my mouth, I freeze. My eyes go wide, and if he wasn't holding me in place, I would have vanished in this moment of horror. Tilting back to look into my eyes, his brows curve in concern. "What's wrong?"

"Nothing." I try to back away but his hold on my shoulders tightens.

"Tell me what's wrong?"

"I just . . . I don't . . ." I look down, wanting to run away, to hide from the humiliation I feel.

"You don't what, Sara Jane?"

Tears burn hot in my eyes. I will them away before they fall, making me even more self-conscious than I already am. My bottom lip quivers and my inexperience cause the tears to overlap my lids. I close my eyes, and whisper, "I'm sorry."

I'm brought to his chest, his arms wrapping around my back. With my cheek pressed to his chest, I lower my head, and breathe him in to calm my upset heart. "I'm sorry," he whispers with his lips to the back of my head. "I'm sorry. I'll go slower next time." A kiss is placed where his breath just left. "You're so pure, my little firefly. Happy birthday."

"Firefly?" I ask on a shaky breath that trails into calm.

"That's what you are to me."

I must look a complete mess with mascara running down my face, but his words comfort me and make me feel cherished. Good or bad, I like the way he makes me feel carefree and loved, like I matter. Not holding back anymore, I look up and ask, "Why me?"

. . . Squeezing me tighter, he kisses me on the head.

Good and evil sometimes blur just like black and white, leaving us in the gray. It doesn't matter if he's going to heaven or hell because the night of my eighteenth birthday, I decided I'd be right by his side, happy to live in the gray as long as I have him.

7

SARA JANE

For as much as Alexander has shared with me over the years, he's kept a lot hidden. I often wondered if he'd done that because he wanted to protect me or if something worse was lurking in his sadness.

I lie still, so still, as he slips out of bed and walks to the French doors that lead to a large balcony overlooking the grounds. He has a ritual. Time on the balcony in the moonlight—I used to think he found peace under the stars, but his unrest overtook most nights and soon he started leaving for a few hours. Not every night, but three or four, depending on his restlessness. I was rarely asleep, but I pretended to be. Just like now.

He moves with assurance, every step taken with purpose. When I met him, he oozed confidence, but I discovered that he didn't know who he was. It was as if his mother's death had caused him to lose track of himself. He made me feel safe and secure, taken care of, and loved. He was never unsteady around me. But I would catch him lost in his own thoughts when he assumed I was studying. I remember a night when music played softly in the background, a fire flamed in the fireplace, my books were scattered on the coffee table, and his room was dim with the heaviness of his mood, he stood in the open doorway that led to the balcony. The anguish seemed to cover him like a cloak, his shoulders sagging and his head seeming too cumbersome to hold up. Alexander leaned against the railing and closed his eyes . . . *"Kingwood Enterprises is the only thing left of my mother."*

"You're left of her."

"No." He laughed, looking up at the night sky. "I'm all bad, just like my dad." Glancing over his shoulder back at me, he sighed. "When are you going to see the real me, Sara Jane?"

"I see the real you every time I see you. This is who you are. I don't know why you think you're so bad when all I see is the good."

With a smile on his face, he turns around, and crosses his arms over his chest. "You're the smartest decision I ever made. You know that?"

"Yes," I say, feeling sassy. "Now come and kiss me."

"You're so demanding when you get compliments."

"You like it."

Hopping over the arm of the couch, he lands with a thud next to me sending my textbooks to the floor. "I do like it. A lot."

That was a good kiss. A kiss that went from chaste to more in seconds. I still remember it so clearly.

Alexander may not have known who he was at the time, but he knew who he was going to be. I often wonder if it was a self-fulfilling prophecy or falling into a trap set long before he was born. There are a lot of ghosts haunting this manor and I don't intend to let him be the next.

Tonight, his secrets are protected by a solid wave of muscle that rolls over broad shoulders, crashing down strong arms. I turn over to get a better look at him before he disappears outside. He's been working out a lot more lately. He says it's to get rid of pent-up energy. I think it might be preparing for battle.

I'm tired after a long day of school and studying late at the library. Making love wore me out even more after we had dinner in bed. I move up so my back is against the head-board and my arms around my knees. The sheet covers most of my body, but my shoulders are exposed and cold. Just when I'm about to sink back down under the covers, I look up to find Alexander watching me. "I thought you were asleep," he says.

"You weren't here."

A wry grin lifts the right side of his mouth, and he comes back to me. "Since when do you need me to sleep?"

"I always need you, Alexander."

Coming around to my side of the bed, he sits, resting his arm around my legs. "My father is selling Kingwood Enterprises."

"What? Really?"

"I thought it would be mine one day."

Leaning forward, I rest a hand on his leg and kiss his shoulder. "I thought you didn't want it."

"I want it. I don't want to run it, but I want it. It's my legacy."

When I straighten my legs, he moves down until his head is resting on my lap. I stroke my fingers through his hair. "Why is he selling it?"

"I don't know. He blindsided me in front of some guys he's hired to help restructure and sell it off in pieces."

"I'm sorry," I say, failing to find anything that will reassure him.

"I've been thinking about why it bothers me when I've never liked being there. My mother gave him her trust fund to start the company." I don't realize I had stopped moving my hand until he looks up at me. "I feel like she's slipping away from me."

Running my fingers gently over his temples, I whisper, "She's with you, Alexander. Always."

"She gave everything up for him. Her last name. Her money. Her love. And I hate that it was never enough for him. He always wanted more, like all her time, her attention, and everything she had. It was never enough for him. He consumed her like a drug he couldn't get enough of. And then she was gone. The photos went away, her items disappeared from view. The curtains were drawn, and I was left on my own."

"You had me."

The smallest of smiles appears, but I catch it. "Yes, Firefly, I had you."

"You *have* me."

He kisses my bare leg while the feel of his arm tightens around me. "Since she's been gone, the company is the only tangible part of her in this world."

"There's still Kingwood Manor."

"She hated this place." A small, but discernible smile creases his mouth before disappearing again just as quickly. "She complained it was too big for two people, and when I came along my father used to demand she stay in their room when all she wanted to do was stay in mine."

"Your father's room is in the other wing." Alexander looks at me, a shared understanding passing between us. "You had to live in this part of the house by yourself?"

"I had a lady who worked nights to tend to me."

His choice of words startles me. *Tend*, not care. "Tend to you? I don't even know what that means Alexander."

"She would cry as he pulled her out the door and made her take a pill to calm her down."

"That's awful." I look around the large room he calls his quarters. A family could live in this room it's so big. It's made up of a huge walk-in closet, an even larger attached bathroom, a sitting area with a couch and large screen TV, and the bed with a nightstand flanking either side of the bed frame. A vision of a crib here instead and a child, Alexander, being separated from his mother brings tears to my eyes. "Why would he make her leave?"

"Because *he* needed her."

"You needed her," I reply, a harsh demand in my tone.

He nods. "I will never do to my child what he did to me." His fingers run over the skin of my inner thigh. "*My* family, my wife and kids, will always come first." Anger seeps into his tone as if he's threatening the world with a long held vengeance.

Maybe he is.

A tear slips down my cheek—the sadness of his story and the fate of mine clashing in the middle of the night. "My heart hurts, Alexander. Tell me something happy."

"When my father would leave on a business trip, which was frequent, my mom would come in here and we'd make a pallet on the floor, watch movies, eat candy, and fall asleep. She used to sleep with a smile on her face."

"Because you made her happy." I smile listening to the lightness in his voice. "It's clear she adored you."

"I wonder if she smiled with my father. She used to tell me she wanted me so badly that she didn't want to miss a minute with me." He sits up, looking toward the open doors of the balcony. "I think my dad felt competitive with me. Jealous *of* me."

"You were a baby. He didn't have to compete."

"My father will win, or he'll annihilate anyone that threatens him or his empire."

"Was he always so mean?"

"Mean? I'm not sure I'd use that term when describing him. Malicious, unforgiving, insecure, but mean seems a little light." His eyes meet mine, unyielding when he says, "I'm a lot like him. I'll push you away, and if you're strong enough to stay, I'll destroy everything I once loved about you while destroying myself in the process." A harsh breath is sucked in, and his expression softens. "Just like he did to my mother."

Fear presides over me as he watches my reaction. My chest feels hollow of beats until I release a shaky breath. *I am strong. I am strong. I am strong.* "You tell me your family will come first, then threaten me. Your scare tactics won't work, Alexander. I see you, the real you. I know where your heart, where your love, lies. You can believe that you're bad, that all the good in you died when your mother did, but you're a lot like her. You've just forgotten. You need to find those qualities and hold on to them. They're the ones that will save you when you need it most."

"I thought you were here to save me?" He kisses my neck.

"I can't save someone so determined to die."

"I don't want to die, sweetheart." He chuckles as he gets up and walks to the end of the bed where his clothes were discarded earlier. "Our fairy tale is just beginning."

Never had I confessed the dreams I've held captive in my heart. One day we might get the life that seems so distant from the one we're living now. I'm not naïve. I know there's darkness in the lightness of Alexander's eyes. It's always there even when his mood contradicts it. Despite that, hearing him talk about our fairy tale gives life to my dreams.

"Where are you going?" I ask, even though I know he won't tell me.

Slipping on his jeans, he keeps his tone casual as if this is an everyday conversation. "I have business to take care of."

"It's two thirty in the morning."

When his shirt slides down over his head, he says, "You should get some rest."

"You should too."

A smirk plays on his face. "If I asked you not to worry about me, could you?"

"I don't worry about you," I say, lying. "I worry about the other guy."

His laugh befits the dark room. "What if I said there isn't an *other* guy?"

"Well, I know there's not another girl."

"How do you know that?"

"Because I know how much you love me."

Pulling me by the ankles, I'm left flat on my back as he crawls onto the bed over me. Playful Alexander is my most favorite.

"You see right through me. You always have." He kisses the tip of my nose. "Go to sleep, Firefly." When he stands, he grabs his shoes from the floor and heads to the door.

"Alexander?"

"Yeah?"

"Be careful."

"I always am."

One shoe is slipped on and then he does the other as I roll to my side and prop my head up on my arm. The door's about to close behind him when he opens it back up. "Sara Jane?"

"Yes?"

"I wasn't threatening you. I was warning you, so you can save yourself."

I had accepted my fate the day I met him. "Like you once said, it's already too late for me."

Our eyes hold long enough for reality to sink in. He bows his head as he ducks out, his gaze falling with his expression. The door is closed as he leaves me in the quarters built for a king's prince, with ghosts of his troubled life keeping me company.

I close my eyes and pull the covers tight under my chin. The bed feels too big without his presence filling it. My worries are bigger. Can I save him before he destroys himself and me along with him? Will he ever feel true happiness, soul-searing joy in the life he's living? Or will I always be left with these unsettled emotions twisted in my gut?

He's always kept secrets from me, but now they seem too big for him to suppress. This mansion hidden behind a long drive and expansive lawns, wrought iron gates, and security cameras, holds the key to Alexander's peace of mind and I'm determined to find it before his past overshadows his future.

8

SARA JANE

W hen I wake up, the space next to me is still empty. Alexander hasn't returned. I glance to the clock and it's just past eight. The sun is shining and I can't sleep anymore. I take my phone from the nightstand, text Alexander, and head into the bathroom to take a shower. I love days when I don't have classes until late morning. Not having to rush lets me ease into the busyness that will be this afternoon.

After my shower, I head for the closet where I've taken over a small section in the corner. But I stop on the way when something white catches my eye by the door.

An envelope.

Walking closer, my name is printed, not written, but printed on the front. I bend down and pick it up, curious to what it is. Opening it, I read:

SARA JANE,

Please join me for breakfast at 9 a.m. sharp in the dining room.

With Regards,
Alexander Kingwood III

IT'S NOT A REQUEST. I have a feeling I don't have much choice. *This* is a demand. I stare at the invitation, reading it again and again. I've never spent time with Alexander's father alone. Maybe I won't be. Maybe Alexander will be there too.

Do I RSVP or just show up in the dining room? Butterflies turn to bees in my stomach, and I feel sick. This is so far out of my comfort zone that I don't want to go. *Why now?* After years. Why does he want to speak with me now? I can't let my worries get ahead of me.

Shit. What do I wear? I rush into the closet and look at what's available. There's not much that isn't shorts or jeans with a T-shirt. I find one cute blouse and my nicest jeans with a pair of flats. This will have to work. I rush back into the bathroom, realizing how much time I squandered in the shower when I thought I had a lazy morning.

Once my hair and makeup are done, I get dressed and check my phone. No calls. No messages. *Where are you, Alexander?*

After doing one last check in the full-length mirror, I open the door and head down the hall. I pass by the four guest rooms, which never host guests, and start down the wide staircase. Really, the house, *the manor,* with its ornate wooden banisters that curtain the staircase, the elegant and refined receiving room, and high, elaborately decorated ceilings, is incredibly impressive. It has lost its luster somewhat over the years for me. I used to think it palatial, but now it feels like a mausoleum. *Sad somehow. Like its inhabitants.* I cross through the main entry and pass the living room.

When I reach the dining room, which I've only been in one other time since coming here the first time, I stop in the doorway.

Sitting at the head of a table that seats twenty, sits Alexander Kingwood III. Without looking up from the tablet in front of him, he says, "Please take a seat, Ms. Grayson." My Alexander looks so similar: his facial structure, his light eyes, the broad shoulders. The coldness I've seen frequently when Alexander interacts with others, has never been directed toward me.

That coldness is in his father's eyes now, though. He gestures to the left to let me know where he wants me. I walk farther inside and reach to pull the chair out, but he rises and says, "Allow me."

He picks up the intricately carved wooden chair and moves it back for me. I quickly slip in and am tucked neatly under the table. When I look at the space between my legs and the arms of the chairs I feel small and wonder if he picked this setting to intimidate me or to actually get to know me.

The door from the kitchen is gently swung open and a lovely looking woman with chestnut eyes and shiny brown hair walks in. She wears bright red lipstick, and I consider complimenting her on the shade. But I'm too nervous to even speak, much less act like I belong here.

Plates are set in front of us—an omelet, strawberries, and wheat toast. Juice has already been poured and coffee steam wafts above the mug in front of me.

"Is there anything else you require?" he asks. When I reply no, the lady disappears and he picks up his fork. "Please eat before it gets cold." He sets it down again and a smile that reminds me of my Alexander's shows up, my guard going down. "Where are my manners? A pretty woman joins me for breakfast and I forget them completely. Good morning, Ms. Grayson. Thank you for joining me."

"Thank you for the invitation, though I must admit I was surprised by it." I study his reaction while cutting my omelet.

"Sometimes this house gets lonely. My son is rarely home anymore. I heard you were here and decided to take the opportunity." He takes a bite of fruit as if we eat every meal together, as if we know each other at all.

"Speaking of Alexander, will he not be joining us?"

His eyes flash to mine, an eyebrow ticking up. "I sent him a text earlier, but he is too busy apparently. I would have thought you'd have spoken to him."

I will be now—for putting me in such an awkward position. "He was letting me sleep in. I had a late night." I add, "Studying."

"How are your classes going? Are you on track to graduate next year?"

"Yes, my course load is heavy, but I'm doing well."

"Alex tells me you're intellectually gifted, that you make good grades without cracking a book."

"Your son is too kind, but it's *he* who does well without much effort."

"He always did take the easy way out."

"I didn't mean it that way."

"I know what you meant. Alex is . . . a lot like his mother. He has so much on his mind except what he should."

After hearing last night how his father would make his wife leave Alexander, I inwardly growl. But wanting so desperately to know more about my boyfriend, I ask what I know I shouldn't, "In what ways?"

Mr. Kingwood looks at me, but in the corners of my eyes I see his grip tighten around the silverware in his hand. "His heart. It's too soft. He'll end up getting hurt if he's not careful."

"Hurt by what?"

"Not by what. By whom." He takes his napkin and wipes his mouth. After leaning back on his throne, he says, "I think you're well aware that this is not as casual an invite as I'd like it to be."

I mimic his actions, sitting back. "I had hopes it would be."

That brings a smile to his face that's more relaxed. "You've been dating my son for many years considering how young you both are. Was it at the holiday party where we first met? Even after seeing you several times since, I don't really know you, Ms. Grayson. I assumed you were a mere passing fascination. One Alex would get over." *Fascination*, not *fancy*, like the phrase. "But here you are in *my* house, even when my son is not, as if you're a resident here."

"I'm not sure what to say."

"I'm not looking for answers regarding your sleeping arrangement with my son. That is between the two of you. What I am looking for are answers regarding your future with my son. That involves me."

"I didn't know you were involved with your son at all."

"He said you were feisty. You look so meek that I didn't believe him. I owe him an apology."

"I don't mean to be disrespectful, but I'm not going anywhere. If you need confirmation of that, you'll have to speak to Alexander."

"My wife used to call me Alexander when everyone else called me Alex or Mr. Kingwood." There's a distance in his eyes as if he's looking right through me at the ghost of his wife.

"I'm sorry for your loss."

His eyes focus again, the earlier smile has vanished. "I worry about my son."

"So do I."

"Loving him has never been easy."

"I hear the same about you."

His palm flattens on the shiny surface of the table, the silverware clinking together from the motion. "I'm going to be very blunt with you, Ms. Grayson. I love my son despite what he tells you. He is my only family, my only blood relative. As such, I've afforded him the lifestyle that a Kingwood should have. You're smart. Pretty, but what keeps you coming back? What is it about my son that keeps you tied so tightly to that relationship when he's out most nights destroying it?" *He knows? He knows Alexander leaves me most nights?*

I gulp, my weakness under his glare evident, but I stand my ground because I know the answer in my heart. I know why Alexander would never hurt me despite the accusation from his father. "Love."

"That simple? It's a foolish emotion."

"Maybe to you. To me, it's everything. I love him, but there's nothing simple about it."

He lifts the electronic tablet that had been discarded to the side of his plate, and pulls out an envelope, tapping it three times on the table. "I know you think I don't care about Alex, but I do. Very much. He's the last tie I have to my wife."

"I thought that was Kingwood Enterprises?"

"You know more than you let on."

"I only know what Alexander shares with me."

"You're better off, unless pillow talk is a regular occurrence."

"Any secrets he shares with me will always remain secret."

"If I've learned anything in life, it's that secrets are never truly kept private unless you never tell anyone. The second is that everyone comes with a price. What's yours?"

My offense comes in the form of a sucked-in gasp. I refuse to let him rattle me anymore though. "I suppose you don't know much about me or my relationship with Alexander, but money has never been a factor that tied us together." I watch as he crosses his arms over his chest and listens intently. "My family isn't poor."

"Your family makes a modest income compared to Alexander's."

"My family makes enough to pay for my schooling," I reply defensively. "I went to a private school and although I've earned scholarships for my college education, my parents easily bridge the gap in finances. We may not live in a *manor*, but our home is nice."

"Your home is nice. Your father works hard and is quite respected in town. How's his practice?"

An ache fills my hands, and I look down to find my knuckles white from squeezing the arms of the chair so hard. I scoot it back, toss my napkin on the table, and stand. "I should get to class before I'm late."

"You and I both know you don't have class until eleven."

My lips part but I stop my jaw from dropping. "I'm trying to be respectful, Mr. Kingwood, but I'm not comfortable being interrogated about my family."

"My apologies," he says, standing up. "Please stay. I would like to talk to you about Alex."

"I may be young, but I recognize a trap when I see one. Did you really text Alexander?"

"I did." He chuckles to himself. "I actually would have

liked him here. By your reaction he's really sold you his story, but there're always two sides."

"I agree, but I trust him."

"Would you like to hear mine?"

"Not without him here."

He chuckles to himself. "You don't need a protector from me."

Our eyes hold steady though my hand shakes under the pressure, and I lose when I look down.

"I'm not the enemy, Sara Jane." My gaze darts up when my name is mentioned as if we're friends. "I hoped my son was smart enough to not involve you where he shouldn't." He sits back down when I do. "It appears he's involved you. Your insider knowledge could be costly."

"I would never betray him."

"What about me? Will you betray me?"

Not knowing if it's a rhetorical question I let it lie like the crumbs from the toast on the shiny wood surface.

"I'm selling the company. With that, I need every part of my life in order or investors will expect to bargain. I don't bargain. I want full value."

"And what do I have to do with your business?"

"Alex is pivotal to this transaction going smoothly, or if we section it off into several transactions. As my son's girlfriend, you play a part. Whether you're willing to do that or not is your choice, but I need to know by the weekend. We're hosting an event." He hands me the envelope. "Here's your invitation." He stands all the way up this time, looking down on me. "Please consider the ramifications if you decide to stay in my son's life. They're bigger than you might have imagined when you were seventeen and falling for the bad boy. There are skeletons that need to remain hidden behind closed doors. I can't afford to have"—his cough interrupts him—"any weak links." Walking to the door, he turns back. "Good luck on your test, Ms. Grayson. Good day."

With the envelope in my hand, I watch him walk out of the room. I'm not alone for long. The woman from earlier enters again, and says, "No rush to leave, and let me know if I can get you anything."

"Thank you, but I think I've lost my appetite."

Understanding brushes across her features as she reaches for my plate. "He can be quite kind, but when it comes to his family or business, he's the hardest they come."

I stand with the envelope held in my hands. "He doesn't scare me. I love Alexander too much to be scared away that easily."

"I know. Everyone knows, including Mr. Kingwood, or he wouldn't have invited you to breakfast."

"So this is his way of welcoming me into the family?"

She laughs. "No, but its one step closer." Holding out her hand, she smiles at me. "I'm Neely."

While shaking her hand, I introduce myself, "I'm Sara Jane Grayson."

"Nice to officially meet you."

"Have you worked here long?"

"Long enough to understand his motives."

"And what are those?"

"Money and blood."

"But at what cost and whose blood?"

"I can't answer that."

"Why have we never met?"

She smiles with the plate in hand and the door to the kitchen pushes open with her foot. "My job assignment is to take care of Mr. Kingwood's every need. We have staff to run the rest of the house and to care for Alex."

Every need? I look at her bright, wide-set eyes and the

fullness of her red lips, the white blouse with the top button open and the tight black skirt. I shouldn't assume, but my mind goes straight to salacious. "His needs?"

The grin on her face broadens. "Almost."

Okay. It's not my business and after what just happened with him, I don't want to know more. Extricating myself from his line of sight is the best thing I can do. Focus on school. Focus on Alexander. Forget the rest. Block it out. Be strong and just forget this morning. I walk to the entrance of the dining room. "Thank you for breakfast."

"You're welcome."

When I reach the top of the stairs, I dash down the long hall to Alexander's room. With the door closed behind me, and my back securely against the wood, I rip open the envelope and pull out the invitation, my eyes scanning the details.

Black Tie.

Saturday night.

Kingwood Manor.

Why would Alexander not tell me? *Is he going?* Why would he not invite me? I tuck it inside my backpack and zip it closed before changing clothes and hurrying out of here as fast as I can. I never felt unsafe here, until now. The walls, *it seems,* have eyes and ears. I need to find Alexander immediately.

As soon as I reach my car, I lock the doors and start the engine. I quickly type a text to him to meet me on campus in front of the business building in thirty minutes.

It doesn't take long to find a parking spot, but it's not close to the main campus. I park anyway, hoping the walk will give me time to calm my nerves. After hiking up a steep hill, I take a deep breath and let it out before crossing the quad. *Alexander.* The man I love, the man who wasn't in his bed this morning when I woke, the man who didn't bother to text me back, is here. *With some girl. Standing too close for my liking.* When I approach, Alexander looks up and raises his chin, standing tall when he sees me.

I struggle to keep my jaw from dropping when I see Maya. Her hand is on his chest and she's laughing. Why? Why is she here and why are *they* talking? They don't even know each other. Was it not just yesterday when she saw him for the first time? The coincidence seems a little too uncanny. Did he not connect the dots and realize she is the girl I said had called him cute? He would flip out if I were hanging out with a guy who had shown interest in me the day before.

After the confrontational breakfast with his father, I'm in no mood to fight off her advances when she knows he's taken. All my twisted emotions from this morning tighten and coil. I'm a viper ready to strike. My eyes meet Maya's and her hand drops quickly to her side, but when I look at him, Alexander's eyebrow quirks and his head tilts. *He thinks this is funny?*

Like the guilty always do, Maya speaks too fast, "Hey, Sara Jane. I'm late for class. Nice talking, Alexander. Maybe I'll see you around." She ignores me completely and leaves.

With five feet remaining between Alexander and me, I stop. "We need to talk."

"Rough morning?" When I scowl, his smile is instantly gone. "Whoa! Settle down."

"Don't tell me to settle down, Alexander. I've had a shitty morning and then I find you talking to her. What the fuck?"

Anger shapes his eyes as he stares, his body following suit as he closes the gap and leans down so only I can hear him through pursed lips. "Don't swear at me, Sara Jane. Now tell me what's wrong."

There's a breathable pause though neither of us takes one. My body is stiff under his hands, so he kisses me as if that will change anything. I turn my head, causing his lips to land on my cheek. "Don't."

He doesn't move, except his mouth against my ear. "Don't you ever turn away from me again." The threat is whispered but it doesn't make it less powerful. "Do you understand?" His voice is not one I recognize as the grinding of his teeth is heard.

I push off him, but his grip tightens. "We're in the middle of campus with dozens of eyes, if not more, potentially watching this exchange." I tuck my arms between us, keeping him away from me without being obvious. "Let go of me, Alexander."

I'm released and given a cold, hard glare in exchange. "What the fuck is going on?"

"Where have you been all night?" Everything I've ignored, everything that has built up over time is spat in his face.

"Don't talk to me like I've done something wrong."

"How do I know you haven't?"

"Because you know me. Better than anyone. You know me, Firefly. I don't tell you certain things to protect you."

"From what?" I take a step back. "What are you protecting me from?" His brow bunches in the middle, a more defined line that's formed in the last two years. "I've let you have your secrets. For years, I let everything go and have given you the privacy you've wanted. Yet today, you've been gone all night, don't bother to answer any of my text messages, and when I *do* find you, it's with another girl's hands on your body." Moving closer to him, I touch his chest. His shirt is fisted in my hands and I plead, "Please let me in."

"If I let you in, I'll lose you. That's what happens to people I truly love."

"Who is after you? Who will hurt me because you care about me? Please, Alexander. I can't live in the dark any longer."

He takes my clinging wrists and moves me back until I release his shirt. "You think you'll find happiness if you know everything, when I know you'll only find misery." Stepping away from me, he releases my wrists and they drop to my sides. "I'm not fucking anyone else if that's what you're worried about. I wouldn't do that to you."

"Then why did you let her touch you at all?"

"I wasn't *letting* her. She did it right when you showed up. What you didn't hear was when I told her to not touch me. That I have a girlfriend. That's the part you missed."

He turns to leave but doesn't get five feet before I beg, "Alexander?"

"Sara Jane, you okay?" I look to my left and find Cal from my study group standing nearby.

I turn to him, but my breath catches when I see Alexander in my peripheral storming toward him. Jumping in his path, my body is flung as I hit the wall of muscle. Just as I'm about to hit the ground, I'm caught and my scream lodges in my throat.

Looking up into the intense eyes that caused me so much pain a moment earlier, a small smile tilts the corners of his lips, and he leans down for a kiss, but instead whispers, "I said I would never hurt you."

"Then let me in." He sighs, and then shakes his head slowly. Gone is his façade of fury. *He's frustrated, but not with me. It's as though he's wavering. How I wish I could read his mind, understand fully the shadows that lurk inside him.*

"You're in. Way deeper than you know, but I guess it's

time you know more." He lifts me to my feet and glares at Cal. "Carry on with your day. I've got this."

The warning is clear in Alexander's tone, but Cal asks me, "You sure?"

My throat hurts as much as my heart, but I manage to reply, "I'm sure." Because we're both in too deep to walk away now.

And I wouldn't even if I could.

9

SARA JANE

Looking back over my shoulder, Cruise is standing by the car. Seeing things in a new perspective, it appears like he's standing guard. *Am I paranoid or has my whole world just flipped upside down?*

Back in the coffee shop, where I sit, Alexander arrives with a coffee in each hand. After setting them down on the table between us, he sits across from me in a leather wing-back and rests his forearms on his legs. "I want to know who killed my mother."

Caught completely off guard, I ask, "What?"

"I can't just let a murderer roam the streets. She was killed, and I need to know why and by whom."

"The newspapers said why."

"I don't care what the papers or the media said. It's lies. It's a cover-up."

My heart beats harder, pounding against my ribs, as I stare at the man who's being eaten alive by his anger. Reaching over, I wrap my hands over his clasped ones and whisper, "Alexander, she was mugged. She tried to fight the attackers, and they shot her."

His pain is evident when he looks down, that line between his eyebrows prominent. "It wasn't over a fucking necklace and a wedding ring." His eyes lift to mine quickly.

"Her jewelry was very valuable."

"Her life was worth more than fucking jewelry."

"You're right. It was, but not to them."

"Don't say that."

"I'm not saying it to hurt you. I'm saying it because I've seen you changing over the years, and I'm not sure I like what you're becoming."

He shakes my hands away and sits back, out of my reach. "You can leave then."

"Don't say things you don't mean."

I've seen Alexander happy, turned on, mischievous, angry, but the dark, brooding expression on his face isn't one I've ever seen directed at me. Until this moment. When he doesn't respond, moments from our three-year relationship start to flash through my head...

"Why me?" I've only spent a small amount of time with him. When I look at him, how handsome he is, how strong he is, I can't see it, what he sees in me.

Touching my cheek, he presses his forehead to mine, and whispers, "I want to see you again. I want to see you every day." Leaning back, he looks into my eyes. "Do you want to see me again, Sara Jane?"

It was such a loaded question for an innocent girl, especially one already so blinded by love. We've fought, we've made up, we've laughed, we've fucked, and we've made love over and over again. Our relationship has been a roller coaster. But my answer will always be the same. *Yes, I want to stay.* But he's not asking me to stay here. He's asking me to leave ... *if I want to.* "Alexander?" I wait, my heart aching in ways I've never felt. Will he actually let me walk away?

He rests his ankle across his knee and looks eerily similar to his father sitting at the head of the table this morning. I stand, and he finally speaks, "Sit."

Our stares are guns, ready to fire and weighted with pain and anger as we silently challenge each other. Again, he says, "Sit down, Sara Jane." Crossing my arms over my chest, I shake my head, unable to speak with the same authority in which he speaks to me. He stands before me, reaching his full six-foot-three height, and towers over me. "Please."

Taking in a jagged breath, I relent and sit down. I'm not sure if I'm losing a battle or winning the war by doing so, but with the years I've invested, I know my heart is not my own. I'll sit another minute. I owe him that much. "That's twice today you've taken a tone with me as if you own me."

"I do own you. You can't argue that."

"I can argue that you'd be lost without me."

"I was lost when I met you."

My emotions are exposed instantly when my eyes begin to water. I feel as though I've been slapped. "Why are you talking to me like this, like I don't mean anything to you?"

He leans forward again and looks around before turning back to me. "You mean everything to me. Everything, Firefly, but I have enough bullshit to deal with. If you're not happy, I'm not going to make you stay." *Not going to make me stay. He knows he could though, yet he's abandoning that position. A lot like how I feel right now. Abandoned.*

"Why do you sound relieved from the thought of me leaving?"

"You know, deep down, it would be better for you to go. Both of us know that. Doesn't mean I want you to, but I don't know if I can make you happy any longer."

Or maybe he just doesn't want to try anymore. "You sound like your father."

I'm met with narrowed eyes and a curious crease in his forehead. Tilting his head, he asks, "And what would you know about my father?"

"For as long as we've dated, it's interesting how little I know about him."

"Then what are you talking about?"

I pull the invitation from my backpack and drop it on the table between us.

He grabs it and without even opening it asks, "Why do you have this?"

"You know what it is?" His silence answers my question. "Why, after all these years, is your father inviting me to one of his parties?"

I see his Adam's apple bob with a thick gulp, and he glances to Cruise just outside the dusty window. When he looks back, he asks, "What's going on?"

"I had breakfast with your father, though I lost my appetite early enough I'm not sure I can say I actually ate anything."

His left hand begins to shake before his other hand covers it. Any of the kindness I'm used to seeing in his eyes has disappeared. "Were you going to tell me?"

"That's why I texted you to meet me. I just didn't expect to find you flirting with Maya when I arrived."

"I wasn't flirting. She came over to me."

"If that had been some guy talking to me, with his hand on me, you would have been furious."

"There was a guy. Who the fuck was that?"

"Nobody that matters."

"He knew your name so he's obviously somebody."

"He's a guy from class. Like I said, nobody. So don't turn this around on me." I sit back tucking my legs under me, trying to physically pretend this conversation is not an argument. "I had every intention of telling you about breakfast and this invitation when I arrived on campus this morning."

"Tell me now." His lips are tight as he stares at me like he's seeing me in a new light.

"I don't want to talk to you right now." I grab my backpack and swing it over my shoulder before snatching the invitation out of his hand.

My wrist is grabbed before I can walk away. He stands again and steps as close as he can to me, his chest pressed to my shoulder. "I'm tired. I didn't get any sleep—"

"Then maybe you should have stayed in bed with me."

I'm released and he turns his back. His breath is harsh, his temper hidden from view, and I walk out. When I see Cruise, he says, "See you later, SJ."

Keeping my head down when I pass, I hide the tears in my eyes and reply, "Later."

I don't know how I manage to hold it together all the way back to campus. Maybe it's the humiliation I feel inside, the same feeling I want to hide from the world. He's never spoken to me in that way, in that tone, or looked at me as though I was duplicitous. *Until now.*

I'm late to my first class, and as per my professor's rule, I'm locked out. "Damn it." I sigh, defeat dropping my shoulders. I head outside and across the quad to sit on an open bench. I'm not sure if it's the weather that's turned chilly or the fight I just had lingering in my veins, but I shiver in response.

Looking around, I'm relieved he didn't follow me. My thoughts are all over the place, and I can't seem to pinpoint why we're even fighting. I lie down on the bench and close my eyes. When was the last night I had enough sleep? *When was the last time he stayed through the night?* Walking out of that coffee shop replays in my head. Everything with him is an enigma leading to more buried secrets. I still don't have the answers I want or need and it doesn't seem Alexander's ready to share.

At one time, I was okay with him having a life outside the one he had with me. He wasn't cheating and I was busy with school, so I let a lot slide. But after this morning, I can't pretend like I used to . . .

The tips of our fingers come together with the blue sky as a backdrop. My head rests on his lap while he leans against the base of a tree and the spring air fills my lungs. I love the simple times with Alexander the best. Being at the park today reminds me how busy our lives have become since I started college last fall. He takes my hand and brings it to his mouth, then confesses, "I miss you sometimes."

"I miss you all the time."

"I'm here whenever you need me."

"I always need you, Alexander." I sit up and face him. "But tell me where you go when you leave me?"

"I would never leave you. You will be the one to walk away. Not me."

"I don't think I could."

"What keeps you here?"

"My heart."

"You're speaking through emotions." He spins a silver ring in the shape of a crown around my finger. I don't wear it all the time, but I have been lately, missing him. He gave it to me last year, telling me I would always be his queen. "What does your rational side say?"

"My emotions are rational."

"You're nineteen, Sara Jane. One day you'll be too smart to give your feelings so much power." He kisses me, soft and gently, like every time he kisses me. "When you wise up, promise you'll leave me."

Surprised, I ask, "Why do you want me to leave?"

"Because you deserve better than I'll be able to give you. And one day you'll discover that too. You'll see me for who I am instead of who you want me to be."

"I think your emotions weigh down the better parts of yourself."

"You wear rose-colored glasses, Firefly."

"I wear my love for you, right here in the open."

"You'll regret that one day."

I kiss him first on his cheek then on his lips and whisper, "How could I ever regret something that feels this right?"

His fingers weave into the back of my hair and he holds me close. "I love you. Till the day I die, I'll love you."

"When did it get so hard?"

The warmth of his voice blankets the chill inside me. I open my eyes, slowly adjusting, and find myself buried in his shadow. "When was it ever easy, Alexander?"

I sit up and he sits down. "I'm sorry." Vulnerability, not something I often hear, but I can now in his tone. It draws me to want to touch him, to hold him, to give him time to say what he needs to say. He runs his hands through his hair and I notice how much it's grown when the locks fall back over his eyes. "When I stood over my mother's casket, I vowed I would find the person who murdered her. I won't stop until that person pays for what he's done."

"Pays by having justice served by the police or like a vigilante you're going to take matters into your own hands?"

Tucking a section of my hair behind my ear, he says, "Why can't it be both?"

"Because it's not healthy to seek revenge, and it's not safe for you to hunt for a killer."

"When you put it like that—"

"You'll stop?" I ask, hope foolishly filling my chest.

He chuckles. "No, I can't."

"You're not Batman, Alexander. What you're doing is dangerous and irresponsible."

"How is it irresponsible to want to stop a murderer?"

"It's irresponsible to my heart. If anything happens to you—"

"You wanted to know what I do with my nights. I've now told you, so I'm not going to continue this conversation."

Frustration sets in again, and I spit out, "What are you doing with your days?"

"I go to work. I'm with you or my friends. There's no great mystery to solve here." He shrugs. "I'm an average kind of guy."

Now I laugh. Average guy. Ha! "There's nothing average about you."

When his arm comes around me, he pulls me close and kisses my head. "That's why you love me."

"I love you endlessly." Leaning on his shoulder, I add, "But sometimes I worry that I also love you regardless of what my instincts say."

"Your instincts are always right. I want to tell you everything, Sara Jane, but I also want you to be happy. It's a line I struggle to toe."

I kiss his temple and take in his intoxicating scent. "I wish things were that easy."

"But like you said, it's never been easy for us. So maybe we just accept our fate and, like Bonnie and Clyde, live on the edge."

"I used to dream I was Snow White and I would meet my Prince Charming."

"You can still have that dream, but I don't think I can give you the ending you want."

"You mean a happy one?"

"Any that involves that easy life you want."

Running my fingers over the veins on top of his hand, I say, "I'll take Bonnie and Clyde if it means I get you."

"You have me. You always did, Firefly." Leaning forward, he says, "I don't want to change the subject, but we need to talk about my father."

"Okay." I lick my lips, and then tug the lower one in when the memory of the confrontation comes back. "Why did he invite me to breakfast?"

Alexander scans the area before replying. "I don't know, but I don't want him near you. He's dangerous."

"He's your father, Alexander."

"I don't want you near him. This isn't a discussion."

"Is it a command?"

"Yes." Running his hand through his hair, he shakes his head, and then says, "Yes, Sara Jane. This is a command. I've never made another of you, but I don't trust him. If he suddenly wants to see you, there is a motive. Don't get caught in the crossfire."

"I can't just ignore him."

"Ignore him anyway."

"What do I say?"

"Anything that keeps you safe."

When I move in front of him, he takes me by the hips, and I look up. "You told me you want revenge. Now tell me the rest."

He drops his head and rests the top against my stomach. "I can't."

"Why not?"

"Because I love you too much."

"You're living two lives. Don't you see?"

When his steel blue eyes look up, he admits what I fear, "I only see the justice I want served."

"God, Alexander, you're impossible. We've been together forever, and I feel like I barely know you."

When he stands up, he tilts his head down. "You know me, Sara Jane. You know me better than anyone."

"Then stop lying to me."

"You're maddening."

"I'm maddening? You're the most frustrating man I've ever known. You have a talent for talking in circles but make everyone believe they've gotten answers. I've given you a free pass for too long. I'm not going to sit idly by anymore."

"Think about what you're asking me."

"I have. For years."

"And you're willing to walk away, after all we've been through, after all the time we've invested?"

"You just told me I'd be better off if I left. You've said it before too. But now you're turning this back on me with *after all we've been through*?" My hands hold tight to the straps on my backpack to hide my nerves as I lay down my ultimatum. "I don't want to leave, but you're standing there holding the door open. Close it and tell me everything or I walk out."

Irritation prods my pride into action. I look at him one more time, praying he opens up to me. When he doesn't, I drop my head, disappointed and disheartened. *Devastated.* Do I go back on my threat? Was it just a threat or was it more? "Why are you doing this?" Tears fill my eyes as I look at him, silently pleading with him to throw me a lifeline.

He doesn't. This is it. He's leaving me to accept what he's willing to give, which I know deep down is not enough anymore.

"Goodbye." Alexander has his hands tucked in his pockets and his eyes on me. I turn my back to him and head to my next class early, willing to wait there rather than stand here and fall apart publicly. I try to distract myself by going through the material I'm about to be tested on. Alexander Kingwood IV is a prime study in clinical psychology, but like he warned me, my emotions are too involved to see a clear picture.

I thought I was strong. Walking away with a chip on my shoulder, my heart throbs to go back. When I duck inside the psychology building, I run to the stairwell, my emotions consuming me the way Alexander did before them. I grab hold of the railing and break down.

Dropping to the step, I dig out a tissue from my backpack, trying to stop my makeup from running down my face. I should have known today would be awful. It started that way, waking up alone, eating with the devil incarnate. Like an omen. I hadn't known I'd also go to sleep on my own tonight though. If I'd known I was going to break up with the love of my life, I would have gone home.

10

SARA JANE

" Sara Jane?"

My name echoes through the apartment, but it's not the voice I want to hear.

Shelly calls again, "Sara Jane, you here?"

The covers are pulled tighter and higher, the pillow adjusted over my head. The knock is light but loud enough. I remain quiet, burrowed in my bed, hoping she gives up. When the bed dips, I know I'm going to have to face her, but deep down I wanted to have a few more days before I had to explain.

"Hey," she says, nudging my arm through the blanket. "You in there?" When I moan, she lies down on the bed next to me. "Remember when Chad and I broke up?"

"No, when did that happen?" I ask, moving the pillow just enough to peek out.

"Confession. We never broke up, but it got you talking. So do you want to talk about what happened?"

"Not really, and you're not funny." The pillow returns to cover my face.

Her arm comes around me, and she leans her head on

my shoulder. "He misses you."

"He has a funny way of showing it."

"He's showing it, but you've been buried in this bed for the last two days and haven't seen it." She sighs. "I don't know what happened. He hasn't told me or Chad, but I want you to know I'm on your side."

"You don't even know my side."

"I know you and you're my best friend, so that means I'm on your side." She tries to move the pillow away from my head. At first I resist, and then I let her. I'm greeted with a warm albeit sympathetic smile. "It really sucks how pretty you are even when you're depressed."

I give in and laugh. "Shush it. I probably look horrible."

"Nope. I'd tell you. Happily. 'Cuz that's what friends do."

Rolling my eyes, I move to my side and face her. "My chest hurts and I feel like I can't cry another tear, and then they reappear, and I cry all over again."

"What happened?"

"I can't live with his secrets."

"He's always been mysterious. You can't deny that's not one aspect of what attracted you to him in the first place."

Looking down, I nod. "He's change—"

"Changed? No, he hasn't, Sara Jane. He's exactly the same guy you met years ago. It's *you* who's changed."

I sit up, trying not to be offended. "Geez, thanks." Before I can really get my pout put on properly, I consider what she's saying. I don't want her to be right. But deep down, I think she is. "I met Alexander the day of his mother's funeral. Any parent's death will shape your future, but his mother's case was never solved. He won't rest until he has answers, and his father won't discuss it." Staring up at the ceiling, I add, "I may have been young when we met, but I knew what I was getting into."

"It doesn't mean you have to stay. It's a delicate matter, but it sounds like you're either supporting him or moving on without him. And by the looks of you lying in this bed, although pretty, you look pretty damn stagnant."

"I love him." Resting my head on her shoulder now, I sigh. *Love is tricky. Worth the risk?* Alexander is not just a man who completes me as if I can't be whole without him. He's the man who sought me, pursued me, patiently but persistently waited for me. Enthralled me. He said he was lost when he found me, as if it was a state he believed he'd forever stay in. He'd just lost—brutally—the one person in his life who cherished him. *But he's also the man I said I would always love, cherish, and accept.* Worth the risk to my heart to stay? To continue to adore and relish? "It is worth it. He's worth it, but like his mother's death changed him, *he's* changed me." *I am the strong woman he believes me to be.*

Grabbing the pillow and hugging it to my chest, I look at Shelly. "He's right. He owns me. There is no *me* without him. There never was."

———

Taking one last look in my mirror, I make sure every hair is in place, and that my dress has no wrinkles. I grab my purse and leave my apartment for what might be the first time in days. I'm not sure what I'm doing is the right thing, but two days without Alexander is more than I'm willing to live with. I miss him. I miss his moods and clandestine behavior. I miss his smile and that damn twinkle in his eyes when he wants to make love. I miss his arms around me and the way he holds me so possessively, and his hands on me intimately. I miss the way he makes me feel like me.

I miss him.

The living room was full of flowers, giving Shelly the perfect opportunity to say I told you so. He had been showing it—one white flower after another—each a flag of surrender filled with his apologies.

The valet opens my door and takes my keys. "Good evening, Miss."

"Good evening." My family has money, but like Alexander Kingwood III so rudely pointed out, not on this scale. That uncomfortable feeling twisted in my stomach causes me to place my hand flat against my belly over the black satin of the dress. I walk around the car and to the base of the stairs. Kingwood Manor looms in front of me offensively, momentarily cementing my shoes to the pavement.

My love for Alexander and all of his sides—complicated and mysterious—makes me take the first step. My excitement to see him, to apologize for walking away two days ago, propels me to the door. My thankfulness that he sent flowers to remind me of his love, urges me to walk confidently toward him. I'm greeted with a tray of champagne and take one for courage, drinking half before I reach the main living room.

It's crowded, but not overly so. There are many women and a few men in their twenties by their appearance, but no comfort is found. Lifting up on my toes, I don't see Alexander, but I do make eye contact with his father. He excuses himself with a charming smile and pat on a man's shoulder, then turns to me and comes my way.

I do not like that man. I used to defend him because he was Alexander's family, but like his son, I now despise him.

With a kiss to my cheek in greeting, his hand slides onto my lower back. "It's good to see you, Ms. Grayson. I'm glad you could make it."

Moving out of his hold, I look down, wishing Alexander were here. "Thank you for inviting me."

"Thank you for coming. You look very beautiful this evening."

"Thank you," I reply, daring a glance his way. "Have you seen Alexander?"

"I have. He said something about fresh air, and then I saw he was with a young woman on the terrace. Not sure if they're still there. Maybe they retired to his quarters. You know how restless young men can be."

"How can you say that to me as if that won't hurt? Is that what you're trying to do? Are you trying to hurt me, Mr. Kingwood?"

"I don't want you hurt, Ms. Grayson. I want you well aware of what it's like to be with a Kingwood. There will be times when Alex will be needed to help ease transitions or seal deals. Taking advantage of all of his talents is necessary and wise in business. My apple didn't fall far from the tree. We're more similar than you think."

If it weren't for the classical music piped into the room and the chatter of guests around us, he would hear the shatter of my heart. "The only similarity between you and my Alexander is your gene pool. Nothing more."

His smile is wide, victorious in its expression. "You speak as though I'm heartless. I'm not. I just don't bother with games of the heart. It's a fault my son struggles with."

"It's that trait that makes him human. It's that trait that makes me love him."

"Love is for the weak. As for tonight, I have a house full of investors. Let's hope at least one makes an offer. I want you to fall in line. Kingwood Enterprises comes before family. You want a good life with my son, then help us close some deals." With a smile I know holds no kindness on his face, he says, "Now if you'll excuse me."

I am not equipped to deal with a man of his stature, of his mind games, but I must hold my chin up and face him. "Yes, please *tend* to your guests." We walk away at the same time. I move forward, trying to keep from running. I catch my breath after being under the intensity of his gaze, not realizing how stifling it was back there. I turn my attention to the doors that lead to the large granite terrace over-looking the gardens.

As I approach the picturesque windows that give a full view of the grounds during the day, I can see just enough in the dark to make out Alexander and a woman by his side. A sickness fills my stomach while I maneuver around a few guests and set my glass down on a table before opening one of the doors and walking out.

"I'm not fucking anyone else if that's what you're worried about. I wouldn't do that to you."

Wouldn't do that to you.

But if I left him . . .

His words come rushing back. He told me he would never hurt me but seeing him with this other woman is feeding doubts to my developing insecurity.

It's much quieter out here, only the sound of the music and a private conversation heard. Any other time, I'd love it, but my nightmare has come to life and I stand there, my mind fumbling for reasons to justify what I'm seeing, playing right into the fears his father planted. When I come up empty-handed, I turn to leave, to run, to escape back to the shelter of my apartment, where I should have stayed in the first place.

What was I thinking?

What am I trying to prove?

That I can be strong? That I can handle his secrets? That I can pretend he'll change? That perhaps what I've always felt so sure about—that he couldn't live without me—*was just wishful thinking. Foolishness.*

What am I doing?

What have I become?

"Sara Jane."

With my back to him, I focus on breathing. *Steady. Inhale. One. Two. Three. Exhale.*

His voice is much closer when he asks, "What are you doing here?"

I am strong. I am strong. I am strong. I turn around and see pain written in his brow, the same pain I saw when he was talking about his mother's death. His expression confuses me, and I falter. "I, uh, I . . ." My gaze shifts to his right and I see the tall, beautiful woman looking at me—head to toe and back up again.

She walks past us, and says, "We'll talk soon, Alex."

He nods, but his eyes never leave mine. "Yes. Have a good evening." Stepping closer, he asks me, "Why are you here?"

"I was personally invited."

"No, Sara Jane, *why* are you here?" he grits through his teeth.

"For you. To apologize for walking away the other day."

He raises his hand as if to touch my arm, but restrains himself and lowers it. "You don't owe me an apology. You don't owe me anything. Don't you understand? You're not supposed to be here."

Stupid tears. Stupid damn tears. "I can see I've interrupted. I thought—"

"You didn't *think*. You *felt*. What did I tell you about emotions? What have you done, Firefly?"

"What do you mean, Alexander? I've cried for days. I thought you'd be happy to see me. Don't you love me anymore? Did you ever love me? I came here for you."

"I love you more than you'll ever know. That's why it kills me that you're here." I can't keep the distance between us. I need his arms to hold me, to tell me we'll be okay, to keep me safe, and to warm me from the chill his father left coursing through my bones. As soon as my body touches his, he does just that. Strong arms wrap around my body and his head leans on top of mine. "You shouldn't be here."

"Why?" A cry fills the question. "Why are you being so cryptic?"

"I'm sorry. But you fell into a trap. *His* trap. He wanted you here and you came. Just like he knew you would. Just like I hoped you wouldn't."

Angling my neck, I look up into his eyes that carry the burden of his grief so prevalently. "Your father?"

"He doesn't spend his time on someone unless he wants something from them."

My cloudy thoughts clear, and I step back. "You pushed me away on purpose, didn't you? What does he want from me?"

"Why are you so stubborn?" The pain on his face morphs into something else, something I'm not familiar with seeing on him. "If I hadn't, you would have come tonight. I didn't want that."

"You didn't want me," I reply, my arm rising to the side, "so you could have her?"

"I've tried my best to shield you from this life, but you're not a little girl anymore, so stop acting like it."

"I haven't been a little girl in years, Alexander. You made sure of that."

"You're better off because of it. You're not naïve like you

were. I was helping you. The world is dangerous—"

I take another step back. "I'm starting to think the danger lives here in Kingwood Manor."

"Good. Keep thinking that and leave before it's too late."

"Too late for what?"

"For us."

The grip on my purse loosens and it falls to the ground. Alexander's quick, his hand reaching it just as mine does. We stay there, eye to eye, my breath becoming his and his becoming mine, and then he whispers, "I love you, Firefly." Mesmerized by the sincerity that fills him, I start to speak, but he beats me to it, "Now leave and never come back."

We stand slowly, our hands still touching. Our eyes confined to each other's. With no argument left to give, I take my purse, and he lets go. I turn for the door, and once again, allow *him* to let *me* go. Three years. For this. To be pushed away *in the name of love. "I love you, Firefly."*

Tears don't come this time, anger and shock too potent to let the weaker emotion in. The party carries on, the music playing as a backdrop to the gossip and deals. Even the white glow of candles and flowers filling the room don't mute the ominous dark walls that harbor more buried secrets. I turn back to see him one last time, but Alexander's gone, as if he were a dream all along.

This huge house is filled with haunting memories and sin that wants my soul. My hands begin to shake, an early winter filling my veins, but I dismiss the eeriness. *I know better.* I know Alexander, and he loves me. That's why he tries so hard to protect me. What he doesn't realize is that I will sell my soul on the altar of this manor if I have the chance to stand by his side.

No matter how hard the Kingwoods attempt to scare me away, Alexander is worth the fight. His father may be long gone to the manor and his grief, but I won't let him drag Alexander down with him.

I turn in a circle looking for any sign of him, but none is found. Rushing across the room, I step up the staircase for a better view. That's when I see him just before he disappears down a hall. I hurry, working my way through the guests and down that same path. But when I arrive to where I think he disappeared, I'm alone with extravagant rugs and expensive looking artwork hung meticulously on the walls. "Alexander?" Slowly, I start walking down the long corridor, looking and listening, for any sign of him.

The party fades as I step deeper into the hollows of the mansion. Then I stop when I hear Alexander: "And if I refuse?"

"Don't be daft, Alex. This benefits you as well as me." The hairs on my arm stand when his father speaks.

I move closer until I'm next to an intricately carved wooden door with a large brass lion knocker centered in the middle. I've never been to this part of Kingwood Manor, always too scared to explore on my own. I have no idea what lies beyond it, but my guess is an office by the sounds coming from inside.

Alexander says, "I won't sign."

"You will. You have no choice."

"Seems I have all the choices."

"Not if I cut you off."

"I have my own money."

"What about Ms. Grayson?" I lean closer when his father says my name, his tone disconcerting even and controlled. "She's perfect, Alex. You did well, son."

You did well.

She's perfect.

You did well.

11

SARA JANE

Silence penetrates the thick wood dividing me from *them*—the Kingwoods. I steady myself, my hand against the wall.

"You did well."

I feel dirty.

I feel used.

I feel . . . I'm not sure what I feel. Was it a plot, a ploy all along to lure me in and then what? What was the plan for me? Pushing off the wall, I shouldn't have been eavesdropping, even if they were talking about me. My feet are moving. I need to get out of here, get air that's not polluted with their contemptuous secrets and destructive lies. What did Mr. Kingwood mean? Alexander warned me—he said I fell into his father's trap. Did I? Were they in this together? *That has to be one of the most ridiculous thoughts I've ever had. Surely. Three years is a long time to play some sort of game.* There has to be a logical explanation, but I'm just hurting and need to clear my head. *I hate that I don't really know where I stand.*

Weaving back through the party, I restrain my emotions,

something I should have done years ago. Just as I pass the staircase, I'm grabbed, hand over mouth, and swung around into a dark corner. I know who it is without seeing him. I know the feel of his body against mine, his scent as it fills my lungs, the taste of his skin against my lips, and his voice as he whispers, "So beautifully stubborn."

"Let go of me."

"No."

"Damn you."

"I was damned the day I was born."

"This isn't funny, Alexander. Let go of me."

"We should talk."

"Go talk to your girlfriend outside."

The laughter bellows deep and loud, echoing unabashedly. "Like I said, we should talk." Alexander whips in front of me, leans down until he's eye level, and says, "Let's go to my bedroom."

My body battles between the adrenaline I'm feeling and the heartbreak from overhearing a conversation I was never supposed to hear. "A few minutes ago, you told me to leave and never come back. Now you want me to go to your room to talk? Which is it, Alexander?"

Taking my hand and holding it so tight I can't free myself, he starts walking with a cocky smirk set on his face.

I tug. "Let go of me, Alexander."

"No. We're going upstairs, and we're going to settle this once and for all."

"Once and for all?"

He stops, narrowed eyes landing hard on my saddened blues. "Yes." After taking a breath and releasing it harshly through the air above us, he swallows and shakes his head.

I've loved this man for years. I've loved him since before he was a man. "Fine. Let's talk."

As we wind around back into the party, Alexander raises his chin acknowledging some man and smiling at some woman. I want to claw my way out of this party and hide under my covers. It was warm and cozy there, made me feel safe. The opposite of how I feel here. When we reach his room, the door is shut behind me and we still to the spots where we stand. "You've told me to leave countless times over the years, but when I do, you want me to stay. I don't know what you want from me. I don't even know what I want anymore, except for the pain of doubt to go away."

He's quick and comes to me. Touching my cheek with his free hand, I don't flinch like I should, like my better judgment tells me to. I turn into it involuntarily as if my fate was sealed long before now. "I want you, Firefly." The struggles of his heart capture his expression and the different emotions flicker across his handsome face.

"This isn't healthy for us," I reply on broken emotions.

"I know I told you to leave and never come back, but I can't let you go." Shame falls over him and fills his tall frame. "I haven't cheated on you, but I tried. I tried to destroy us—"

It's not tears that come, but a shiver surging my spine, my hands turning to ice. "You tried to destroy us? You tried to cheat on me? What have you done, Alexander?"

"Nothing. I failed. I've failed you, and I've made that monster proud. Can't you see I will never be good for you?"

"We move in circles—"

"No. We move in figure eights."

"Infinite," I whisper, looking away.

When I tilt my head up, he says, "I can't let you go. The minute you showed up tonight, our fate was sealed."

"You can't stop me."

"I'll try."

"Like you tried to cheat?"

"I'll succeed this time in stopping you." His voice is eerily calm, his gaze fixed on me.

A matching glare is sent right back. "I can't take anymore."

"I can't live without you." His expression wrinkles in confusion. "I would never hurt you, Sara Jane. I'm fucking everything up. I need time to sort through this shit. About the company. About the future. About every fucking thing."

"I don't know anything anymore. I don't think I even know you anymore." I sniffle, hating that damn weakness showing up before I have time to hide it. "I just want to go home."

"I said I would stop you, hoping that was enough to keep you here." Stepping to the side, he adds, "I know it's not. Firefly, I don't want you to go. But if you stay, you have to trust me until it's safe for me to give you everything you need."

"Trust you?" My eyebrows shoot straight up. "You told me it was wrong to come tonight. I still don't know why. I heard what your father said. He said you did well. I've been a pawn in your wicked game."

His eyes tighten closed and his hands go to his side. Stepping away from me, he says, "I—" He stops, the words appearing to break him, harm him in ways that make his shoulders sag as he looks down. All it takes is a moment—to process what's happening, the fact that he's losing me. Resiliency surges when his eyes meet mine again, a passion burns inside like the day I met him. "You haven't been a pawn. Not to me. If you stay, I'll love you until my dying day."

My heart is conflicted. I know he loves me, and that is the balm that coats the inside and heals the wounds. *I just wish I knew what was really going on.* "You say that as if you can keep that promise."

"I can."

"You say that now."

"I say that always. Today. Tomorrow. Now and forever."
He's said that before, but tonight . . .

His struggle to touch me comes in the form of shaking hands in a tight fist. His head falls down, his eyes closing. I want to help him. I want to heal him, but I stay. "I don't know what to think, Alexander. I don't know what to believe."

"Don't believe what you heard, what you've seen, or what you think. Believe in me."

"How?" I whisper. "You haven't been yourself for a while and then when I heard you talking . . . Why would your father say that about me?"

"He thinks you can be useful to him, but you've got to understand, I would never let that happen. I would never let him take advantage of you."

"I need you to be more than some guard against your dad—"

"He's not my dad. He's my father. There's a difference." He sags against the door, his fight leaving his body. "I'll be whatever you need me to be, baby."

"How about honest?"

It's small, but it's full of pride and love when he smiles. "Always so damn feisty."

"I'm serious, Alexander. He said you did *well* in reference to me. What did he mean?"

The smile is wiped clean from his expression, and I'm not sure if it's because I'm holding him accountable or because I've brought the conversation back to his father. Maybe both. "I told him not to speak of you again."

"What is going on?" I move closer, hoping my plea can be seen as easily as it's heard. He licks the corner of his mouth, the heaviness returning, so I say, "Please. With love comes trust. I will never betray you. I swear on my life. You say you'll love me until your dying day, now trust me the same."

"I do." I move closer to him, bridging our troubled waters. Reaching for my hand, he takes it. "It was never about a lack of trust in you, Sara Jane. Please believe me. I never wanted to place my burdens on you. Your heart is too big and you would try to fix something you can't. You try to fix me, and you can't. But if you know that, you'll leave, and I never wanted to lose you. I'm sorry."

"I would try to help you because I love you. Don't you know how helpless I feel when I see you in pain and don't even know what causes it?"

"You know already."

"Your mother's death."

He nods. "I think Kingwood Enterprises is involved."

The weight of this bombshell drops my mouth open. "Oh my God, Alexander. Your father?"

"I'm not sure about my father. My mother was his reason for living. Her death destroyed him. He was always cold, but her death turned him to ice."

"Then why do you think the company is involved?"

"Cruise and I found a lead a year ago that we followed into the district along the river. Two drug dealers were selling to two Kingwood corporate execs. Beyond the problem that we had execs strung out, they were blackmailed into dealing inside their division of the company or risk being exposed."

"What happened?"

"The execs were fired and the dealers . . . we've made a

few enemies in the search for my mother's killer. They plea-bargained their way out of a sentence after we tipped off the cops anonymously. They know who I am. They know I'm involved. They took a deferred sentence in lieu of community service and rehab."

My fingers drag into my hair in shock. "What are you talking about? Are you involved in a drug ring?"

"I'm not using, and I'm not selling, if that's what you're asking."

"But you're involved?" I turn around and close my eyes, hoping this nightmare will go away. Unfortunately I only find the darkness behind my lids, the same as when they're open. I tug my bottom lip under my teeth. My thoughts are rampant, unsettling at best. "What have you done? What have you done to us?"

"I'm sorry."

"It's too late for that. You're in danger. That's what you're telling me, right?"

"You're in danger, Firefly."

Me? I rub my temples and across my closed eyes willing the tears to stay pocketed away. Turning around, I ask, "Is that everything?"

"Last week, one of the execs got out. Cruise contacted him and learned new information."

"About your mother or the company?"

"My mother. He told Cruise he had come across a woman a few times down in the Lower Banks district."

As much as I don't want him involved in anything illegal or worse, something that could get him hurt or killed, I now know the truth. He's not going to give this search up until he has the answers he wants. "And?"

"She was mumbling my father's name and crying. She

was also high as a fucking kite and the last thing she said before passing out was Madeline Kingwood."

"Why would she say your mother's name?"

"That's what I need to find out."

My body bristles. "No, you can't do this. Alexander, you and Cruise are not the police, and it's not safe." I sigh. I can see the resolve in his eyes. His mind is already made up. "Why would he tell you this? I have a feeling it's not out of the kindness of his heart."

"Money. It always comes back to money. If his information pans out, I'll give him ten thousand."

"There's nothing worse than a person with money and a vendetta."

"Actually, there are lots of things that are worse than being rich."

"You can't justify this vigilante behavior to me. You're going to get yourself killed and where does that leave me? Alone and broken-hearted. That's where."

His eyes shift past me. "This is why I tried to protect you."

"You mean keep it from me. Don't be like your father. You're better than him, Alexander. You're better."

"I never promised it would be pretty or normal. I can't give you that 'normal' you want so badly. I can't give that to you. I can't even promise you tomorrow."

"You're scaring me."

"That's why I told you to walk away. To leave me."

"You say that as if I can, as if I could ever walk away from you. I didn't the day I met you, and now I'm three lifetimes buried in too deep." I go to him, not able to keep from touching him any longer.

"I'm a selfish bastard when you deserve a generous soul."

"You are my soul."

Fingers tentatively touch, his hold tightening around me with each passing second that ticks like hours. "I'll never be that guy who works a nine-to-five and home for dinner by six. Kids. God, Firefly, I'd suck at being a dad. I'm so fucking screwed up. I'm willing to put my life at risk. I've put yours at risk to settle the anger inside me, an anger that may never subside. But most of all, I worry I'm like my father. You deserve better."

Cupping his face, I force him to look at me. "But what if you're like your mother? What if I can love you enough to make you forget the anger? What if you can sleep through the night, wake up to me every morning? What if you're the only one I want to be with?"

"Then I'm sorry I ever looked your way. I'm sorry for following you and parking, for making you cross paths with me, for kissing you that first time and not being able to stop myself every time after. I'm sorry I fell in love with you, but I'm more sorry that you fell in love with me, because there's no happy ending to this fairy tale. There's only a means to an end. When that ending comes, you'll be the only one I'll ever regret meeting."

"Don't say that, Alexander." His words cut deep, tears falling from my eyes.

"It's true. Without me following my heart, my stupid fucking emotions that day, you could have had a happy life. But you see, I'm a Kingwood through and through, and being a Kingwood means I'm a bastard bent on going to hell and you're going to pay the price for it."

The side he's been hiding from me was always there, our world revolving around it when my eyes were closed. *I didn't need to fix him.* He's not broken in ways that need bandages. But with my eyes wide open, I know what I need to do. I need to love him. *Fully*. Without reservation or judgment. I need to accept what he's shown me, what he's tried to tell me all along.

I am strong.

I am strong enough to love him.

And I will as if I was born for the job.

Looking at him—his jaw tense, his eyes grayer in his honesty, his heart exposed to me in ways that scare him. He's stunning in his agony, beautiful in his strength, and confident in his love for me. This is the man I fell in love with. Knowing if I go now and leave, this lion of a man would be brought to his knees—the power is intoxicating. This is what he's trained me for—to be the woman strong enough to love him.

"Our relationship may not have been the easiest route to take in life, but it's the only one worth traveling. So bring on your darkness, weigh me down with your burdens, but don't assume I'm that same little girl you met years ago. I'm a woman, and I can handle the truth. I can handle your secrets and I'll keep them safe, but if you lie to me, you'll be the one paying the price."

A brighter blue returns when a spark of light reflects in his eyes. A lustful smile rolls across his lips, and he leans forward. "Do you know how amazing you are?"

His gravitational pull draws me in. I move closer, brushing my lips against his but not kissing them. My tongue dips out, and I run it along the light stubble that dusts his jaw. When I reach his ear, I tug his earlobe between my teeth and bite just hard enough to elicit a reaction. "We're more amazing together."

His breathing deepens, his fingers flexing around my hip. "Don't tease, Firefly."

"I never tease." I slip out of his reach and walk to the

couch, putting distance between us. "I can't live in a web of lies. I'll only stay on one condition."

With eyebrows raised, his gaze softens in curiosity. "From tears to negotiations. You're not that little girl anymore. You grew up when I wasn't looking."

"Should have paid more attention."

"I guess so." His lips quirk up on the right side. "What is your condition?"

I lean back and rest on the arm of the couch. "If you confide in anyone, you confide in me. If you make a major decision, you discuss it with me first. I'm in this relationship, but I'll only stay if I'm an equal in your eyes."

"Will you never understand? You were never an equal. You have always been more. You are everything." Walking to me, he settles between my legs, his hands rubbing the outside of my thighs. "After all we've been through, you're choosing to stay. Why?"

I slide my hands around his middle and pull him closer. "Because you're a part of me, and I'm a part of you. There's not one without the other."

Kneeling before me, the hem of my dress slides up. He pushes my legs apart and kisses my inner thighs. "Say it again."

Hot air coats me, and I repeat, "You're a part of me, and I'm a part you. There's no me without you and no you without me. There never will be." My head falls back and my eyes fall closed. My breath deepens and my chest rises. "Bring on your troubles and lay your darkness down. I'll take it all if it means I get you."

"You have me, Firefly. You will always have me."

Because, love is risky.

And it's worth it.

12

ALEXANDER

It wasn't her stubbornness, though I found that intriguing in the most devious of ways. It was the change I saw in Sara Jane, the one I knew was deep inside her all along, waiting to be born, that reaffirmed what I knew the moment I saw her.

Meeting her at my lowest was something I should feel bad about. It didn't matter though. For whatever reason, she chose to love me. What she didn't realize was I loved her long before we met. My soul was seeking something deeper, something pure, something it could twist within, molding it to mine. There stood my sweet angel, her halo straight and beaming, a guiding light calling me to her. Her innocence was mine for the taking, and I took.

And took.

But now she's rewarded with the strength I urged her to find, rampantly coursing through her veins. She would never bow to any man, and would be above all other women. I did that. For her.

Selfishly, for me.

Sara Jane Grayson, the girl, will wither.

Sara Jane Kingwood, the woman, will rise.

The transformation has begun. Last night, she shed her childhood wish of the white picket fence and the predictable husband. I want her by my side to become the man I need to be to take on the life I've been given. When I look at her, my beautiful sleeping angel, I know she'll be right there, as she was meant to be. The day I met her, fate had played its hand, and I won. Now it's time I return the favor. Leaning down, I slide the hair covering her neck, and kiss her bare skin. "Wake up, Firefly."

A smile lies lazily on her lips, her eyes still closed. "I think I prefer queen."

I smack her ass. "Not yet, though you will be. I have no doubt." Rolling over until my feet land on the carpet, I stand. "Time to get up."

When her eyes open, I see her search out the clock. "It's three in the morning." She rolls over in protest, putting her back to me.

"You said no more secrets."

"I meant in daylight hours." Walking to my closet with a smile on my face, I laugh when she catcalls me. "You have the most amazing body."

"You do. Now stop staring at my ass and get dressed."

The covers fly from her body, and she sits up just as I disappear to pull a sweatshirt from the shelf, jeans from a hanger, and start getting dressed. When she appears in the closet doorway, she leans against it in a way that makes me reconsider leaving altogether. The curve of her ass, the full-ness of her breasts, her hips are womanlier these days. Dirty thoughts run rampant until she asks, "Is something wrong?"

When I look into the depths of her eyes that hold my soul captive, I reply, "Nothing is wrong. Everything is right."

Her smile outshines the sun at dawn, and she comes to

me. Everything I love is wrapped in my arms, naked and bare for me, exposed to the thunderous elements of my raging heart. I'm hoping her goodness far outweighs my bad.

I hate the guilt I feel when I look at her. I met her when she was young enough to fall in love with me. I made her leave me, pushed her so she'd walk away and give herself a chance at happiness. I was cruel, but wanted her to see me for the asshole I was ... I am ...

"This house is huge," Sara Jane notes as we park. I get out. She's been to my home. She knows my friends have money. Lots of money, but she still seems surprised by the wealth when gawking at the house.

When I take her hand in mine, my fingers wrap around it, reminding me how small she is compared to me. A sinking feeling fills my stomach as I lead my innocent, intelligent, and beautiful girlfriend to the slaughter. I've put this off for a long time, but she insisted on meeting my "friends."

A warning was not enough. They may have money but they aren't sophisticated. This world is a real life cruel, teen drama. Everybody wants something and is willing to barter, steal, or trade to get it. That includes sex, drugs, and other dirty dealings that would shame their family name if it ever got out. I have a feeling, like me, they didn't fall far from their family tree. Their parents are just as devious as we are.

I fucked Lanie Monroe's mother a couple nights before my mother's funeral. She came over to bring me comfort food but had forgotten the food. She was in her late thirties at the time, and hot as fuck. Her advanced yoga practice was put into use that night. I was a fucking punk and bragged to everyone the next day. Lanie found out and approached me after class. She was waiting at my car, pissed. Not twenty minutes later, I had her bent over a large rock in the woods near campus. I fucked her without regret, never even kissing her. She begged me to tell her she was better. I lied and told her what she wanted to hear.

We're all fucked up in some way or another, the privileged lives our families afford us dooming us to seek thrills and attention in new ways. I regret how I treated Lanie that day because now I know it was never about her need for attention or the competition with her mother. It was about me and my need to ruin not just my life but everything that came in contact with it. I've used my gift in looks as a weapon too many times to count. A great face is like a free pass to destruction.

The moment I laid eyes on Sara Jane, I knew I would never be the same. She's better than this, better than us. Although she's gorgeous, it wasn't just her looks that drew me to her. It's not just how clever she is that keeps me on my toes. It's not even her patience, which she seems to have in spades when it comes to me. It's everything. How do I expose her to this seedy side of people who've lost their way, sold their morals for the next hit, and will eat her innocence alive, spitting her out for entertainment?

My feet stop just before we reach the front door. "Let's go. I'll take you to dinner and for ice cream after."

Her hip kicks out and her head tilts as she smiles. "Are you nervous to introduce me to your friends?"

"Barely. They are barely my friends. You've met Cruise. You already know Chad. Those are my friends. You are my best friend, so let's go. Anywhere you want to go I'll take you."

"You're my best friend too, Alexander." She takes the last step, and nods toward the door. "Come on. I want to see this part of your life."

... I should have never done what I did to her that night. Does heaven operate on credits and debits? Can her kindness wash away my sins? Or am I destined to burn in hell?

She makes it easy to believe I'm not too far gone.

She is still too soft.

Too vulnerable.

Too good.

I kiss the top of her head, knowing I'm not going to stay, although I wish I could for her. The habits are too ingrained in me. A worse one forming now that I'm bringing her with me. It's a habit I could get used to. "Get dressed," I say, releasing her and leaving the confines of the closet.

Sitting on the couch, I wait for her to finish getting ready. My attention is drawn toward the bathroom when she asks, "Are we going to be out all night?"

Standing, flaunting my feathers like a damn peacock in pride, I smile. "Not with you looking that edible."

I receive a smile as reward. "You sure can be charming, Mr. Kingwood, when you want to be."

"I can be lots of things. Some are just more acceptable than others."

"It's too early in the morning to try to decipher your riddles." She heads for the door. "Come on. The suspense is killing me."

Meeting her at the door, I open it and wave my arm, gesturing for her to go first. We make it to the top of the stairs before she stops, looks back at me, and says, "I used to love this place. I thought it was fancy."

"And now?"

"Now there's something sinister seeping from the walls. I'm starting to think danger lives in Kingwood Manor."

My firefly was too smart for her own good. "So you don't want to live here one day?" I ask, smiling, thrilled the shine has finally worn off. Now she can see things for how they really are. I need to know she's staying for the right reasons.

She starts down the stairs. "I don't need all this." As much as I like her flexing her newfound strength, I like being able to protect her too. I want her strong, but I also want her to need me.

My smile grows. One thing I know about Sara Jane Grayson is that I can offer her the world and she'd only want an acre. One of the many reasons I love her. My smile is wiped away when I hear, "It's late to be sneaking around, don't you think, son?"

We both stop a few steps from the bottom and turn toward the living room where the monster himself sits, a tiger baiting his prey.

I take Sara Jane's hand and reply, "If it was broad daylight, I wouldn't need to sneak."

"You're twenty-two. Sneaking out is for children. You know you can come and go as you please." His eyes are set on Sara Jane. "I was disappointed you left the party so early."

She glances to me then back to him, questions in her irises. "I was tired."

My father looks dissatisfied with her response. Turning his attention back to me, he says, "There were people I wanted you to meet—"

"I brought you Scotch on the rocks, just how you like it." A woman stops short when she sees us. The lights are dim, but I can tell who it is. She stands between my father and me, and says, "Alex?"

Snapping his fingers, he brings her eyes back to him. "You should go, Carinna."

Sara Jane's hand tightens around mine. It's obvious she recognizes her too. The woman I was talking business with during the party sets a glass down on an antique table next to him. I know he won't be able to leave it there for long. He reaches for it and says, "Thanks for the drink, sweetheart . . . and the company," effectively dismissing her.

"You want me to leave at three a.m.?" I'm not surprised she's insulted.

Sara Jane looks up at me, waiting for me to make the first move. I move down two steps until we're even and then we walk the rest of the way down together. "Good night, Father. Carinna."

Behind our backs, Carinna says, "We just had sex, and now you're kicking me out?"

"It was good. It wasn't good enough for me to want you to stay."

I whisk Sara Jane out the front door not wanting her to hear how my father treats the people in his life. I'm not willing to risk her realizing what I'm made of, although from the interactions she has had with him, I think she already knows. Taking her to the garage, I input the code and the sixth garage door rolls open. We stand there side by side in silence. Then she takes a step forward and a few more until she's standing in front of my newest purchase—a base Harley-Davidson Iron 883 with custom everything. Down to my name, King, embossed into the leather seat. Whipping around to me, she asks, "Is this yours?"

Nodding, I hope she doesn't kick my ass for not telling her sooner.

She touches the matte black chrome and leather seat, then takes a step back. Closing her eyes, she rubs her temples. When she reopens them, she asks, "I thought the bike was a phase?"

"No." I keep it simple.

"It looks new."

"My old bike was run-down, so I replaced it."

"It looks expensive. This will make you a target for thieves, which doesn't thrill me, Alexander."

She thinks riding a motorcycle is risking my life on the

regular. We agree to disagree on this, or so I thought, but now she's throwing in the robbery card. "It was custom-made for me. I couldn't have designed a better bike."

Her hand goes to her hip. "*I couldn't have designed a better bike.* Alexander, do you hear yourself?" Her sass is bordering between cute and annoyance.

"You think you're invincible, but you're not. I don't want to lose you."

"You'll never lose me unless you leave. Although, you're too damn stubborn to take good advice when it's given."

The fight leaves her voice, and she moves closer to the bike. "Have you hidden this from me not feeling you could tell me?" *Yes, but I can't tell her that.* My firefly always worries about me, my safety. Why would I give her more to worry about?

"I'm trying, Sara Jane."

She sighs and walks the length of the bike, inspecting it. When she looks up, she asks, "Are we going?"

There's my feisty little woman. I go to the cabinet, flip my keys from my pocket, and open it. When I turn to her, I present the special helmet I had made for her, approaching with care. She never liked riding a motorcycle, so we always took her car. This time, she doesn't protest. I slide the shiny black helmet down over her head, and snap the band under her chin. I kiss her nose and then adjust the bike up, lift the kickstand, swing my leg over, and settle on to the saddle. "Hop on." She does, and readjusts until she's comfortable and flush against me. Her arms come around my middle. "Hold on tight, okay?"

"Okay." She leans her cheek against my back and asks, "You still refuse to wear a helmet?"

"I don't need one."

"But I do?"

"Yes. I won't risk your life on a thrill."

"What about you?"

"I need you to stop worrying about me."

"That's not going to happen." Her response comes quick and definitive, making me smile.

"Hang on tight, Firefly." I start the bike.

"I've been doing that since the day we met." Despite the rumbling of the loud exhaust, she's not scared. Her body is relaxed around me, and I cover her hand with mine.

Moving my hands to the handlebars, I wrap my fingers around them firmly, and then take off down the driveway. The gate at the bottom of the property opens wide for us, and we're off into the night.

Sometimes trust comes in ways that aren't earned. There's no reason for Sara Jane to be with me right now. There's no justification for all the secrets and lies I've told her over the years that explains why she shouldn't dump my ass for good. But something inside me knew she was meant to be mine, something so innately good in her to take the chance. I have no doubt that my mother played a part in putting Sara Jane in my path that day. She has loved me since, without limits, without expectations except to be loved in return. Her forgiving heart allows me to work toward forgiving myself.

When I park a short time later, she sits up, and looks around. Let's just hope once she sees what's really going on, she can hold on to that forgiveness.

13

SARA JANE

oly Shit!

"I can explain," Alexander says. He's smart to keep a safe distance behind me.

"You better, and fast because my mind is spinning to assumptions you're not going to like."

Surrounded by floor-to-ceiling glass walls overlooking what seems like the entire city as their backdrop, my mouth has fallen open from the view, and from the technology that fills this spacious penthouse apartment. Alexander touches my lower back, but I step out of his reach. He knows I'm pissed without the obvious gestures, but I want it to be clear to everyone here. I feel betrayed. I feel betrayed by everyone in this room.

Cruise, Chad, and Shelly remain quiet as they stare at me with wide eyes.

Alexander says, "It started as a small operation and has grown."

"Grown?" My mind struggles to piece together the puzzle before me. I turn to Shelly, her betrayal and lies cutting me as deep as Alexander's. "Why are you here?"

The answer doesn't come fast, her cautiousness taking over. "It's not what it—"

"It's not?" I strike back. "Because this looks exactly like everyone I know was in on whatever this is except me."

She replies, "I'm only here because most nights this is where Chad stays." *This is where Chad stays. Shelly had the choice to stay with her boyfriend, knowing that night after night, mine left me. What the hell?*

"How did I not know about this? How could you lie to my face?"

Standing behind Chad, she looks worried. "I was alone in the apartment anyway. You weren't there. You were at the manor."

At the manor—secluded, protected, deceived by everyone around me who I thought were my friends, and by Alexander who I can't even look at right now. "Locked away like Rapunzel." I look her in the eyes, but she looks away. "I trusted you. You were my best friend."

"I still am, Sara Jane. Please," she says, grasping my arms. "I'm your best friend. Everything was to protect you."

"While everyone else lived in reality, I've been living a charade."

Shelly knows this is going to take me time and walks away. "I'm sorry," is mumbled.

Alexander takes my hand and though I try to pull away, he doesn't let me this time. "You weren't locked away or living a charade. You chose to see what you wanted."

"I was blind, but now I see the big picture, and I'm not sure what to think."

"Don't jump to judgments."

"Alexander, stop. Just stop. I don't need you to fill in every silent second. I need to process that you have some kind of *operation* setup that could rival the CIA." Four large desktop computers anchor the room, with three smaller laptops open and running some scanning program. The furniture is leather and sleek, the stark-white kitchen is off to the side with a clear glass table covered in photos laid out like an investigation. Cruise sits quietly in the corner, looking as if we interrupted something but wise to not speak.

Chad sits at a desk near the kitchen. I'm so confused why the three of them are here in this makeshift computer lab, so I ask the one person who owes me nothing, but will be honest—Chad. "Why are you here?" He's never been able to lie to me. Friends since high school, I'm hoping that trait is still intact, but who knows since he's been hanging around Cruise and Alexander. My annoyance is at an all-time high. The fact that I have been kept out is sobering and irritating.

Chad looks worried. He should be. He thinks Alexander is tough. Well I'm tougher. His voice is quiet, but he replies, "This job helps me pay for school."

"Job?" My eyes turn to Alexander. "What is he talking about? What is this place?"

Alexander looks much too relaxed for someone whose girlfriend has just found out more lies he's been hiding. He smiles that wry grin that usually gets him out of it just as quickly, but it won't work on me now. I'm way too fired up. He says, "Babe, this is where we conduct our searches."

"What searches? Your mother's murderer?"

"Not just that, though that is a priority." *In the middle of the night?*

"Alexan—Never mind." I'm so hurt. I can't think of anything rational or kind to say. One bombshell after the other has been dropped tonight. I am strong, but at what point do I say enough? With questions swirling around my head—How long has this been going on? Can we continue our relationship under this new revelation? Can my heart heal?—I realize they can't give me the answers. They don't have them. That's what this is about. And like Alexander said earlier, I'll get what I need in time. Hopefully we all will. I have to trust him until then. But the room feels warm, and with my vulnerability exposed, I need a minute. "I'm going to get some fresh air. You guys can get back to whatever it is you're doing here."

I walk out onto the large balcony, leaving the sliding glass door open. The frantic, but hushed voices drift outside, though I can't understand anything spoken, except when Alexander says, "Don't worry. She'll be okay."

Will I?

I take a deep breath. *Yes, I will.* If nothing else, the one positive I can find instantly is that when Alexander is here, he's safe. There's comfort that comes with the answers I've found tonight.

Looking out over the city, I didn't pay much attention to where we were going or when we arrived. I had no idea whose building this was, or who lived here. It's clear though. Cruise is from a wealthy family, meeting Alexander when they attended the same prestigious private school when they were younger, but his parents cut him off when he got a job at Kingwood Enterprises. I don't know what he does there, but I know he can't afford a penthouse in the middle of downtown. Nor can Chad who goes to school on scholarships just like he did back when we were at our private Catholic high school.

Alexander can.

He can afford to indulge any whim he has, especially his life's mission.

A shiver runs up my spine and the breeze fills my nose with his scent. I don't have to turn around. I know he's there.

Before he can downplay the situation, I say, "First the motorcycle, now this." Turning my back to the railing, I hold on to it for support. His body is a silhouette with the lights from inside haloing him. "This seems more like an obsession. I'm trying to understand, but this is so much more than I could have imagined. This is about your mother?"

"That's my priority, Firefly."

"I thought I was, but seeing this, having everyone know except for me . . . I'm not sure what you're really doing or how I fit into the big picture. Your picture. Our picture. Our future. We just made declarations that I meant."

He sighs. "I meant mine too."

"You've said you trust me."

"I trust you with everything that matters."

My head jolts back. "This really seems to matter to you by the lengths of deceit you've gone to keeping me out."

"We work with people I don't want you around. These are the people leading us to the answers I want. You don't realize the role you've played, but you being here for me has been everything. I couldn't have done this without you, knowing I had you to come home to. You've given me the strength to do what I needed to do."

"I feel betrayed, Alexander. I felt crazy before, paranoid that you were up to something behind my back, and maybe cheating."

"I hope this gives you some relief then. I only hid it to protect you." *From what? And why . . . how could Shelly lie to me so easily?*

"You always say that. Am I that fragile?"

"You have so much going on in your life—"

"That doesn't mean I don't want you, all of you, being a part of it. I can handle more than you give me credit for."

Signaling inside to the others, I say, "I can handle this. If you have my friends involved, I should be involved."

"Chad is a damn good programmer and hacker. I needed him because I needed information. He's paid well. Don't be mad at Shelly. She wanted to tell you. I kept her from doing it."

"How?" Rubbing my temples, I lower my gaze to our shoes. "She's my best friend, and you had her lying to my face."

"She wanted to be with Chad. Chad works most nights because of his school load. Shelly was around enough to where she just started helping out where she could. People trust her."

"I used to trust her," I reply, looking him directly in the eyes.

"You still can. Don't take the anger that should be directed at me out on Shelly. She wanted you to know. We've struggled with this for a while, but she doesn't know what Cruise and I know. She's been a good friend to you."

"And a better one to you." I won't get anywhere with him or any of them if I make accusations. I'm willing to listen to learn what they do know. "What about Cruise?"

"He's like my brother. My mission is his mission."

"What does that mean? Is what you're doing legal, Alexander?"

"No. For the most part."

So matter of fact, so without care for repercussions. No beating around the bush. He just lays it out there that he, my boyfriend, is the head of some investigative syndicate, and I had no idea. Until now. "This is doing my head in."

He steps closer, and I lower my head, letting him cage me in his arms. His voice is low, calm, reassuring, though

I'm not feeling the effects. "My life is wide open for scrutiny. You've now seen my truths."

"Have I?" I ask, looking up into his eyes. "Or is there another bombshell in your back pocket?"

"I started this to find out who killed my mother. I needed to know. I didn't know this would grow, but the deeper Cruise and I searched for one murderer, more criminals were identified. Including my father. He turned a twenty-million-dollar company into a two-billion-dollar corporation. Nobody does that keeping everything legal."

"Bill Gates did."

"We can volley back and forth all night if you want, but I'd rather show you what we're doing." He tugs the belt loop of my jeans and says, "Come back inside."

I stay still. "How much are you going to show me?"

"Anything."

Crossing my arms over my chest, I correct him, "Everything, Alexander."

"Fine. I'll show you everything." He tugs again, and I finally relent, and we go inside. I sit down on a chair in the center, and he grabs a bottle of water from the fridge as if we're hanging out any other night. Maybe he is, but I'm still in shock by the setup. After taking a long gulp, he leans against the counter. "Two years ago—"

"Two years ago?" I ask, my question coming out an octave higher.

"I'm sorry," he says quickly.

Looking down, my hands twist in my lap. "You've kept me in the dark most of our relationship."

Making his way over, he sits on the steel table in front of me and takes my hands in his. "I didn't want you involved."

"I'm involved because I love you. I thought you loved me."

"Don't say that. You know better because you know me."

"I don't know anything anymore, but here we are, so tell me the rest."

He moves to the couch and says, "We went to where she was killed and started from there. You know the rest."

"So you're searching for druggies to give you answers?"

"Yes. More or less. The problem was, the more we dug the more we discovered a singular connection. Kingwood Enterprises."

My chest burns and I release a long slow breath. I feel the crinkle in my forehead as I take in the information. "You keep saying this but I don't understand how it comes back to him, why this woman you found will have the answers you need."

"I don't know. I just know I need to follow my gut and that tells me to talk to her. I have to have more information."

"But you know this isn't safe. That's really why you didn't tell me."

"I'm not scared, Sara Jane."

"You should be, Alexander. You don't know what you're walking into. This is not a caped crusader game you're playing. These are bad people you're dealing with, so if I have any say in the matt—"

"You don't. You're not going to argue with me about this. I've dealt with bad people. You met my friends from high school. You saw how they treated people. Sometimes people just abuse the life they've been given."

"Yes, spoiled rich kids and their privileged lifestyles can lead to bad things, but it's not the same kind of people who make their money off the pain of others."

His eyes narrow on mine. "I can read between the lines. You think I do this because I can. It's not that."

"You're going to get yourself killed, and for what? An answer to someone's death?"

"Not someone's death. My mother's."

"And then you leave me, here on earth, to avenge *your* death. We can continue this vicious cycle over and over. Please. Turn the information you have over to the police, and let them follow the lead."

Standing abruptly, he turns his back to me. "I can't. You know this. I've told you. Her case has been buried and bought, and they will never find the killer because they've been paid to drop the search."

His pain drips into his words. She was the only person who he felt loved by. The only person who intentionally spent time with him just to love and adore him. *I don't know the pain he's feeling, but I know it would eviscerate my heart if my mom died, though.* I stand up to hug him from behind. With my cheek to his back, I say, "Okay, Alexander."

His hands and arms cover mine, and he releases a breath. "Thank you." Slipping from my grasp, he walks away and looks over Cruise's shoulder at the monitor on the desk.

I'm not sure what to do, so I sit on the couch and observe. Shelly's quick to sit next to me, but I keep my eyes forward. She must feel terrible, and she should. We've never had secrets. Never. Not even when Tuck Bennice groped my ass under my skirt in the library in ninth grade. The second I saw Shelly at lunch, she cornered me in the girls' bathroom, seeing I was not my normal self, and gave me a look. The expression on her face was both intimidating and reassuring if that's even possible. But I told her what happened because I knew I could trust her. No one ever found out about the groping just as I planned, but Tuck took a nosedive in the school parking lot two days later, breaking his nose on the curb. She deserved an Oscar for that performance. To this day she claims he fell, but I know better because I know her and what our friendship means to her. Or did . . .

She says, "Please don't be mad."

My gaze slides over to her. "How can I not be?"

She sighs and leans back. "I haven't been involved for very long, which I know is no excuse. Would you believe me if I told you that it may seem illegal—"

"Not seem. *Is.* What you guys are doing is illegal. If it wasn't, there would have been no need to hide it or 'protect' me."

"Fine. You say potato. But I look at it like the show *Dexter*. He's doing it for the greater good."

"Don't be fooled, Shelly. The benefits to society aren't as great as you think."

"Why are you being so hard on him?"

Pushing off the soft, gray leather, I reply, "Because it's a house of cards. When it falls, he does. And there will be nothing I can do to stop it."

"I don't want you to stop it," Alexander says brusquely. "I don't want you anywhere near this. What I want is for you to go to school, get the job you want, and be happy."

"With you?"

"Yes, because I'm not doing this bullshit back-and-forth dance with you anymore, Sara Jane. This is it for both of us. We made promises, and we're going to keep them."

"I won't be part of anything illegal."

"I don't want you a part of anything illegal either."

Cruise's eyes are set on me. He says, "He didn't want you to know. I don't know what happened to change his mind or why he brought you here tonight. You know I like you, Sara Jane. As Alexander's woman, I'll give you the respect you deserve. But you're not cut out for this. I'm just wondering if you can keep this to yourself, because if you can't, we *all* go down."

"Careful, Cruise," Alexander cautions.

Cruise is not one for soliloquies, but when he stands, he speaks as if I'm not here at all. "She's a liability, which is why you kept her in the dark." His arms rise. "What the fuck were you thinking? Let me guess, your dick made this decision?"

He's grabbed so fast that I'm startled. Alexander pushes him backward by the chest and has him pinned to a wall, holding him eye level in seconds flat. "Don't. Don't ever fucking talk about her like that again." His voice is a growl, violence in his words. "Or I will end you."

Cruise shoves Alexander off, and then straightens his shirt while eyeing him. "Fuck you, King."

"King," Alexander snarls. "Remember that."

Walking away, Cruise knocks a lamp off a table as he passes, heading down a dark hall. A door slams, and my gaze is directed back to Alexander. His anger is flared through harsh breaths. His eyes hardened as he stares at the hallway.

I stand but stay, worried I've caused them to fight. "I'm sorry."

"Don't apologize, Firefly," Alexander snaps. "You don't owe anyone an apology."

Twisting my fingers together, I whisper, "I don't want you fighting because of me."

"We're not. We're fighting because he's forgotten what affords him his life. And to be clear, *I do*."

I glance to Shelly who's sitting quietly in the corner. Chad's eyes return to the screen in front of him. Pretending everything is normal seems like a good plan right now. He has a luxury I don't. Moving closer to Alexander, I place my palms gently on his chest. Standing toe to toe, I say, "You don't have to prove anything to me."

Grasping my face in his hands, he sighs heavily. "When are you going to figure it out? This is for you, for us. Cruise will be fine. He's tired. He'll be fine."

"Will your friendship?"

"I only need you."

Holding him by the middle, my fingers pressing into him, I plead, "I can be your safe place to land each night. But you need your friends, too. You need more than me, Alexander. Don't throw away what's important to hold on to me. I'll be here. No matter what." His lips press to my forehead, and he lingers there. My eyes close as I savor the gentle touch. "I don't want you fighting with him or anyone over me."

Pulling back, he says, "Without you, I have nothing left to fight for."

"Fight for your future. Fight for your mother. Fight for your family's company. I can take care of myself."

Cruise returns and stands at the other side around the couch, away from us. "I'm on your side." His eyes flicker between us. "Remember that."

Alexander stands tall, power strengthening his spine. He turns away from me and heads for the balcony. One nod tells Cruise to follow him, and he does without a word.

When they're out of earshot, Shelly says, "His temper is going to be his downfall." When I look at her, she's watching them through the window. Turning back to me, she whispers, "You'll either save him, or he'll take you down with him."

"That's ominous." Sarcasm . . . not the best choice.

"The truth is ugly, but *you* still wanted it." This is not the Shelly I've known for more than half my life standing next to me. "I've lied to you. I'm sorry about that. Now that you know everything, I won't do it again, not even if the lie is easier to tell."

"What do I do?"

Chad looks up when I ask the dreaded question. "Sara Jane, I'm working for Alexander because I believe in his pursuit of justice. But also, I'm angered by the corruption and obscene crimes we continue to uncover. You've known and trusted *me* for a long time. And I trust him." I nod my head. Part of me feels chastised by both Shelly and Chad, but I also feel justified in my anger and hurt.

The truth is ugly, but you still wanted it.

And I trust him.

I look to Shelly who says, "Follow your heart."

"That's what got me here."

Alexander and Cruise catch our attention when they shake hands, then bring it in bumping chests. With no smile in sight, Alexander says something and they both glance at me. He's biting his lip when he comes back then releases it with my name rolling off his tongue, "Sara Jane, I need to head out for a while." I feel instant panic. "I'm taking you back to the manor."

"Wait. No. You brought me here for a reason." I hate the plea in my tone.

He heads for the door, ending the discussion.

I cross my arms over my chest, and figuratively dig my heels in for the battle. "You promised, Alexander. You promised me I could trust you, and you would be open about what's going on."

Whipping around, the fury in his eyes penetrates parts of me and causes me to gasp in astonishment. His presence is menacing as he returns to me in two large strides. "Sara Jane. You're not my keeper. This is a business I'm running here, and I need to tend to an issue that has arisen. Period. I won't ask for permission. I will include you to the point I can, and that is to keep you protected from the bastards out there who don't give a fuck about our lives." He points to the others in the room so I know he is not just talking about him and me.

Despite the humiliating tears in my eyes, I find my own power and cross my arms. "Okay, but I will not go back to the manor. I'm not leaving."

Leaning even closer, tilting his head, his gaze hits mine hard. "What are you doing?"

"Facing the facts. I'm in now. But I feel safer here than at your home, especially after spending time with your father lately." Taking his hands in mine, I add, "I'm your friend. Your soul mate. Your family."

"I need to know you're safe." He looks down. "That's the only thing that allows me to pursue these leads."

"Nothing's going to happen to me. You've made sure I'm safe. But look at me." When he does, I whisper, "I can take care of myself. Part of not shutting me out is trusting I can be more to you now that I have some idea of what you need. I love you, both the dark and light."

"Why are you so difficult?"

"Because I let things slide for too long, and like you, I'm in too deep. So I either keep threatening you, which obviously does no good, or I join you."

"I don't want you to join me. I want you to be safe, by my side. But safe."

"I can do that."

"There's no going back once you do."

Resolve traverses around my heart, sealing it in strength and momentum. "There's no going back already. If I've caused discourse by being here, too bad. I'm staying. For us, Alexander. It's for us."

"It's not saf—"

"No one is going to hurt me. As long as we're together, I'm fine."

"I won't survive if I don't have you."

"That's why I'm staying. We're a team."

A smile appears, one that tends toward amused. "I always loved how feisty you are, even if it drives me crazy at times."

I shrug my shoulders. This is not new information, but I feel settled somewhat. "I'm going to make sure you have your happy ending, Alexander."

"Why?"

"I know you're good inside, and I'm going to help you find it again."

And there is the smile I fell in love with. It's a mixture of vulnerable boy and cocky man. Mischievous, adorable, and sexy all in one. "You're willing to fight for me?"

I wrap my arms around him, leaning against his chest. His arms come around me, and I whisper, "We're more than people in love. We're souls entwined in eternity."

"Thank you, Firefly. Please always fight for us."

Tilting my head up, I look at him. "I will. That's a promise I'll keep."

Strong arms hold me tight. His chin rests on the top of my head. I close my eyes. I have to be brave. I can sense that his hurricane is brewing. I just have to ride out the storm along with him.

Everything he's taught me—free-thinking, wanting me to be strong—shows me what matters: love. This is it. This is the time I must be the person he believes me to be. This is the time I prove how strong I am.

14

ALEXANDER

Pulling the piece of paper from my pocket, I double-check the address and look up at the door. The painted letters are faded. Bricks are covered in soot and garbage litters the ground. The alley I face has a working light, but it's dark between the other end that's lit and me. I rev my bike and glance at Cruise. He nods and takes the lead, riding ahead of me. Once we reach the end, we stop under the lamp rigged to the side of the building.

I cut the engine and pocket my key. "This is it," I say, looking up at the dark red door. A paint job couldn't save this door. The wood is rotted, the handle barely hanging on by a screw. There's not a lock in sight, so I open it before I can talk myself out of it. Cruise follows me inside, but his hand hits my arm and he takes the lead.

The building appears abandoned as reported by the guy who tipped us off, but I'm not dumb enough to believe that. My gut feeling says we are not alone. The screech of a cat causes Cruise to jump, but I remain steady on our quest, as I know this tip will pay off.

A lamp on the far side of the room illuminates a worn-out sofa with exposed springs and spider webs. A woman lies on top of it in a ragged dress. I would wager she's no older than my father, but with skin that's peeked into death's door, she looks well over seventy. Staring at her eyes, they're wide open but vacant. "April?"

Her light-colored eyes pivot my way as I shine my phone down, using the flashlight to get a solid look at her. She mumbles, "Did you bring me something?"

"What do you want?"

"Anything to take away this feeling."

"What feeling is that?"

"Life." She sits up, hunches forward on her knees, but keeps her eyes on me. "I've seen you."

"You know me?"

"No. I've only seen you."

"Where?"

"You look like your father when I knew him."

"You know my father?" I ask, shocked.

Sitting back, she laughs as well as an empty shell of a person can. "I know him. Why are you here, rich boy?"

I'm intrigued that she knows anything about me, much less seems to actually know my father, when I just heard her name recently. "I was told you might have some information on my mother."

Her smile disappears, and she drags her dirty forearm across her lips. "I don't know anything about her."

"How do you know my father?"

"You got anything?"

In high school, I had friends and made connections between buyers and sellers, though I was never a dealer. That knowledge helped when I started searching for my mother's killer. I was around addicts enough to know what she wants. "No." I hold firm in front of her, needing answers.

She stands and walks around the couch. Her hair is matted and hasn't been washed in a long time; the stench is either coming from her or the sofa. It's indistinguishable. "Did he send you here like the last guys?"

"Last guys?"

Leaning against a broken doorway, she faces me, but her eyes shift quickly between Cruise and me. "He tried to kill me. More than once."

"Who?"

"You look so much like him. What's your name?" I hesitate. She holds her fingers to her mouth like she has a cigarette between them. She doesn't. With a grin that lifts easily on one side, she says, "You don't have to tell me. I know already. I know. I know you. I used to see you as a baby. He even let me hold you once."

Reason is hard to hold on to when you're looking into the eyes of a crazy person. "Why would he do that?"

"You should ask your father." She taps her imaginary cigarette, and asks,

"Why are you really here, Alex? Do you go by Alex like your dad?"

"Why did my father try to kill you?"

"For your mother." Her voice is too steady, too comfortable, speaking of my mother as if she would harm a fly much less a human. "I need money." She slinks closer. "You're so handsome." When she tries to touch my face, I back away. "Discount for your friend if you have cash."

I dig out a hundred-dollar bill and toss it on the couch. "Don't waste it. What is your last name, April?"

"How did you find me?"

"Your drug dealer."

"Kingwood," she replies, her eyes growing heavy as she slumps back down on the couch. "I know you. Alex Kingwood." *Alex Kingwood*. She knows my name. "Bring me food." For someone so drugged, she certainly seems to have lucid moments.

Cruise hits me on the arm. "We should go."

I should be mad over the lack of real answers, but she's a mess and I'm lucky I got what I did from her. "I'll bring you something next time. Take the money and get yourself something to eat."

I turn and start for the broken door but stop when she says, "She said you were a good boy."

When I turn back, her eyes are closing, her body sinking onto the couch until she falls sideways. Running back, I try to catch her before she passes out, but I'm too late. Her chest is rising and falling. Her sleep is deep. "Fuck." I ask Cruise, "What do I do?"

"She can't ride a bike in that condition."

Staring at her, I run my fingers through my hair. "I need to get home and talk to my father." I have to leave her here, even though the place is every shade of vile. "Send her some food tomorrow and every day after."

"I'll take care of it."

My Harley hides in the night—the matte black sleek, the price point just as high-end as the custom-built bike. It's not meant for neighborhoods like this, neither are Cruise and I. It makes me wonder if we're in over our heads, or in too deep, like I told Sara Jane.

Sweet Sara Jane. She's going to be the death of me if I don't get myself killed first. The woman's got me by the balls and heart, and I think she's finally figured that out. I speed down the alley and round onto the street. Cruise is next to me as we head to the bridge.

Looking over, I see his smile and roll my eyes. That situation may have been a mess, but after years of research and dead-end leads, it's good to have something to chase down. I feel victorious. I enjoy the wind blowing through my hair, the chill of the night coursing through my veins, and the anticipation of returning to Sara Jane.

Shelly took her to the manor when I left. She wanted to go to bed, be there for me when I return. Maybe that's how we are now—open and honest—with everything out on the table. No more secrets. A weight has been lifted from my shoulders. I float toward the light, allowing the weight to sink to the dark.

I like this feeling. Floating to the surface instead of drowning. Peace. It brings me peace that I don't have to do this alone, behind a cloak of deceit. *Together* we're strong enough to make it. My father was so wrong. "*Part of not shutting me out is trusting I can be more to you now I have some idea of what you need. I love you, both the dark and light.*" Fuck, I'm a lucky bastard.

When we cross the bridge, I lift my left hand and wave once. Cruise nods and takes off down a side street that leads to the penthouse. I drive straight. I have a lot of shit to deal with when it comes to my father, but that's nothing new. Our relationship is complicated, and I don't see that changing anytime soon.

Fifteen minutes later, I've entered the prestigious neighborhood that my family's manor anchors at the end. The gates of the driveway open, and I speed up until I reach the garage. It opens and I pull inside, parking the bike.

I hurry inside, my anger tempered by thoughts of Sara Jane. Taking the stairs by two, once I reach the top, I rush down the corridor to my quarters. The house is quiet, the hour just going on five. I open the door quietly. My sweet angel is asleep on the bed, the room tinted blue from the moonlight filling it.

Unzipping my leather jacket, I let it slide down my arms and toss it on the couch. I toe off my shoes while unbuttoning my shirt. I drop it on the floor and walk into the bathroom. Whipping my undershirt off, I toss it to the hamper, and miss, but I don't care. I leave it and strip down my jeans. After brushing my teeth and taking a piss, I walk back into the room and climb into bed, hoping I don't wake her.

I'm too restless, my body wide awake, my mind reeling with everything from confessing to Sara Jane to April and her connection to my father and me. *"I know you. Alex Kingwood." What did April mean?*

Lying next to Sara Jane, I see the freckle she has just above her upper lip on the right side near the center. She didn't have it when I met her. It's something that became a part of who she is, a lot like me. A lot like she is to me as well.

When I was little, I once caught a firefly and ran to the terrace to show my mom. When I opened my hand, it was dead. My mother took the bug from my hand and held it in her palm. She cupped her other hand around it and said, "Life is delicate. Hold your hands together but not so tight that you smother it. Let it breathe. Let it live." We walked to the closest flowerbed and buried the bug. I remember her closing her eyes and saying a silent prayer.

The next night I caught another firefly and cupped it in my hands. When I opened them, the firefly flew away, and I started to cry. My mom held me, and told me to open my eyes. When I did, the light of the firefly was within reach. I didn't try to catch it, though I could have. Instead, I stayed in my mom's arms, watching it do what it was made to do— create magic. *Fly freely.*

I cup the delicate skin of Sara Jane's cheek, and her eyes open. The hazy look in her eyes only adds to her peaceful beauty. Her hand grasps my wrist and she turns to kiss my palm. My firefly has brought beauty to a life that had lost it, created magic by showing me how to love. I have to let her breathe to let her live. And if she strays too far, I have to trust she'll return.

She whispers, "You came back to me."

"Always."

A sleepy smile graces her lips.

"Go to sleep, Firefly." I kiss the freckle, her lips, each one of her eyelids, and the softness right under her left ear.

The hold on my wrist loosens, and her hand rests against her chest. I pull the sheets up and cover us to our necks. Though my thoughts weigh heavily, my heart is light just from being near her.

The alarm rings too early. Sara Jane ends the torture, but she begins a sweeter hands-on one when she rubs my cock. Her breath blows across my skin when she whispers, "You want me." Not a question. A fact. Tender lips kiss my face and down my neck before she goes lower, under the sheet, dragging her nails along the inside of my thigh while taking my boxer briefs with her.

Her lips embrace me, her tongue caressing, the whole of her engulfing me. "Fuck," I moan, my eyes squeezing closed as my head presses back into the pillow. I find the top of her head and steady her as she pulls me into her warmth.

The pressure intensifies, and her hair is wrapped around my fingers. With each suck, lick, bite the tension is twisted tighter and tighter. I don't make announcements. She can tell when I'm going to come. Her mouth grips, her hand covering the gap, and the speed picks up as my body jolts beneath her.

Both my hands hold her as she takes me, swallowing around my dick until she's drunk me down. My body gives in, and my muscles relax. Sara Jane lifts and crawls up my body. Her lips are swollen with desire, red tainting them like I've tainted her. She kisses me, and I kiss her back twice as hard.

When she falls to the side, and lets out a sigh, I say, "Oh no, baby. My turn."

I don't bother with the sheet and let it fall to the bottom of the bed. I like seeing her naked and exposed, sexy and squirming just for me. Her body is open, her pussy delectable as it glistens for me. With two fingers, I spread her open and dip down to taste.

"You're fucking incredible."

"You like to tease."

"No, baby, I like to savor." I don't bother with fingers. I fuck her with my tongue. Her body wiggles in reaction, so I pin her down by her hips.

"Alexander," she moans, her back arching off the bed.

I can't handle it when she sounds so taken, when my name rolls off her tongue in so much pleasure. When her legs trap me in place. I do this to her. I. Alone.

Fuck.

My pleasure from power overcomes me and I lift her leg up and rest it on my shoulder. I'm not able to resist the calling of her body to mine and drop down to kiss her tits and collarbone. Pressing into her core, even deeper, I look up, and into her eyes. The depth of trust found in her gentle blues pushes my pride down while I press into her. I'm overwhelmed by the privilege that she's mine and she only wants me. "Fucking hell you feel amazing, Sara Jane."

"Say it again," she pleads. "Say my name like it's the only name that matters."

I stop thrusting, my body stopping from her request. My breath comes harsh, but I look at her, making sure she's looking me in the eyes. "You are all that matters, Sara Jane. All. Everything. The only thing." *The only good thing.*

Her hands slide up over my shoulders and neck until she's holding me by the face. "Will you give up this search? For me?"

Searching the flecks in her eyes, the wings of her words as they fly like a whisper to my ears, my gut reaction responds, "I can't."

She lets me remain in my unrequited stance. "Will I ever be enough?"

I drop to the side and roll onto my back. My arm drapes over my eyes, and I release a long, deep breath. "You and my need for answers aren't one and the same."

"But we're equal."

"No, but it's parallel."

Lying back, she sighs. I've disappointed her . . . or hurt her feelings. I could smooth the crinkle in her emotions I've caused, but that damn promise about no lies needs to be kept. She needs to know where my loyalty lies and that's in two places—in the past with my mother and the present with my firefly. "What are you thinking?" I dare to ask.

"I'm thinking if you can't give this search up, then I'll just have to help you."

"How?"

"By supporting you." Lifting up, she strokes my cheek. When I move my arm, I cover her hand, and she adds, "I may not be able to help find who killed her, but I can be here for you." Her kisses come and I devour her, just like I consume her each and every time I'm with her.

She's the sky.

I'm the earth.

Together we make up our own universe.

Capturing her orgasm, I kiss her lips and fuck her until I

lose myself to the blackness and bright flashing lights. Sitting up abruptly, I hold her even closer by wrapping my arms around her back, and kiss her so hard she never has to wonder what she means to me again.

Our union brings a deep blush to her cheeks. Lying back, I bring her with me. She's wrapped around my body, her heart pounding against my side. I chuckle at how much she enjoys sex. Takes control even. "I think I've created a monster."

She sits up, her hand against my chest. Not laughing, but instead, determination owning that glint in her eyes, she says, "You didn't create a monster, Alexander. You created a queen."

15

SARA JANE

I could lounge here for hours longer, content in body and mind, smiling like a loon. My relationship with Alexander has shifted, deepened. With our souls exposed in new ways, my trust in him has strengthened.

He's shared his darkness with me, letting me carry part of his burden. His mother's murder has always been troubling. I suspect most unsolved cases are, but it was his mother. Her death, like her life, will always stay with him. I know this. I see his pain so clearly even when he tries so hard to hide it from me. I can be there for him. I can help however he needs. I will do anything to ease his anger and help him find the peace he's so desperately seeking, the peace he deserves.

Unfortunately, I have class. I flip the covers from my body and sit up, glancing to the empty spot beside me. Alexander left for the office an hour ago, leaving me with a kiss and bones of jelly from our morning activities. Making my way into the bathroom, I start the shower and then head for the mirror. He's right about me. I've changed. I see it in my face and how it's slimmed. I see it in my body—my breasts are fuller, my hips wider, my waist tapered in. I like what I see, but I like that Alexander sees the real me too.

Grabbing a fresh towel, I hang it on the hook and step under the shower spray.

I feel rejuvenated after days of discourse. We've broken down walls between us and he's shown me his secrets. I'm not willing to lose him over his need to find the truth, so I'm here to stay.

I dry my hair with the towel and hang it up before walking out of the bathroom.

"You've become a beautiful woman."

I jump when I hear the male voice, the timbre sending shivers down my bare spine. My eyes meet his, and I cover myself and run for the bathroom. "What are you doing here?" I yell with the safety of a wall between us. I grab Alexander's robe from the hook and swing it around me, tightening the belt.

"I came to see you, and I got more than I could have asked for."

My heart is racing, my skin crawling beneath the soft fabric. He saw me. That rat bastard saw me naked. I grit my teeth and swallow my embarrassment. Looking out through the doorway, he sits smugly in a chair by the fireplace. "Why do you want to see me?"

Gesturing toward the sofa, he raises an eyebrow. "Sit down, Ms. Grayson."

"I'm not dressed."

"Sit down anyway." His tone leaves no room for argument and while I debate in my head if I have any say in the matter, I know deep down I don't. I take a breath and exhale slowly. Tightening the robe over my chest, I walk to the sofa and sit. The reality is he scares me to death. I wish Alexander were here.

I don't bother with questions. He has his own agenda, so I wait. He's not a man to keep someone in suspense, always ready to tell exactly what's on his mind. "I didn't think much of you when Alex first brought you around." *Wow, thanks.* My grimace can't be restrained, but he continues, "I had dated the best society had to offer. After all, I'm not unaware of how important good looks are in life. I was gifted from both sides. My mother was a model when she met my father. He was considered a catch in looks and last name. Together they were the toast of the town." My heart sinks as he brags of something so superficial. "Alex's mother was the most beautiful woman I had ever seen. She wasn't from around here but came here for school. I never thought she'd give me a chance. She didn't know my family or our position, but I asked her out anyway. She told me no." He laughs to himself, lost in the memory. "I asked her out every day for a week. She finally said yes. I won her over. Whether it was my charm, or good looks, my persistence, or maybe she found out who I was. I didn't care. I was in love with Madeline the moment I laid eyes on her, and I loved her until the day she died."

This man's moods are as unpredictable as he is. "You only loved her because she was beautiful?"

Looking back at me, he says, "Beauty is not in the eye of the beholder. It's precious and rare. But above all it's expendable."

"So it never mattered what she looked like—"

"She was taken from me anyway."

"Why are you telling me this?"

"Because beauty is also a commodity. It's bought and sold every day. Just like I knew, Alexander knows the benefits of having great genes. It will help him in business and in life. He needs someone equally his match."

Alexander has always made me feel incredibly beautiful, but now doubt sinks in. Why *did* he choose me? I hope I'm reading him all wrong, but I ask, "Are you telling me, looks wise, I don't fit?"

His eyes spark with challenge. He tilts his head in confusion and says, "Quite the opposite, as I first said. You're stunning. I see why my son finds you so desirable."

My head jerks back. "Please don't talk about us in that way." I close the gap in the robe that exposes my calves.

"I'm not hitting on you, Ms. Grayson. If I were, there'd be no question in your eyes. You'd know. Out of respect, I've kept my distance. Out of respect for my son."

"You don't respect him."

"You have made up your mind so decidedly against me already. Let me put things to you more simply. If I wanted to fuck you, Ms. Grayson, I would have. So yes, out of respect for my son, I have kept a polite distance."

"You're so sure of yourself, regarding me. I would have never—"

His head is shaking. "Never say never."

Standing, I move around to the other side of the couch. "Lines have been crossed. This is inappropriate on every level. I'm sure Alexander will not be happy to hear about this."

He stands and buttons his gray suit jacket, a roguish grin surfacing, reminding me of Alexander when he wants to have sex. "You won't be telling Alex anything about this meeting. My son and I have a few wrinkles to work through, but you wouldn't want to be responsible for ruining the relationship we have built. Right, Ms. Grayson?"

Fisting my robe at the neck, I ask, "Why did you come here? To threaten me, to get me in line with whatever scheme you have going on?"

"I came here to offer you a job. I think you'd be an asset to me."

My mouth falls open. "Doing what?"

"You have a way with people."

"You don't know anything about me."

Sliding his hands into his pockets, he replies, "I know quite a bit about you. I know you're often late to psychology on Thursdays because you stop for your weekly treat—a coffee at the campus coffeehouse. You were late paying your car insurance two months in a row recently. The teaching assistant last year in history hit on you twice, and you never told Alex. And your dad's stroke two years ago happened after you told him you wanted to live with Alex." He looks pleased with himself, his arrogance dripping from the corner of his devious grin. "You may stay in my house, but you don't live here. Why is it that you and my son never followed through with that move-in plan?"

I gulp, his words, the memories hard to process. "Are you following me?"

"Follow might be too narrow of a word. Information comes my way and who am I to deny it."

"You're a horrible man."

Sighing, he says, "I expected more from you."

"If I'm such a disappointment, then why would you want me to work for you?"

"I'm glad you asked. We'll be transitioning as we begin selling divisions of the company. Although no one should know, I understand that Alex has confided in you. Since you know, your skills could be utilized through various departments that struggle with change."

"Nothing with you comes easy. What are you really offering?"

"A chance to be a part of this family."

"I don't need to be a part of this family. I only need Alexander."

He steps closer, and by instinct, I want to move back, but I stay to hold my ground. Reaching for me, he touches my cheek. I cringe and turn away, but his fingertips stay and move slowly down my cheek until he's grasping my neck. "So beautiful."

My breath freezes in my throat. I can't take it, and I move away. Hating that I give him power, I walk to the door with my head down. I open it, and with my back to him say, "Leave before Alexander finds you here."

"I've made sure he's preoccupied. You might remember Carinna? The woman from the party."

My head whips to the left, my gaze over my shoulder hitting his. *Lies. Don't believe him.* "I've never failed a test, Mr. Kingwood, and I don't intend to now."

"Carinna said the same thing. She was quite taken with my son, and he for her, and yet, I still took her from behind while she was bent over my desk, her lipstick smeared across a contract she was so sure I would sign."

My fear swells inside. With my hand shaking, I grip the doorknob tightly to hide the emotions Alexander told me to bury for protection. "You raped her?"

"I think you've missed the point of our meeting, Ms. Grayson. Carinna Halifax wanted something. She used her assets to obtain it. I benefitted from both—the deal and the assets. To be blunt, no, I did not rape her. She'd be in my bed now if I allowed it, but I have other ideas for my bed." He moves behind me. His breath creeps along the back of my neck, making the hair stand on end. "I wasn't hitting on you earlier, but that was before I saw the dampness on your skin and wondered how wet you were between your legs."

Spinning around, I put my hands up as a barrier. "You

need to back up, or I will scream at the top of my lungs." He chuckles, his amusement angering me. "Leave."

Reaching forward, I flinch, my eyes squeezing closed. "Now, now, Sara Jane. I can call you Sara Jane, right?" His knuckles brush against one of my breasts. My hand goes flying, knocking it away as I stare into his sinister eyes. "Don't you ever touch me again."

He licks his lips. "I see the way your nipples respond to me, so sharp against the fabric. Your breath is deepening. Your eyes are dilated. You're wild and yet can be tamed. Alexander has done well with you. Your compliance is necessary, Sara Jane, but your beauty is a bonus." He takes a few steps back and shoves his hands in his pockets. "You fair very well under critical tests. I wonder if Alex will."

Carinna. She is Alex's setup. How dare he. My heart still races, but my head is in the game. "Before testing people, you should study your opponent's strengths and weaknesses. I'm no damsel in distress, and I refuse to believe the lies you've concocted about Alexander."

"I'm well aware of your strengths *and* weakness. What I'm surprised to learn is that you're my opponent. I mistakenly thought with Alex as a common denominator, we could be allies."

I open the door wide and move to the side. "I won't sell my soul for a paycheck," I say adamantly, but I'd sell it to protect Alexander.

Stopping next to me, he eyes me from the side. "My apologies for making assumptions." He walks into the hall. "Good day, Ms. Grayson."

I shut the door and lean against the thick wood, locking it under my arm. My breath is shaking like my hands. If there's anything I must do, it's to make sure Alexander doesn't become his father. Yet, I can see him slipping into the role so easily.

Pushing off the door, I go to the closet once my breath is calmer, more even. I have no idea how I went from a school girl to the woman I am now—determined to do anything to save the one I love—but I know I'm ready to take on the role.

I can't tell Alexander about his father. He's too volatile to handle it rationally. No, I must keep this under lock and key, safely inside of me. He must never know. The situation has been handled. It's over. I'm good. Stronger for it.

While I get dressed, I realize the answer is right in front of me. Staring at a photo of Alexander and me, a simple black frame wrapped around the innocence of a black and white photo, it's easy to see how we were once such different people. He looks youthful, something I never noticed when we were teenagers. Carrying both his mother's death and his father's spurning, he was already older than his years when we met. What I thought was a carefree smile still lights up my world, but it's something I haven't seen in too long.

Walking out, I finish getting dressed and ready for school. How can I bring that smile back?

————

I'M TAPPED on the shoulder. "Are you okay?"

My daydreams were getting the better of me. I turn around to Cal, who's sitting behind me in the auditorium, and ask, "What?"

He leans down and whispers, "Are you okay after the other day?"

"I'm fine." There's no conviction to my answer. Even I

don't believe me. I turn back to face the Smartboards up front, hoping it's enough to end the questioning.

"Was that your boyfriend?"

I nod slowly. "Yes."

"Look, I'm not trying to pry or anything, but you should be careful. I've seen guys like him before. It never gets better."

Turning around again, my eyes narrow, and his goes wide. Whispering, this time with conviction, I set him straight, "I appreciate the concern, but I've known him since I was seventeen. I don't have to be careful around him."

"That's a long time."

"Yes, it is. Why are we still talking about this? I'm fine. Really."

"It was just something in the way he looked at you—"

Losing patience, I struggle to keep my voice low. "How did he look at me, Cal?"

"Like he'd rather kill you than let anyone else have you."

My lips part in shock from his answer. "You think he'd kill me?"

"I didn't say that. I said he looked at you in a way that said you were unmistakably and solely his."

"You could tell that by the way he looked at me?"

"Everyone on campus could tell that."

Oh, Alexander. My sweet, determined man. "Our relationship is complicated—"

"Clearly."

Now annoyed, I'm quick to add, "I was going to also say, but there's no one I trust more with my life."

He glances to the front of the room and back to me. "I'm not judging. My sister was in a *complicated* relationship, so I understand more than you think. If you ever need to talk to someone, you can talk to me, Sara Jane."

"Thanks for the offer, but I'm fine. We're fine." When I turn around, I vow to ignore him the rest of the semester. I don't need outside observers causing me trouble or putting strange, misconstrued thoughts in my head. Anyway, I'm not so sure that I don't look at Alexander that same way.

———

"HELLO, I'm here to see Alexander Kingwood." I need to see him. I need to talk to him, to touch him, to hold him. To cement myself to him in ways that I never felt I had to before today. Others have done this to me. Alexander and I are just fine.

"You're Sara Jane. Hi, I'm Kimberly. We met very briefly at a holiday office party two years ago."

Her welcoming smile and warm greeting elicits mine. "Yes, I remember now. How are you?"

"Very well. Thank you. How have you been?"

"Busy with school, but good."

"Alexander talks about you all the time." Her smile softens. "You've got him wrapped around your little finger."

My cheeks feel hot from hearing he speaks to others about me. "I don't know about that, but things are good."

She stands and looks through the glass door toward the cubicles that fill the next room. "That's great to hear." When she sits back down, she says, "He was in a meeting, but I think he's out now. You can go back."

"Thank you; good to see you again."

"Yes, you too." I open the door and enter the large space. I've been here several times, but it's been a while. Weaving my way toward the back, I see Alexander.

He's on the phone with his back to me. I overhear him say, "I'll be there. Nine sharp."

A throat is cleared and Cruise says, "Hey Sara Jane, what brings you around?"

Alexander spins in his chair and when he sees me, he stands up, looking all kinds of guilty. "Hey, Firefly." Taking me by the upper arms, he brings me in for a kiss. It feels like a distraction from the phone call, but I don't want to lay into him right off the bat. After all, trust is a two-way street.

"I couldn't stop thinking about you today, so I wanted to stop by and see if you wanted to grab dinner before I have to meet up for my group project."

"Yes," he replies, grabbing his suit jacket from the hook of his cubicle wall. His eyes hit Cruise, a silent message exchanged.

Something's going on, and I'm about to find out. "Do you need to wrap up or anything?"

"Nope. Let's go."

When he turns to shut down his computer, Cruise takes a call. I look around at the employees on the phone, closing up for the day. But then my eyes meet the ones I've tried to forget. Mr. Kingwood stands in his office, glass dividing us, and stares straight at me. His hand comes up in a small wave before I look away. "I can wait out in reception if you need more time."

"No, I'm ready." Alexander peeks back at me and smiles again. I dare to glance up one more time. This time his father is gone, and I release a breath in relief.

"Are you okay?" Alexander is staring at me, looking concerned. I can tell from the way he searches my eyes, he knows something is up. But he drops it. His hand covers my lower back and guides me toward the door. "Talk later, Cruise," he says as we pass.

"Later."

16

ALEXANDER

I thought we'd make it to the restaurant before the barrage of questions hit, but I should have known better. With Firefly, there's never just one. "Where are you going at nine?"

"It's good to see you, too."

She laughs. It's light, but I'll take it. "I'm sorry." She wraps herself around me, and I put my arm around her. "It's good to see you." Lifting up on her toes, she kisses my neck. "Now where are you going at nine sharp?"

"You really shouldn't eavesdrop on people's private calls."

"I wasn't. You were speaking loud enough to be heard from where I was standing. Now stop evading and answer the question."

When the elevator dings, I escort her, leading her to the car. "If you really want to know, I'm meeting a drug dealer from the lower four quarters who apparently sold to a woman I met the other day. When Cruise saw her today she remembered this guy once used to work for some Kingwood execs."

"And what do you expect to learn from this meeting?" We reach her car and the alarm clicks off. I open the door for her, but before she gets in her expression changes. It's different, a shrewdness knotted in her brows adding to the expectations building between us. She leans against the car and turns to me. "I'm a part of this now, Alexander. I want to know where you go and who you're meeting. I want to know everything."

I touch her cheek, searching for signs to see just how serious she is. "I never thought you'd accept this so readily."

"I haven't, but you have, and I support you."

"That simple?"

"No, completely convoluted and complex, but I know you're doing this so that means I'm doing it."

"Remember when I said I'm in too deep?"

"Yeah."

Kissing her, I let my lips remain long after and then whisper, "So are you."

She leans back to look in my eyes. Touching my cheek, she replies, "I always was."

When I get into the car, the need to touch her is too strong to deny. I reach over and take her hand. Bringing it to my lips, I kiss the top. "I want you to move in."

"Alexander—"

"I'm only asking that you think about it. You're there most nights anyway."

"We've been here before."

"You weren't quite twenty last time."

"Alexander."

"Please consider it."

Her gaze disappears like her hand from mine. "I don't know about the manor."

"We can look around for a new place if you want. It's not

about the manor, it's about me."

She's quick, her eyes pleading like her words, "I would for you. I would do anything for you. Haven't I proven that already?"

"You have, but you don't have to prove anything to me, Firefly. You're here, and that's enough if that's all I get. But please know I want more with you."

The add-on at the end makes her smile. "I want more with you too. I promise I'll think about it."

"That's all I can ask. Oh, except, what do you want for dinner?"

"I'm thinking Italian food."

"Your wish is my command."

At the restaurant, I love when she orders with big eyes and a hearty appetite. It's entertaining watching her scarf pasta down like someone's going to steal it from her. "So good," she moans in pleasure.

The sound does things to me, my body awakening for her. "It was good, but not as delicious as you. I think I'll have you as a midnight snack later."

"Are you ever not horny?" She bumps her shoe against mine under the table.

"Not when it comes to you."

"I hope you always feel that way."

"I have no doubt I will. You get more delectable with each birthday."

Her fork is set down, and she sighs with an amused grin. "You know how to work me over too easily. I need new tricks."

"Your tricks are fine. I just know you."

The plate is pushed away. Resting her chin on her anchored arm, she smiles. "What's my favorite color?"

"Blue, like my eyes," I reply with a wink.

She rolls hers. "What's my favorite movie?"

"The Notebook because you like sappy love stories where the protagonist dies."

Sitting back, she laughs. "What's my dream car?"

"A black Range Rover. Loaded—sunroof, automatic, Bluetooth, leather seats, dark tinted windows. I'm batting a thousand."

"You're not doing too shabs." Her tone turns more serious. "Where's my favorite place?"

Shit. My mind searches for the correct answer, but I'm left with nothing, so I try for charming her. "In my bed?"

She shakes her head. "I love it there, but I was thinking of somewhere else."

"Are you going to tell me?"

"No. I think despite all that we've learned about you lately, it's good for me to have a few secrets of my own."

"So you're going to keep it from me?"

"No, I just want us to get to know each other again. Do more than have sex and eat dinner together."

"I'm quite partial to those," I say, reaching over and taking her hand.

"Me too, but you'll find out where I go when you need to know."

"I think you like having secrets."

"Don't we all?" She pushes away from the table. "I need to get going. I'm already going to be late."

In the car, holding hands with her reminds me of more innocent times. We used to do this a lot, and I'd almost forgotten. When did life become so hard?

It doesn't take long to get to campus. I wish it were longer as I'm not ready for this ease to stop. On the drive over, she says, "If you're going out tonight, I'm going to stay at my place. I pay for it, and I'm never there."

"Because I'm not there."

"You're not at the manor much either, so this should make no difference."

My eyes flicker to her. "We just had a good time. Are you starting a fight?"

"No fight."

"I would like to come home to you."

"I'd like that too." Her hands tighten around her seatbelt and I turn back, gripping the steering wheel when she adds, "You know where I live."

"This isn't going to become a habit, is it?"

"It might. Sometimes I don't feel safe at your place."

"It's a fortress. Way safer than your apartment, and it comes with cleaning and room service." When she stares out her window in silence, I say, "That was supposed to be funny. Although it's true."

"I'm sorry." She puts on a smile that feels put on for me, and shrugs. "The perks are nice, but . . . I don't know."

Pulling to the curb in front of the library and putting the car into park, I ask, "Why do I feel like you're keeping something from me?"

"I don't have anything clean over there anyway."

The distance seen in her eyes spreads between our bodies. I hate it. "I'll return to your place tonight."

Her hand moves to my thigh, her whole demeanor lightening. "You will?"

This time the smile I wear is put on just for her. I need to give her this comfort. "I will."

Leaning over, she kisses me on the cheek. "Thank you."

"You're welcome."

The passenger door is opened and she steps out. Before it closes, she leans back in and says, "I've been thinking about why you think I like The Notebook. You're right that it's my favorite movie, but you've got the reasoning all wrong. It's not about being sappy or the protagonist dying. I love it because they fought to be together. Against all odds, they made their way back to each other and loved with every fiber of their being." Her gaze falls as her chest rises quickly. When she looks back at me, she adds, "I didn't love it because of the ending. I loved it because of the journey. Every love story has its burdens to bear. It's how they survive it that makes it great."

The meaning in her words isn't hidden, but I don't want to leave on a heavy note. "Maybe we can watch it this weekend."

A soft smile appears on her gorgeous face. "I'd like that."

"I'll bring popcorn."

Her smile grows. *It's a smile I've missed.* "Don't forget the chocolate-covered raisins."

"Never."

When she exhales, a few of the demons holding her happiness hostage escape, and her eyes catch the setting sun. "I'll catch a ride from Shelly since you're borrowing my car."

"Thanks for loaning her to me."

"Take care of her, and I'll see you tonight."

"Tonight." I nod and she steps back. I watch her as she walks away, my hands gripping the wheel tightly. I want to keep that promise of the movie this weekend. I love her so fucking much and want to give her that true love ending she wants so badly. The alternative would only cause her more pain.

"Every love story has its burdens to bear. It's how they survive it that makes it great."

I desperately want ours to survive.

17

ALEXANDER

Kingwood Manor is portentous with its ivy-covered walls and black spires reaching for the dark skies. The red brick masonry was laid years before we took up residence, but remains pristine. I skid to a stop, trying to leave a mark before I park next to a familiar beat-up, forest green Maxima. The car is parked, but idling.

When I get out, I tap on the waiting car, and tilt to look inside. The window is rolled down and Chad looks over. I say, "I'm going to change clothes. I'll be right out."

When I get back in, I tease, "Your car is a piece of shit. You know that, right?" Reaching over, I lock it just in case it decides to fly open while we're driving.

"Not all of us can live in the splendors and spoils of wealth."

"They call me King for a reason."

He backs the car up, and we head into the world where it's always felt easier than living behind these brick walls. "And here I always thought it was just a coincidence with your last name."

"Ha." I click my seat belt into place because Sara Jane

would kick my ass if she found out I wasn't buckled in properly. She's cute like that.

Reading my mind, he asks, "How is Sara Jane after last night?"

"She's fine," I reply. "She adapts well to change. Anyway, I don't think anything I do anymore surprises her." I laugh.

"She made valid points."

Looking at him, my brow furrows. "Not you too, Chad. I need your help. No one's better than you."

"Sometimes I wonder if what we're doing is right."

"It's not legal."

"I didn't say legal. I said right. There's a difference. I'm not hurting anyone by digging up information. It's what is done with that information that keeps me up at nights."

"Don't worry."

He looks over at me. His hair shaggier than usual, the wire arm of his glasses slightly bent. Shifting eyes between the road and me. "I'm worried. Shelly's involved—"

"I won't keep you if you don't want to be a part of this anymore."

"I need the money."

"Shit, Chad. I get it." My temper flairs, but it's hard to be mad at one of the nicest people I know. He never argues, so this conversation surprises me, but I get it. "This is not your battle."

"You're my friend. I want to help you."

The high-rise looms ahead. "I'll give you the money you need for school whether you stay or not."

"I can't do that."

Staring out the window, the misery I've dragged my friends into envelops me. "You can." Taking a deep breath, I calm the anger that could be unleashed too easily these days. He doesn't deserve to bear the brunt of it. "We're friends, Chad. You're one of my best friends. If I can help, I will."

When the car is stopped and I notice my bike alongside it, I turn to Chad. "You do what's best for you."

"Thanks. Hey, good luck," he says when I get out.

"I don't need luck. I have this." I flash a wad of bills and a snarky smile.

He shakes his head in disapproval. "Like I said, good luck, King."

"Thanks for the ride."

"Anytime."

Once I'm on my bike, I drive out of the nicer part of the city and meet Cruise by the bridge.

Word got out.

The welcome wagon is waiting for us when we arrive at the dilapidated building where April has taken up residence.

Four bikes and a car.

Fuck.

Why do I have a strong suspicion this isn't a friendly welcome?

We stop at the other end. To my left, Cruise waits for me to make the final call. I ask, "Do you think we were set up?"

"I don't think we'll know unless we go for it."

I'm hesitant to drag him into a situation that shouts danger. "I've got a bad feeling about this."

"We've come this far."

Nodding, I say, "We've come this far."

We held our own . . . in the beginning, but being outnumbered and with a gun to our heads, we both fell fast. I protected my ribs and head the best I could. The large beef-heads converged and just enough damage was done to send a message. It's times like these that I wonder if they know who I really am. They must. If I weren't under the Kingwood name, I have no doubt we'd be dead. My ears are still ringing from a blow to my right side. I spit pooling blood from my mouth, and squat down, my side hurting. "Fuck, Cruise. What are we doing?"

"We're getting close."

"How do you know?"

"Because if we weren't, they wouldn't have been hiding behind their fists." His head rolls to the side and he spits. "It will only get worse the closer we get to the answers."

Pushing myself to my feet, I walk over to him. "They're trying to keep us from finding out more than we have."

"Yup. Ow." He grabs his side.

When I reach him, he's lying on his back and looks like he's in a lot of pain. He takes the offered hand, and I pull him to his feet. Our hands flip into our regular greeting, our fingers anchored together. "Thanks, brother."

"Got your back, man."

"Yeah. Got yours, too."

"Yeah, let's not get mushy over this shit. My jaw fucking hurts." He wiggles it back and forth so I know it's not broken. *Thank fuck.*

I help him lift his bike off the ground, and he does the same for me. They kicked in my exhaust, denting it. *Fuckers.* They'll pay for that, and I don't mean monetarily. Picking my wallet out of a puddle, I see they took five hundred dollars and my credit cards. I don't worry about that shit. Those cards have trackers, and they can't use them without a fingerprint to activate them. Kingwoods aren't going to let their black cards be used by just anyone.

After picking up the pieces of my phone, I toss the remains in a dumpster. "Fuckers will pay for this."

"Shit, they scratched the paint. Stupid fucks." He swings

his leg over and starts his bike. "Looks like the ties between them go back to before April, but we need her to get the details. You think she'll show?"

Settling onto the leather seat of my bike, I smile though it hurts. "I'm sure 'cause you'll make sure of it."

He moves forward until he's even with me. "I had a feeling you'd say that."

"We can't back down now."

"One way or the other. But no matter what, we'll be prepared next time."

Reaching out, we fist bump. "Let's get out of here."

We take it slow to analyze the damage done to our bikes. I think they got it worse than we did. Fuck the blood. I'll heal, but damn, my bike. *That* pisses me off.

I just hope my face isn't too bad or Sara Jane will freak out and my dad will kick my ass tomorrow night. We clean up and buy a Gatorade at a gas station. Fighting always wears me down, which is why I never did it unless necessary.

Tonight it was necessary.

We hit an all-night diner, needing fuel. "I'm starving," I say when we slide into a booth across from each other.

Cruise laughs. "Damn this light is not flattering. I don't think I've ever seen your pretty boy face look so fucked up before."

"That's because I usually win."

The waitress pours coffee for each of us without saying a word. She takes our orders, and when she finally looks us over, she asks if we need ice.

"Is it bad?" I ask.

"Nah, but I'll bring it anyway so you don't swell."

We eat our eggs and bacon, pancakes, and potato wedges with one hand, holding icepacks to our cheeks with the other. When she brings the ticket, she asks, "What do the other guys look like?"

Cruise works his charm and lies, "Worse than us."

"Good for you."

———————

MIDNIGHT.

When I open the door to her apartment, Sara Jane is asleep on her couch. Some old sitcom is on the TV and her kitchen light is on. Taking the remote, I flick the TV off and hit the light switch off, too. I kneel down in front of the couch and watch her. She's troubled, a little wrinkle in her forehead giving her worried mind away. Her body is restless, and I count her breaths. Every third breath is punctuated with a sigh.

Her eyes slowly open, but she's not scared. She actually looks more at peace looking into my eyes. "When did you get here?"

"Only a minute ago," I reply as I stroke her head gently.

Reaching out, she touches the corner of my mouth. I thought I'd cleaned up the blood, but her peace turns to turmoil, and she lifts her head. "What happened? Why are you bleeding?"

"It's no big deal. We should go to bed." I start to stand, but she grabs hold of the sleeve of my jacket.

"Alexander, what happened?"

"It was handled, baby. Don't worry." I twist my arm so my palm is open to her.

Her gaze goes from my hand to my face, and then she accepts the offer. When she's standing, all five feet four inches, bare feet, and tiny pajamas, she wraps her arms around my middle. "I always worry about you."

"It's a bad habit you need to break."

When she looks up, her lips are twisted to the side. "You've got a few of your own."

"Truer words were never spoken. Come on."

In the bedroom, I strip off my clothes after leaving her in the bathroom, happy to be going to bed. "I'm exhausted."

She comes back into the bedroom with a towel, a washrag, and a cup of water. "Lie down."

"Are we playing nurse and patient?"

Her laugh is music, the melody one I know by heart. "You wish."

"I do, on every star."

Sitting next to me, she asks, "You waste your wishes on role play?"

"No. I spend all my wishes on you."

"I hope they all come true."

Kissing her on the cheek, I whisper, "They already have."

"You're very charming when you want to be."

"I always wanna be with you." I lie back as instructed. She dips the washrag in the cup. When she touches it to my face, she's careful, but I still protest, "I'm not hurt."

"You're bleeding. That means you're hurt." I wince and get a hard glare. "What happened?"

"Some guys needed to flex their muscle to prove a point."

"On your face?"

When I laugh, I wince again. "Fine. Maybe they did a little more damage than I first thought."

Her gaze dips down my body. "Is that bruising on your ribs?"

"It doesn't hurt that much. Surface bruising."

"Did you get what you were after?"

"Guess we'll find out tomorrow."

She wipes across my forehead, keeping her eyes on the job at hand. "What's tomorrow?"

"A party at Kingwood Enterprises. I want you to be there. Will you come?"

Her hand stops, the rag still pressed to the side of my eye. "I'm not sure I can make it."

Taking hold of her hips, I wait until she finally makes eye contact to say, "I need you there, Firefly."

"You'll be fine."

"Okay. I *want* you there."

She sighs. "I have my group project."

"Then come after." I wiggle her hips. "Come to the party. Please."

Setting the rag down and taking the towel, she pats my face. I open my eyes to find her searching my expression. "I'll consider it."

"That's the second thing you're having to consider. Any thoughts on the previous?"

She smiles, and I smile in response. "It's only been a few hours."

"And?"

"I need more time."

"I want you with me. Every night. Every morning."

"I practically am now."

"Practically isn't all the time."

Her smile grows. "You make it hard to say no. You know that?"

"Actually, you're the one who makes it hard." I take her hand from my face and move it lower until she finds something harder to hold on to.

"How are you always ready for sex?"

"I was born for action."

"I'm starting to believe you." She stands with her nurse supplies in hand. "I think you'll live. I hope the other guy got worse."

"It was three of them."

She scoffs. "Good God, Alexander. You're lucky this was the only damage they did."

"My bike got worse." She rolls her eyes at that one, as I knew she would.

"Your bike can be replaced." She walks to the bathroom. My pretty firefly floats like an angel back to me. The light is turned out, and she slips under the covers, careful when she slides against me. She whispers, "You can't. Take care of yourself, okay?"

"Yes, ma'am."

That earns me a poke to my ribs. "Ouch."

"Oh damn, I forgot. I'm so sorry."

As panic takes over, the apologies roll off her tongue, so I grab hold of her, welcoming the touch of her warm and soft skin. "I'm fine. Really. It's okay."

Laying her head on the pillow next to mine, she says, "I'm sorry."

"You said it yourself. I'll live." Her lips warm my chest. My arm tightens around her. "Be with me, baby. Be with me always."

She rolls to the side and looks at me. "I'm with you, Alexander. We're one. Always one." Rolling onto her back, her shoulder pressed to mine. Her hands are like a prayer as she rests her cheek on them. "I want to live with you."

I'm tired. I'm delirious. I must have misheard, my ear still slightly ringing. I'm mentally and physically exhausted. "Really?"

"Really," she replies with a solid smile, one stuck on love. I suspect mine's similar.

"Best news I could get." Looking at her, I lean over and kiss the tip of her nose. "What changed your mind?"

"You came over tonight."

"That's all it took?"

"Why did you come over?"

"Because you were here."

"That's all it took." She kisses me gently and leans back again. The tips of her fingers run along my neck and over my shoulder before she rests her palm on my arm. "I shouldn't say this because Lord knows you don't need your ego inflated, but I'm going to anyway."

"Hit me with the compliments, woman. My ego is the only thing not bruised tonight."

"You're more thoughtful than you let on. You're gentler than you like to show the world. You're not as tough as you want people to believe. It's for all those reasons and a million more that I love being with you. So remember, you don't have to wear your armor to bed. I love you, the man before me now."

Her leg swings over mine, and she pulls herself closer.

"Ouch," I mumble, wishing I could hide the pain better.

She lifts up, and strokes my hair from my forehead. "Aww, poor baby. I'll take extra special care of you and help heal my wounded knight in shining armor." Kissing my chest, she rests over my heart, her hand tapping to the beat. "So it's us. Officially now."

I cover her body by wrapping my arms around her. "There was never any other way. It was always together or nothing."

"Seems that way." The tips of her lashes brush against my chest when she closes her eyes. "Thank you for coming over tonight."

"There's no place I'd rather be."

18

ALEXANDER

S ara Jane is so fucking sweet to people who don't give a shit about her. It's me they care about. I'm the one they are more than willing to use. I call them friends, but they're enemies disguised as friends. Cruise is the only one I trust.

I nod when I see him, but I'm not here to socialize. I'm here to make a point. She turns, a mix of worry crossing her face. "There are a lot of drugs."

"You wanted to see how my friends party. This is how they party."

"Some of the kids at school smoke weed."

"Have you ever smoked?"

"You know I haven't." She playfully jabs me with her elbow.

"Let's keep it that way." I guide her through the living room, and into the kitchen where the large island is covered with bottles. "What do want to drink?" Grabbing a bottle of whiskey, I start pouring it into a crystal glass.

"I'll have what you're having."

"Really?" I ask, surprised.

"When in Rome." Looking around nervously, she adds, "C'est la vie."

"That's a lot of clichés you've got going there. You okay?"

"Fine." Her voice pitches, and then frustration sets in, and she clears her throat. "I'm fine. Just give me the damn whiskey."

"Damn whiskey," I repeat, teasing her. "Probably wise. It's the only way to survive these parties." I grab another glass and pour the liquid in before adding a dash of Coke to each glass.

Another drink later, I do what I hoped I wouldn't, but knew I would. Sara Jane is too pure, too good. She's lethal in ways that weaken me. I have to be strong. I can't be with her, and yet my fucking emotions are messing with me. This girl. She fucking owns me—heart and soul, but I still go, leading her reluctantly up the stairs. The alcohol has made her tipsy and her body's relaxed, trusting me . . . so fucking foolish.

Don't do this. Don't do this.

Not to her. She's good and I'm going to ruin her.

I'll ruin her worse if she stays with me. I'm going to use immature fucking psychology tricks on her. Make her leave me because I'm too weak to leave her.

I turn against any good that might be left in me and look into her entrusting doe eyes. She asks, "Where are we going?"

"I've wanted you since I saw you."

A sweet smile appears. "Aw."

"Not aw. I wanted to do things to you, to take things from you."

Her smile fades. "Like what, Alexander?"

"You keep asking if I want you and why we haven't made love."

"Well, yeah. We've dated for months, and we've not gotten past first base. The rejection hurts."

"I want you, Firefly. I do, so much. But if we do . . ." That's it for me. Am I ready to be everything she needs in life? I can't even fucking take care of myself, and she'll need me. She'll need me to protect her because she only sees the good in the world. She only

sees the good in me. I'm about to prove her wrong. "Please tell me to take you home. Tell me you want to leave or you have a headache. Tell me anything that will keep me from taking you up these stairs."

Glancing up the staircase, she asks, "What's up there that you don't want me to see?"

"Some of the bad I want to keep from you."

"You brought me this far. You obviously want to go up there."

"I don't. I thought I did, but I don't."

"But you will?" Yes. Because that's the sorry ass I am.

Nodding, I reply, "I will. So tell me to take you home. Do anything to keep me from fucking you like you're a girl I don't care about instead of the one I do."

Her lips fall apart and her pupils widen. When she looks up the staircase again, she asks, "But you like it?"

"No, but I live in a world where things aren't coming up roses. It's dirty and twisted. I want you to have a better life." I tell her the truth as I touch her cheek. "Because you've changed me for the better."

"We're better because we're together."

Drunk confidence makes her push her shoulders back and tits out, digging deep for some false bravado. "I'm not afraid of seeing whatever it is. I'm afraid of losing you, and if you don't get what you need, that will happen." Wrapping her arms around my neck, she says, "I've been eighteen for months. I want to have sex with you, Alexander." My name is slurred. "I'm ready. Why don't you want me?"

"I do, baby. More than you'll ever know, but I also know I'm no good for you."

"It can't be that bad."

She can't hold her liquor. I like that she can't. Not because I want her drunk, but that she's completely opposite from every girl *at this party. That's one of the more obvious reasons she's better than all of them.*

The class president from my senior year passes us. "Getting lucky, Kingwood?" A girl who used to stalk me in the halls is hanging on him like she's hanging on to his words.

Sara Jane replies for both of us, "He is."

I kind of want to smile with pride, she's off balance and leans a little too far to the right. "You okay?"

"More than okay." Her lips reach my ear, and she whispers, "I've seen porn before. Is it dirty like that?"

"It's dirty like that." Dirtier, but I want her to see with her own eyes. I want to taint her innocence to make her strong. She'll need that strength to be with me. The debate is dead and buried. I was never going to take her home before destroying the last of her innocence. I kiss her hard before carrying her up the rest of the stairs. At the top, I press her against the wall, pressing my cock against her as my tongue invades her mouth. Her lips are fucking divine, her tongue coaxing more than mine to touch her in ways that I've not touched her before. An ounce of guilt strikes, and I pull back. "Fuck, I shouldn't be doing this."

"Don't stop this time. I'm so wet for you."

No fucking way I can ignore that from my sweet, innocent vixen. I kiss her again and her leg wraps around one of mine.

The hall's too crowded. I need to get her out of here alone before I fuck her right here. "Come on." I take her hand and lead her down the hall. When we reach the bedroom, I stop in front of the open door and then place her in front of me.

When she sees inside, she tries to take a step back, but I hold her in place. She attempts to turn away, but with my lips to her ear this time, I say, "I want you to watch." I keep my tone firm, knowing she needs to see this. She needs to see how crass my life can be.

The class president is fucking my stalker on the bed. The girl's tits are bouncing in reaction, but she likes putting on a show, well aware of the eyes on her. People are standing around the room, some watching, some not. Cruise comes from the bathroom and sits on a chair in the corner. The girl he was kissing earlier kneels before him while he watches the action on the bed.

Shifting her over for more coverage from the inside, our bodies are blocked by the door. There's no way in fucking hell I'm letting anyone see my girl get off but me. Sara Jane's breathing changes, lengthening. I slide my hands over her ribs and higher until I'm squeezing her breasts. "Alexander." Her voice teeters between lust and a warning.

"It's okay, baby. Nobody cares what we're doing," I lie. "Touch me." Her hand comes around and rubs over my dick. "Yeah, just like that. Such a good girl. That feels so good." With my cheek to hers, I can tell her eyes have closed. She's letting the sensations take over. The girl on the bed grabs her own tits, pinching her nipples while watching us. I pinch Sara Jane's through the thin satin material of her bra, which elicits a groan filled with desire. "Open your eyes and watch." My voice is gruff, laden with need.

With her eyes open again, she sees the girl looking at her, watching us, and Sara Jane's chest begins to heave, but she makes no move to leave. I slide my hand under the back of her dress and into the top of her panties. When I reach her wet pussy, she bucks back. "People can see us."

"I know." I dip a finger inside her tight pussy. She's so fucking turned on and God, do I fucking want her like I've never wanted anything before. From how wet she is, it won't take long to get her off. I sink deeper receiving a lustful moan in return. I start fucking her with my hand while her hand dives deep into my jeans. "Fuck, Firefly, make me come."

The girl on the bed looks our way. "I've missed you, Alex."

Sara Jane freezes.

Whipping her to the side until her back hits the wall, I press my lips to hers. "I want you so much. Only you." I hurry her down the hall to the nearest bathroom and lock us inside.

My patience is gone, my hands are under her bra, and I have a pert pink nipple in my mouth when she asks, "You could have had sex with her if you wanted?"

A question. "I don't want her. I want you."

"Never?"

"Never what?" Licking the skin between her breasts, my hand fumbles with her dress. I want it fucking off.

"You've never been with her?"

I slow. This is what I wanted, right? To freak her out? To turn her on? Why the fuck did I bring her here? "No way, but every guy back in school was. She always got off on people watching."

"And you've watched before?"

Stopping, I stand up so she can see the truth in my eyes. "I've watched. I was high as a kite, but I watched."

"Since we've been together?"

"Yes."

"That's why you didn't bring me here before? To your friends' parties?"

"I told you," I say, sneaking in a kiss, "they aren't people I consider friends, but they're the people I grew up with."

"Cruise is here. He's one of them."

"He would say I am too."

"Are you?"

"I was. I don't want this life with them. I want to spend it with you."

A small smile appears. She looks down, the flush of her cheeks darkening. "It turned me on, Alexander. Does that make me a bad person?"

I caress her cheek and smirk. "God, no. It means you're good." I drop to my knees to fuck her clit with my tongue. "So good, but I'll make you feel even better."

. . . I wake up sweating. I kick the sheet down and look over to find an empty bed.

"You were having a nightmare."

Sitting up on my elbows, Sara Jane is curled in a chair in the corner of the room. "I was?"

"Yeah, you kicked me. Twice. I tried to wake you, but you pinned me down. You're strong even in your sleep." She sips from a mug.

"I'm sorry."

"You were dreaming about that night." She leaves it there. Neither of us needing more to know which night she's referring to.

Looking away from her in shame, I whisper, "Yeah."

She exhales through her nose, then takes another sip before setting the mug on the dresser and crawling back into bed. "And yet I'm still here." Lying back, she pulls the covers over her and then tugs on my arm. "Maybe one day you'll have sweet dreams of us instead."

I've had many sweet dreams with Sara Jane as the star. How could I not? When my head hits the pillow, I reply, "Sometimes wishes come true."

19

SARA JANE

B efore Alexander leaves, he comes to my side of the bed and kneels down. "I need to go to the manor to get ready for work, but think about tonight, okay?"

I'm tired, still sleepy in the six o'clock hour, but I'm honest. "I will."

He kisses me on the head, and whispers, "Have a good day."

"Love you."

Before he leaves the bedroom, he sends me a wink that would make my knees weak if I were standing. When the door closes, I grab the pillow he slept on and bunch it in my arms, inhaling his musky male scent into my lungs. The smell of his sweat turns me on, but I could get drunk on the smell that lingers from our early morning connection.

I take the hour I have left and close my eyes. I've not felt this content in a while. Everything feels right, feels how it should. *Finally.*

THE MORNING HOURS fly by with classes, and then I'm rushing to the library. I reach the second floor where the group usually meets. Maya and Shelly are there. Cal is sitting at the head of the table and Ryan's next to the empty seat I take. "You guys are early."

"Friday night," Ryan says. "My fraternity is having a party. I need to get back and help set up."

Maya asks, "Do you have plans?"

She crossed a line when she talked to Alexander behind my back. "Yes, with my boyfriend. He asked me to move in with him, and we're going to be celebrating all night long. If you get my drift."

"Sara Jane." Shelly's tone is cautioning.

Shooting Shelly a glare, I don't back down. Maybe it's the stress of the last few weeks or the memory of Maya flirting with Alexander that set me off, but we are not friends, and I refuse to pretend we are. If I make claims on Alexander in the meantime, so be it. "What? She hits on my boyfriend, then she asks me a question, fishing for information on him. So I was just letting her know that I plan on fucking my boyfriend all weekend long."

"What the—?" Shelly stands. "What has gotten into you?"

Maya protests, "I wasn't hitting on him."

Cal stands with his hands out. "Let's all calm down."

Ryan sits back and laughs. "Holy shit. Girls play dirty."

"If you only knew," I joke, not really, nudging him like we're locker room buddies.

Shelly steps around the table. "Are you drunk, Sara Jane?" When she walks by me, she says, "We need to talk."

I roll my eyes, but get up and follow her to the corner windows. As we stare down at the quad, she asks, "What in the hell are you doing?"

Irritated, I look her way. "Why are you so upset? I'm the one who was betrayed by my friends."

"It doesn't matter how you feel. You can't act like that."

"Like what? I'm lost on what the hell *you're* talking about."

"You're with Alexander—"

"And?"

"And you're better than what you displayed back there."

"I am so confused. Are you saying because I'm with Alexander I need to act a certain way?" She looks around and if I didn't know her better, I'd say she was nervous. "Shelly? What is going on? First you lie to me for what? Months? Years? Now you're telling me I should be acting a certain way because of whom I'm dating?"

"Look," she starts in a hushed tone. "I shouldn't tell you, but I've hated lying to you—"

"How could Alexander trust you more than me?"

"It's different."

"How? This betrayal cuts deep, Shelly."

"I know. I'm sorry. I really am. Please. It was never about trusting me more than you. It's about him loving you too much to risk losing you."

"Don't defend him. There is no defense for the lies. You were my friend first. You should have never lied to me."

"I had to. For Chad. He needed the money, and I missed sleeping with him."

"You kept massive secrets from me over sex with your boyfriend?"

"No. That's not it. I didn't mean sleeping with him sex. I meant actually sleeping at night together. He was never home, and I missed him. We were drifting apart. I did what I could to save my relationship."

"So you sold our friendship out?"

"Don't say that, Sara Jane."

"It's the truth. You sold me out for Chad."

"You would do the same for Alexander."

"No. I wouldn't lie to you. You know why? Because there's nothing I would do behind your back that I would need to lie about." I move to return to the table.

To my back, she asks, "What about Alexander?"

I pause to absorb her question before turning back around and crossing my arms over my chest. "What about Alexander?"

"What does Alexander have to lie about? Why did he need to hide what he's doing from you if it's all on the up and up?"

She knows how to get my blood boiling. Seething, I come back, so we can finish this. I get closer, and whisper, "You tell me. You seem to know all about what's happening over at that fancy penthouse. What are you doing when you hang out over there all night?"

"*They* trust me."

"So they don't trust me? Whatever you're implying, just say it, Shelly." I huff. "And for the record, I trusted you and got burned. Do I need friends like that?"

The frown on her face arches lower before she pleads, "Please don't hate me. I was protecting you just like they were."

"From what?" I run my hands through my hair in frustration. "I'm so tired of this. I just want to go back to when everything and everyone was normal."

"See, that's the thing. Was it ever normal?" Her tone softens, her own exasperation evident as she sits in a chair nearby. "I've been around that place enough to learn a few things."

"Like?"

Her shoulders are hunched, but she looks up. "Alexander owns fifty-one percent of Kingwood Enterprises." My eyes flash to hers in astonishment. She goes on to say, "His mother's money enabled Alexander Kingwood III to start the company. She didn't want a position, but she remained the majority shareholder."

"So?"

"So I think Alexander is right. I think his mother was murdered, and maybe by his father."

I lean against the table next to her, staring off across the library. The shock of her secret hits me hard. Oh my God. *Poor Alexander.* "What does Alexander say?" When she doesn't respond, I look her way. Her eyebrows are bunched together, and I quickly catch on. "He doesn't know, does he?"

She shakes her head. "He has no idea that he owns the majority of Kingwood Enterprises."

"He has no idea that he's worth millions."

"He knows he's set to inherit millions. What he doesn't know is that he's worth billions."

And it comes full circle. "I can't act like this because when he inherits the money and company, all eyes will be on him. Everything I do and say—"

"Will be used against him."

Sighing, I drop down into the chair next to her. "So you're looking out for me, and I didn't even realize."

"He loves you, Sara Jane. He's made it more than clear he wants to be with you, that he wants to build a life with you. He's been preparing and once asked me about rings and what you'd like. He told us he wants you to move in with him, but you weren't ready. Roommate to roommate and friend to friend, I need to know if what you said back there to Maya is true. Are you moving in with him?"

"You make it sound ominous when it could be amazing."

"Kingwoods die. There are only two remaining, so yeah, I worry about you."

"Everyone dies one day, Shel."

"It's not the same and you know it. I haven't learned much about his life, but I know that family is cursed."

"Don't say that."

"I'm sorry. I don't mean to scare you. I know you love him. I care about Alexander too. He's good to you, but he has a death wish, and I'm scared I'll lose you."

"I'm not leaving him. I tried."

She stands. "Next time, try harder. For yourself. For your family. For me." She takes a deep breath and exhales slowly. "I've told Chad I want to move when we graduate."

"And go where?" I ask, standing.

"Anywhere but here. There's no good ending. We all know this. Alexander knows this, but he throws money at it as if that will make it better. Once we graduate, Chad and I can get jobs. We won't need this dirty money." *If Shelly is defending Alexander, she is certainly not quiet in expressing how disgusted she is about it.*

"You'll be leaving me behind."

"You can come with us." *But that's the thing; I can't leave with her. And she should know this.*

She hugs me. "You'll always be my best friend. I love you."

I wrap my arms around her, willing my tears away. If she wants to leave, I may not like it, but I have to respect her wishes. "I love you, too."

When we separate, she says, "You can't tell him about the company. Not yet."

Wanting to safeguard him from any dangers that might be lurking, I say, "His life could be in danger."

"He's safe. His father could have done something long before now if he wanted him gone."

"You talk about his life so casually when I feel sick to my stomach. Are you sure he doesn't know he owns the company?"

"Have you ever heard him talk about owning it?"

"He doesn't even like it. He hates working there."

"It's not too late for you two. You can leave as well, start your life over somewhere else."

"He won't leave until his mother's murder is solved."

"Then we'll make the most of the last year we have left." Checking her watch, she adds, "We should get back to the project, but I want you to know, despite keeping the penthouse a secret, you can trust me, Sara Jane. You always could. I know it doesn't seem that way right now, but I wanted you happy and the Kingwood family . . . just be careful."

"I've been with Alexander for three years. I plan to be with him a lot longer. I know him. Don't warn me about him. As for his father, I'll need all the good thoughts you can spare."

"Are you okay?"

"I will be." This time I leave her standing there, needing to get Mr. Kingwood out of my head since he already controls my fear.

"Hey."

Turning back, I ask, "What?"

"Go easy on Maya. She's an idiot, but I don't think you need to worry about her."

"She should learn to keep her hands off my boyfriend."

"I've never seen this jealous side of you."

I've never felt this kind of jealousy before. The rage of someone trying to take what's mine away is getting the better of me, considering I've never even seen Alexander's eye stray to another woman. The image of Maya touching him has amplified my irritation. "People change. Apparently."

"Guess so."

We wrap our project up early, all of us anxious to be done for the weekend. I was useless with this new information swarming around in my head. Alexander is majority shareholder of Kingwood Enterprises and doesn't even know it. But I do. This secret is big. Too big to stay buried for much longer. I griped at him for doing what I'm expected to do now. I don't want to lie to him, but until I know more about what his father's plans are for us, I need to tuck away this secret.

I head back to Kingwood Manor with my stomach tied in knots. My feet feel sluggish as I walk up those stairs and down the hall. Once I'm in Alexander's quarters, I scan the room. I'm alone. A rushed exhale of relief comes out, and I lock the door.

Checking the time as I cross the room, I have less than two hours to get ready. For Alexander, I'll go. Only Alexander.

A note is taped to the mirror when I walk into the bathroom. I recognize the handwriting before I can read it. Taking it down, I read: *Please join me tonight, Firefly. Kingwood Enterprises offices. 8 o'clock.*

Smiling, I leave the bathroom and head to the closet to see if I have anything I can wear or if I need to go home to get dressed. When I open the door, a black, satin dress hangs from a hook above designer shoes that must have cost more than a few of my car payments combined. A typed note card is attached to the dress that reads: *Please say yes.*

"Yes, Alexander," I say out loud just because I will always say yes to that man.

———

AFTER PARKING my car in the building's garage, I take the elevator to Kingwood Enterprises. I'm greeted with the shiny gold letters of the company, check my coat with the assistant, and make my way through the glass doors. Past the cubicles, the sound of the party escapes the company break room.

I wish tonight could be different. I wish I could walk right into Alexander's arms and hug like we used to, like we did before his father ruined that dream. I didn't tell Alexander about his father being in the bedroom earlier, or the offer, if that's what it can be called. I might call it black-mail. I won't keep it from him longer than I have to. Knowing his father and his evil deeds, he'll twist it and set me up to look like I betrayed Alexander. I can't have that. I won't. With my chin raised high, I walk forward.

The doors are open and the staff has overflowed into the hall just outside the room. I'm tempted to hit the bar, but I want to see Alexander first. Looking around, he normally stands out with his tall frame, chestnut hair, handsome face, and cut jaw, so it's weird that I can't find him.

Working my way through the crowd, I feel empowered by how men look at me. This dress is flattering to my frame, making me feel pretty. I'm also starting to believe I'm the woman Alexander always thought me to be.

The height of the heel of my new shoes gives me a good vantage point, but I still don't see my boyfriend. A sickening feeling starts to fill my belly though. I feel exposed and vulnerable, like unwanted eyes are caressing me in ways that are a violation to my body. Looking over my shoulder, I see Mr. Kingwood—champagne in hand, smirk firmly in place, eyes on me. I lower my gaze and move past the buffet into a shadowed corner. With my bare shoulder blades against the wall, I examine the room more thoroughly.

He's not here. I check my watch. 8:05. Where is he? Why would he be late, knowing I would be here on my own? With my eyes scanning, I make contact with the one person I would love to avoid. Again. Unfortunately, he's coming right for me. "Good evening, Ms. Grayson." I don't reply, biting my lip to hold in the curse words on the tip of my tongue. "I knew you'd look stunning in that dress when I saw it."

Looking down at my dress in horror, I ask, "You bought this?"

"I did. The shoes are perfection with your delicate ankles and toned legs." *Oh, God. I feel sick.* He *chose this dress for me?*

"Please don't speak to me like anything about this conversation is okay. It's not."

I move to leave, but he says, "Speaking of conversations, we need to have one in private. Let's go to my office."

"You are not my boss, and as someone who is not my boss, you don't get to tell me what to do."

Coming up behind me, his hand wraps around my upper arm as he walks forward, taking me with him. "That was not a question. If you'd like to continue to see Alex, you will grace me with five minutes of your virtuous time."

I stop fighting and walk on my own accord. "Where's Alexander?"

"So untrusting. Were you always this paranoid?"

"Not until I met you."

He laughs. "Good one. I enjoy a spot of humor from the female persuasion."

"Humor? I don't find anything funny about this situation."

He unlocks his office door. "Good. Then we can skip the foreplay and get down to business."

"I want to wait for Alexander."

"He'll be joining us shortly." He holds the door open for me. "If you please."

Standing at the gates of hell, I glance around once more, hoping to see Alexander. When I don't, I push down my fears, and walk straight into the devil's den.

20

SARA JANE

He closes the door behind me. I don't sit. I cross the room and look out the window, at the city lights around us before turning to face him. All my strength stiffens in my muscles. "What business do we have to discuss?"

Mr. Kingwood, the rat bastard himself, takes his seat behind the desk and steeples his fingers. "I was checking to see where we stand from our last discussion."

"I haven't thought twice about it."

"Let's not do this. I'm well aware that it's probably all you've thought about. You're a terrible liar, and I don't have time for it anyway."

"I'm not onboard with whatever plan you're scheming."

Chuckling, he says, "You make me sound awful."

"You're not?"

The smile is gone. "Be careful. My patience wears thin." Alexander's dad is a vile, unpredictable man. Before I met Alexander, I never would have spoken to an adult the way I'm speaking to his father now. *Alexander's influence? Or just how I would have turned out anyway?* He stands, pressing the tips of his fingers against the desktop. "Let me rephrase what I want from you. Consider it a job. You'll be paid very well to continue to appear on the arm of my son, but when necessary, like any other beautiful asset, you'll help close deals."

"You want me to be a whore for you?"

"So crude," he says, shaking his head at me. "What about Alex? Will you be a whore for him if he asks you to be?"

"He would never ask that of me."

"You sure?"

I head for the door. "We're done here."

"I thought we weren't going to play games, Ms. Grayson?"

"I'm not. I don't understand why you want me to do this. There's something more to it that you're not sharing."

"I've been very forthcoming with you. More than I should have been." He leans back on the console behind him. "Please sit. This doesn't have to be uncomfortable. I'll go easy. I understand you're a virgin, in a way."

Affronted, I reply, "Why do you say things like that?"

"Because I can. Just like I control Alex's future."

"I think you and I both know better." It slips out before I can stop it.

"We do, don't we?" His eyes pierce mine, and he shouts, "Sit down!"

Two breaths. I keep him waiting for the count of two long holdout breaths before I move as I'm told, too scared to disobey. The blinds to the office are closed and no one can see in. My heart and mind plea for Alexander to walk in. *Where is he?* I'm in way over my head, and a sob forms in my chest but gets caught in my throat.

Taking the seat across the desk, he stares at me. "You

have been a problem for me. On one hand, you're my son's girlfriend, and from what I gather, one he's quite fond of. On the other, you're distracting to both him and me. What do you think?" *How am I distracting to him? Up until a few weeks ago, he'd barely spoken to me.*

"I love your son."

"I didn't ask that." Sitting back, he sighs. "In simpler terms, I'm not sure if I want to fuck or kill you." My gasp loosens my sobs and tears threaten to fill my eyes. I refuse to show him weakness. "I don't kill people, Ms. Grayson."

Did he not kill Madeline Kingwood after all? Before I can really understand the depth of that, the reality of what he's inferring clenches my heart, squeezing until the ache is felt tight in my chest. "I won't sleep with you."

A smile that is too relaxed for the circumstances crosses his lips. "I'm sure you're aware that my son has become my enemy."

"He's your ally."

"He's on a mission to make me out to be a monster. It's very troublesome."

"You are a monster. If for no other reason, how you talk to me."

"No, Sara Jane, I'm not. And some women find me quite alluring."

"Most people would refer to them as paid escorts."

He laughs. "You're witty." He bites back, "It will make fucking that sarcasm out of you that much more pleasurable."

I stand to leave, his threat fueling my reaction, but freeze when he says, "Sit down if you care about Alex." I glare at him but refuse to sit. "Alex may be my blood, but he's his mother's son."

"You loved her," I say, hoping to remind him of that love Alexander remembers so well.

"I did."

"The woman you loved gave you Alex. How can you hate anything that came from that love?"

The harsh gulp I hear reveals the nerve I've hit. "Love destroys you, makes you weak. I'm fighting the only way I know how. Are you weak?"

"No." Even I can hear the desperation in my voice. I need to get out of here.

"You say you love my son, but how much?"

My chest feels heavy with his implications, my breath hardening. I lower my head and close my eyes. *I am strong. I am strong. I am strong.* When I look back up, he says, "You are, but I'm stronger." *Shit. I said that out loud?* He stands and walks around the desk.

My hands start to shake. "Please—"

"Please what, Sara Jane? Such a pretty name. Have I told you that before? Maybe I have." His thigh is pressed to mine, and he reaches out to touch me. "You're so pretty."

"Don't touch me."

A chuckle lifts his gaze away as he steps back. The relief my body feels is emboldening, and I stand, refusing to stay any longer.

Death, control, and all the power he can gather takes over, and he grabs hold of my arm and squeezes. Hunger for more of all three is seen in his eyes. *The man is a monster.* "Or what?"

My sob finally escapes just when I think I can fight back. *Or what? What will I do? What can I do?*

His laughter deepens but the darkness buried in his soul surfaces. It was so fast, I never saw him coming, much less the large hand when it dropped me to the floor. My knees hit the carpet between his desk and the wall of windows. My hair is grabbed. I start to scream but a large hand covers my mouth, and he pulls so tight that the pain stifles my ability to breathe. My skin stings from the slap against my cheek. *This* is what my gut warned me. Alexander's father plans to rape me to grow the chasm between his son and himself. *What man does that? How can someone be so depraved? Alexander, where are you?*

With his acrid breath hitting my ear, he spins me away from the window to my feet, my back to his front, and says, "We don't have to tell Alex. He doesn't have to know. You have a choice to make. Save yourself or save him, but I will promise you this, if you scream, I will ruin him, and then I'll ruin your family. You will be the only survivor watching as your world falls apart."

My tears are bitter with betrayal, but I have to swallow them. "If I don't kill you, he will."

"Your threats are idle, Sara Jane. I can end him faster than you can call him."

"Why are you doing this?"

"Have you ever looked at someone and seen hate written all over their expression? Try looking at your own child who has looked at you like that for the last eighteen years."

"Because you took his mother away."

I was scared before. Now I'm terrified as his eyes bore into me. "You think you know what you're talking about. My son is weak and has spread rumors to destroy me. He won't win. I will. I'll destroy what he loves most. Now bend over like a good little girl or you won't see the light of day tomorrow."

Pleading for my life, for Alexander's, and my family's, I say, "He's your son. Your blood. Your only heir. For the love of your wife, why are you doing this to Alexander, to me?"

"You can make this easy, or I'm more than happy to oblige and obliterate your world. Is that what you want?"

"I hate you so much."

"That's okay. I've discovered hate tastes sweeter on the lips of the innocent. I take it you're choosing to protect Alex?"

He yanks my hair back until the back of my head is on his shoulder. I grapple for the desk but I'm pulled back too far. Pain fills my scalp, but I refuse to give in to him. "It was your decision, and you've made your choice." His free hand slides over my breasts and squeezes before trailing higher. He holds my neck tightly and I gasp for air. *Is this how I die?* Then he moves even higher, the salt from his fingers on my lips. "Now you'll pay the price. Your tits for Alex's tat. Sounds fair."

He removes his hand, sliding it harshly across my lips while the heat of his other hand caresses my hip, my dress inching up. Then I'm left, my voice stolen with my pride and buried like my strength. I'm forced forward. My hands slam on top of the desk in front of me. His erection is against my leg, soon pressing into me if I can't stop this. Memories and mantras flash like rapid fire through my mind.

I am strong.

I am strong.

I am weak ...

"I'm not leaving without Alexander."

"Alex," the lead bitch corrects, ending his name harshly. "And don't worry, I'll keep him preoccupied just like I have before."

"Before me," I correct, the whiskey giving me courage I wouldn't normally have. He would have never been with me, like he was upstairs, and then move on with a cheap whore, like her. Never. Alexander would never cheat on me.

"No, honey." She pats my head condescendingly. "Like I did a

little while ago while you were preoccupied with the stars outside." She laughs.

"You're lying. He wouldn't cheat on me."

"You're boring me just like your awful hair. Run along, Sara Jane." She says my name with disgust.

"He'll be looking for me."

Her eyes remind me of a cat the way they tilt up at the outer corners. Her nails are painted a deep pink, closer to what I imagine the humiliation in my cheeks resembles. I've known girls like her, the ones who guys trip over themselves to talk to, the ones that put out, but pretend they're virgins. "God, you're annoying. You act like you're somebody when you're nothing. I know about you. You go to St. Mary's, but you're standing in the middle of my house like you belong, like you're one of us—the upper echelon of society." Her arms go wide, her gold bangles clanging together. "Alex is known to slum it every now and then. You're a passing phase, an easy target. You fell for his lines and money, just like they all do." A drunk blonde sidles up behind her, her fuzzy gaze trying to intimidate me. "You can't compete with us."

"I don't have to compete. I've already won. Isn't that what you're really afraid of?"

"Did you really think you'd be able to hold his attention? He's a man, and you're just a little girl who lucked into getting his attention when he was hard up. But don't worry." The words she spews are so easily believed by everyone, even me, when said in such a way as to demean. "He's not hard up anymore. I've made sure of that so you can run on home and play with your Barbies while the adults stay. In other words, he doesn't want you here."

"He wouldn't hurt me," I say firmly. "I know Alexander."

She reaches for the door and cracks it open. "You don't know him well enough, sweetheart, because I just gave him a blow job he'll be thinking about all night and begging for more in the morning."

Doubt fills my chest, but I straighten my shoulders back and face my enemy head on. "He wouldn't let you near him, much less touch him with something that's used as often as a garbage disposal."

I'm slapped, my head jolting to the right. "Get out," she shouts. As soon as she says it, her mouth pops open in surprise. "Alex. I didn't see you there."

I whip around and find him standing at the front door. When our eyes meet, I see the fury flickering in his irises. They divert to the bitch that hit me. "Did you just touch my girlfriend?"

"It was an accident," she replies with arrogance and a small laugh.

Before the laugh reaches her smile, he's in her face, so close she can probably taste what she'll never taste again—his breath. "If you were a man, I'd level you."

"Alexander?"

When he looks my way, the lines in his forehead soften, and he smiles gently. He seems to collect himself, his disposition lighter. "Are you ready to leave, Sara Jane?" He reaches out and turns his palm up to me.

"I'm ready." I rest my hand in his and go to him.

His arm comes around me, protectively putting himself between the jealous whore and myself. We start to walk, but he makes a point of stopping, and turning back. "And Lanie, go fuck yourself. Your mother was better."

. . . That was the first time I ever saw Alexander hurt somebody—purposely hurt someone. Her reputation and pride were more damaged than she was.

The skirt of my dress is hiked to my waist, two of his fingers sliding between my exposed cheeks. "So pretty. So soft. You make me so hard. You've teased me too long. Have you ever been taken here?" I hear the zipper of his pants . . .

"Stop."

I halt when he says to, not sure where to run to anyway. My hurt, my anger kept my feet running, but the burning sensation inside me isn't from running. It's from the truth piercing my heart. "You slept with her and her mother?"

Alexander bends, his hands resting on his knees. His breathing is as strong as the regret that rolls off him. His hands go to the top of his head, and he shifts. "I've told you I'm a fuck-up."

"No, that's an excuse you hide behind so you don't have to expose real feelings. You tell me to bury my feelings, that they'll hurt me, but it's not my feelings that hurt me. It's you."

This is the first time I've ever seen him worried, worried he'll actually lose me. "What do you want from me, Sara Jane? Tell me and I'll do it. I'll do anything to make this right."

My tears were lost to the rain ten minutes prior when I ran away from him. Now standing before me, and me before him, I feel my age. I feel unworldly and inexperienced as the adrenaline drains away. I feel cheap and not worthy to be with the beautiful man whose secrets and lies cut deep. "I want you to love me."

"I do, but I'm bad and you're good."

"What makes you so bad? What makes me so good?"

"Your heart. Yours beats strong while mine only murmurs. God, I love you so much, but love like ours is only meant for fairy tales. We live in reality."

"We live wherever we want to live—fantasy, reality, fairy tales, happily ever afters—"

"Nightmares, horror stories, star-crossed—"

"Star-crossed doesn't have to mean doomed."

Holding my face carefully in his hands, he says, "Don't you understand; that's the very definition of star-crossed? Doomed from the beginning."

"Then we won't be star-crossed. We'll be destined."

"Don't live in a fantasy world, Sara Jane. I will do anything

to be with you. Anything. I love you that much, but for us to be together, I need you to do something."

"Anything."

"Live with hope, but be strong. Promise me you'll be strong when you think you're weak. Promise me you'll be strong when you no longer hold on to hope. Promise me you'll be strong when there is no other way to be. Promise me."

"I promise. I'll be strong when I need to be."

. . . My chest shudders with a cry, my tears puddled on the glass in front of my face. My scrambling thoughts settle. I refuse to be weak any longer. I will not be a victim to this man, so I grab the only thing I can reach. "Stop!"

"Or what?"

Summoning Alexander's anger when something of his is threatened, when something precious that only belongs to him has to defend itself, I push off the desk and turn around. With the expensive gold-tipped pen prodded against his neck, I come face to face with pure evil, but this time I use Alexander's words, his strength, and my power to keep my promise.

"Or I'll kill you myself."

21

ALEXANDER

"We're late."

April doesn't say anything. I'm sure being prompt isn't something she generally concerns herself with. For the last two nights, she's been in a hotel with Cruise checking on her almost hourly. I've not spent much time with her, but enough to want to help her clean up, something she says she wants. Two days—it's working so far, even if she did pull a butter knife on Cruise at two in the morning when he busted her trying to slip out to find a hit of anything.

I've paid for the hotel. I'll pay for her rehab. That's the deal. I've been impressed with her determination to clean up, pretending the one incident didn't happen. Something unexpected did happen though. Underneath the drug-induced filth and toil of her life, she's a stunning woman. And fortunately the usual side effects haven't become the main effects of her existence. I think there's hope when the drugs clear from the striking blue of her eyes.

In the quiet of the elevator, I say, "You look beautiful, April." I say it not because I have to, but because I want to. I have a feeling she doesn't hear many nice things these days. *When was the last time anyone said anything nice to her?*

A smile, though small and shy, makes its way across her face. "Thank you."

"You're welcome."

"You'll still pay for my rehab and set me up with an apartment like you said?"

Stepping off the elevator, I stop to finish this conversation before we go any farther. "I will. Full rehab and one year of apartment rental. The rest is on you."

"Thank you for helping me. You're kinder than your father."

I've visited her twice in the last two days. She wouldn't talk at all the first day. The second she talked about a family she once had. I don't know what it's like to lose everything, but she gave me an idea. What she refused to talk about was my father. It was frustrating, but she doesn't owe me anything. I'm hoping tonight will change things. Remind her of what I need without causing too much pain in the process for anyone. It's a move my father would pull, which worries me. I don't want to be like him, but sometimes we have to be what we aren't to get what we want. I try again by asking, "You seem to know a lot about him. How do you know him, April?"

She looks away from me. "Everyone knows your father."

My father, the famous widowed millionaire—money, looks, and a prestigious name. The full package by everyone's standards. If they only saw what I see, the cunning man behind the myth. Checking my watch, I don't have time to dig into this anymore. Cruise arrived ahead of us to pull my father aside. I want this done before Sara Jane arrives, but we're late. I'll keep her waiting to handle this first, then join her inside the party.

When we walk across the main floor, the lights are dim, the music from the party is loud, and Cruise is waiting on us.

He meets us halfway and does a double take. "She looks different," he says before his eyes shift to me and back again.

"Is Sara Jane here?"

"No. I scoped out the party. Neither is your father."

"Good. Let's go to his office. He's probably in there hiding from his employees."

"He's not exactly liked." Cruise is staring at me, so I finally snap, "What?"

April remains quiet by my side. He glances to her and then shakes his head. "Nothing."

"Then stop staring, and let's get this over with." Cruise steps in line and we take a sharp right and make our way to my father's office. "You're going to take April back to the hotel. The rehab place is expecting her in the morning."

The light is on in my father's office, but the blinds are closed. I'm not surprised. He's probably fucking some intern before he announces the company is being sold off for the price of its parts.

I'm hoping April's my smoking gun and ready to talk once she sees him. I know there's more to their story, and I want to find out. Between April and him, I'm determined to get answers once and for all. My father has despicable people working for him, and I know one of them knows something about my mother's death. His dirty deeds are coming back to haunt him, his sins are about to be exposed, and I might finally get justice for my mother.

Refusing to give him any more respect than I have already, I push open the door. As predicted, he's found some easy target to play his sick sexual games. Her dress is up and her bare ass pressed against his glass desk. He's leaning forward, positioned like he's ready to fuck her. I laugh, loving that I messed up his plans. Though not announced, our entrance wasn't quiet. When he doesn't even bother to acknowledge me, I spit, "Get your whore out."

Typical. He doesn't even bother to turn around as he stands there like a statue, staring at her. "Told you my son would be here shortly." Her hair is messed up, some hanging down, some still up. The woman's body shakes with a sob, and I hear her start to cry. My anger converts into confusion. He shifts and very slowly looks back at me over his shoulder. "Just in time, Alex. I couldn't have planned it better. Oh wait, I did plan it. I just expected to be inside her when you walked in." My world is ripped out from under me. "You might know this whore."

The woman moves her head to look at me and the air is gut-punched from my lungs as my mind grapples with familiarity. Through strands of chestnut hair, black streaks down her cheeks, and red that at first glance is mistaken as blood, I recognize those deep oceanic eyes. They're mine. *Mine.* And they should never look that fucking devastated. My brain stumbles for a split second to make sense of what my father and the woman I gave my whole fucking heart to are doing. "Sara Jane?"

"Alexander," she says, her voice breaking at the end. "Help."

Only a split second. Then I'm there before she finishes her sentence, throwing him to the ground. Sara Jane remains standing, her hand unmoving, a pen held in the air like a knife.

Despite the scuffle behind me and Cruise yelling, I take hold of her wrist and lower her arm down slowly. "I'm here, Firefly." Staring into her eyes, something wild has replaced the kindness I'm used to, her spirit dimmed, but her instincts unleashed.

"Alexander," she says, sniffling. Her forehead hits my chest.

I push her hair back from her face and wipe the black streaks from her cheeks. "I'm here." Sliding her dress down to cover her hips and underwear, I wrap my arms around her. "It's okay. I'm here." I turn just enough to see Cruise out of the corner of my eye blocking the door. I look at my father and make a promise I intend to keep. "When I kill you, you will die a slow and painful death."

He laughs, pushing up off the floor. "I expect no less, but I was just testing to see if she was worthy of the Kingwood name. Like wine, she should be tasted before committing to the whole bottle."

Turning back to Sara Jane, I rest my cheek against her head. My jaw is ticking, my hand shaking from the rage filling my muscles. But she needs me more. Through gritted teeth, I tell Cruise, "Get him out of here before I fucking kill him."

"Don't threaten me, son. If you want the truth, she came willingly. She wanted me. All along. She wanted me. Can't blame her."

My temper spikes. "Shut the fuck up."

Sara Jane fists my shirt, pulling my attention back to her. "Get me out of here, Alexander. Please."

The noise behind me grows, Cruise and my father fighting until his back hits the large window. Shielding Sara Jane with my body, I turn back. My father is frozen with fear. When I follow his line of sight, my gaze lands on April. My assumptions are finally confirmed. She played a role in the Kingwood mystery.

My father stammers, "Wha-what-t is she doing here?"

April stands just inside the doorway, her mouth open and her eyes full of tears as she stares at him. When she looks to me, she says, "He injected me the first time. I trusted him with my life . . . with my baby. I should have known better."

Shocked by this turn, I say, "I don't know what the fuck is going on, but you need to tell me now."

April's cries turn to sobs as she stares at the man on the other end of her hatred. "He turned me into a drug addict. One of his henchmen showed up every day after that first day. Pinning me down and shooting me up until I was the one roaming the streets looking for the next fix."

Baby?

"She's supposed to be dead." My father points at the ghost that's come back to haunt him. "She tried to take you from your mother."

"What? What do you mean?" My gaze darts to April.

"She, she, she needs help. She—"

"I was so happy. I thought he'd be happy. I'd just given birth. I gave birth to the heir that woman couldn't. But he," she screams, pointing back at my father, "he took my baby. He stole *you* away from me."

Blood rushes in my ears, and my head becomes light. My grip on Sara Jane and reality loosens. I'm not sure what happens in the next few seconds. My body along with my mind goes numb. Blackness replaces the air evaporating from the room and my thoughts float like I'm underwater. My body is shaken, my thoughts still racing toward reason, toward some rationale that can help me hold on to the words thrown out so recklessly.

Alexander is whispered, my skin tingling from warmth. I look down into the only eyes I can lose myself in. "Alexander," Sara Jane says, cradling my face with her soft hands. "Alexander, look at me."

"I am."

"Look. At. Me."

My eyes focus on her wide, worried eyes. Her expression breaks what's left of my heart. Reaching out, I brush the pads of my thumbs over her cheeks, hoping to make the lines level out.

The mixture of loud voices and movement behind me drags my attention away from my sweet Firefly. But it's not just my world that's changed. All of ours have changed, forever more. Not sure what happened in the time my mind went numb, but when I scope out the scene behind me, April is crying and Cruise is holding the gun we bought after the attack last night. He's pointing it right at my father, but his hand is steady, and I know his mind is focused, unlike mine. The standoff is amplified when my father stands strong, like a fool. We all watch as he reaches into the cabinet next to him and pulls his own weapon. My instincts kick in, and I shield Sara Jane instantly with my body. I won't just die for her. I will go to hell to protect her without a second thought of my own ending. I tell her, "Get down."

She slips under the desk behind me and both of my arms go wide, trying to stop the catastrophe playing out. "Get out, April," I say. "Cruise, lower your gun." He doesn't. I understand under the circumstances. When I look at my father, I see the change—the fear in his eyes, the concern covering his expression. Looking at me, it's for me, concern for me. "Father, don't do this."

"She's a junkie, son. She lies for drugs. She does anything, says anything to get her next hit." He wipes his brow on the sleeve of his jacket. "She wouldn't leave us alone. Your sweet mother was so good to her, and look what she does. She fills your head with lies."

April says, "I'm not lying, Alex. You can't deny how much we look alike."

My father shouts, "Shut up, you lying bitch!"

Cruise's arms are solid, but he still asks, "What do I do, King?"

"Lower your gun." Turning to my father, I say, "Dad, lower your gun."

April drops to her knees, letting the floor take the blunt blow as she sobs. "I'm not lying. He ruined my life. He's lying."

When she looks up again, our eyes meet and in that moment, I see *her*. I see the truth running through her pained face and pleading in her eyes. "Oh my God, you're telling the truth." Betrayal rushes my veins and I turn in disgust to see the man who claims to care about me. "Is she my mother?"

"He took you from me," April cries, "right out of my arms. They cut me open to save you. I couldn't move. He took you from me and left me there to die. I've been dying every day since. But this is my redemption. This is yours. I'm the one who gave birth to you. You are my son."

My father refuses to look at me, so I say it louder, "You did this. You did this as if this would never come to light." My voice rages like my emotions. "Admit it!"

Something miraculous happens. My father shows real emotion. For the first time in history, I wish I could read his mind, but I think what I'm seeing is his heartbreak, his pain, and his loss over my mother's death. And possibly, his failures with me. "I did everything for your mother. She wanted a child so desperately. I could give her anything she wanted in the world, but that's all she wanted. Son, you've got to understand. I loved her."

"More than yourself? Because that would be deep love."

"I loved her more than anything." *He's forgotten what love means.* "I failed your mother when I couldn't protect her from this bitch." His gun lowers, but wags in April's direction. "I met her when I'd drank too much. She made me feel powerful, not like the failure I did at home, but it was nothing. She was nothing to me. One time and my shame would live with me forever. My shame would not just hate me, but survive me and live on." *He cheated on Mom?*

I stand with my arms hanging down, my life sinking to a new low. "Your shame lived on through me. You made me feel like nothing, nothing worth your time or love."

"No. That's not true. She was bringing my shame to life, to taunt the woman I loved. I begged her not to go through with it."

I scrub my face. "Have I ever meant anything to you?" The defeat I feel seeps through my blood and I lean back on the desk for support. I can't process that my life has been a sham. "My mother was an angel. She had so much love to give and showed me how to give it. I never felt worthy because I was *your* son, but I knew I was redeemable because I was *her* son. Who the fuck am I now?" My disgust seeps out. "You are the cause of her death. I know you're a part of it and I will spend my life proving it. You're going down for what you did to April, but you'll rot in a jail cell for what you did to my mother and for touching my girlfriend." I take my phone from my pocket and flick it on to call the cops. "You're going to pay for everything you've done—with your company and with your life."

"No," he pleads. "I gave your mother everything she wanted. Let me explain. We'd just foun—"

"There's no explaining your way out of this. Say goodbye to your life."

"I'm sorry," he says, his body losing the fight and his shoulders sagging in response. "I love you."

The explosion causes me to drop to the floor, my body covering Sara Jane. Her scream penetrates the silence of the aftermath. I hold her shaking body as tightly as I can. My eyes open when I hear Cruise yell, "Holy fuck."

Daring to look, Cruise shoves the gun in the back of his pants, looks down, and rubs his temples. "Shit, King."

April is a mess on the floor, so he leans down to help her up. I survey behind me. Blood is everywhere from the window to the floor, the bottom of my pants and some on my shoes. My father's lifeless body flat on his back—eyes closed tight in the last emotion he ever experienced—fear. *He fucking shot himself. The coward.* Turning back to Sara Jane, I whisper, "I want you out of here."

"Alexander. Alexander. He's dead?" she asks, crying.

"Yes." I shift to my knees and look over my shoulder. Fucking hell. When the reality of what just happened hits, it's going to hit hard. But for now, I need to get her somewhere else, somewhere safe. "Don't look anywhere but at the exit. Keep your eyes forward, Firefly. Okay?"

"All right." I help her to her feet. When she's standing steady, I wrap my arm around her waist, but she sees the blood on the floor and gasps. "Oh my God, Alexander. We need to call nine-one-one."

"I will, but he's dead. They can't save him. Just keep moving."

Cruise has April sitting at his cubicle when we round the corner. I walk Sara Jane to mine and set her in my chair. Bending down, I spin her toward me, holding her by the knees. "Look at me. Look at my eyes, Sara Jane." Her hands cover mine, and she nods. "Good." When I know I have her full attention, I tell her, "Stay here. Right here. Don't move until I come for you. Do you understand?"

"Yes." She sees me glance to April, but her tears dry and my strong, sweet girl comes back to me. "I'll help her. You go."

"You sure?"

She nods and I kiss her quickly. "Thank you." I lower my voice. "When the cops arrive, don't say anything about April and what she said or what my dad said. Can you do that for me?"

She touches my cheek and I lean into it, needing her comfort. "Don't you know, Alexander? I would do anything for you."

I nod, closing my eyes, absorbing the trust she's given me and stealing her strength. When I open my eyes again, I say, "I will do anything for you. I love you. Remember that."

"I love you. Now go. We'll be okay."

Nodding once again, I stand and dial the police while heading back to the huge fucking scene of a crime that is my life. What. The. Fuck. Just. Happened?

22

SARA JANE

Alexander walks away and I look at the woman in front of me. She's crumpled over, her face hidden by her hands. I stare at her, curious. I heard what was said back there. She's Alexander's biological mother. Moving my chair closer, I reach out to touch her. She jumps, but when she looks up, she releases a long breath, and asks, "Who are you?"

I rest my hand on top of hers. "I'm Sara Jane."

"No." She shakes her head. "Who are you to him?"

"I'm Alexander's girlfriend."

She looks behind me. When I turn, I hear a woman scream and Alexander's voice. I stand quickly, positioning myself in front of April protectively.

Over the tops of the cubicle, I see Alexander trying to calm the receptionist, Kimberly. Alexander had mentioned in passing once that she dated his father. I'm not sure how serious it was, but even if it wasn't, she's now dealing with a horrific loss.

Alexander embraces her as he walks her away from his father's office. His tone is hushed, words whispered in a comforting tone. He handles her with such care, her full trust in his hands. When my gaze shifts to her, I see the way she looks at him, the way her arm wraps around his waist, the way she touches his chest, her hand resting on him like she's done it a million times.

Are they close? He said he's never cheated, and I believe him. Kimberly remembered me when I arrived tonight, so I dismiss the jealousy, and my heart begins to ache in what she must be feeling right now.

Turning around, I sit in the chair across from April again. "Did you look for him?"

Regret. Shame. Disappointment. Her expression floods with emotion while her fingers twist. "A couple times, but I was in no condition to continue."

I see tissues on a desk two down from us and grab them. Offering her the box, she pulls a few and wipes her face. I take several and drag them under my eyes and across my cheeks.

She says, "He loves you. What he did for you in there, how he protected you. Love should always be that pure, that easy."

"I'm not sure love is ever easy."

"Then save yourself while you can. If it's not easy now, it never will be."

I dab my tongue to the tissue since I don't have any water, and wipe lightly under my eyes, her words rattling me. Getting up, she says, "Hold still." She takes another tissue and gently wipes under my lips. "Your lipstick is smeared."

My spine bristles, the hair on my arms standing up. "I . . . I fought—"

I was nearly raped. Alexander's father nearly raped me. Knowing Alexander would see.

"He didn't get the best of you."

The best of me . . . "My body's not the best of me. My heart is. That's what I protect the most."

"Wise. I was dumb enough to fall in love once." An actual smile, though very small, appears. "It didn't turn out so well."

"I'm sorry."

"Don't be." Looking out the window next to her, she says, "Just don't repeat my mistake."

"And what would that be?"

Her eyes meet mine. "Getting too involved with a Kingwood."

Too late.

I don't bother saying it though. There's no point in defending my feelings. Cruise comes down the aisle where we're sitting and hands me my purse. "King wanted me to give this to you. The police are on their way. They're going to want to talk to us." Looking at me, he asks, "How's she doing?"

I stand and we lean on a cubicle divider away from her. "I guess okay, considering."

"How are you?"

"When did you start carrying a gun?"

"After we were jumped."

The blood on Alexander's lip. I remember and retort, "It's not considered *jumping* if you're looking for trouble."

Cruise smiles. "You're probably right. Guess we'll keep those details from the cops."

"Alexander wants to keep most things from the cops."

"How do you feel about that?"

"It's not about my feelings. It's about Alexander." I walk past, bumping his shoulder on the way. "And I'll do anything to protect him."

I hear a whistle. "I'm not sure what you did with that little Catholic schoolgirl, but damnnnnnn, The woman's a badass."

"Don't forget it."

"I won't."

Security rushes by me, running toward the office. They're on their phones the moment they see what's inside. I join Alexander and Kimberly near the door that leads to the reception area. She's crying on his shoulder as he holds her, rubbing her back.

I tap him. "Alexander?"

He looks up and his arm drops down. "Come here."

I take a step, but it's not close enough for him to reach me. The line between his brows deepens and his eyes narrow as he tries to read me. My indifferent expression is enough to spur him to come to me. "Are you all right?"

"I'm fine, but what are you doing?"

Taking me by the elbow, he moves us away from Kimberly. "You don't have to worry. She's a good woman."

"How good?" *Shoot.* Why'd I say that?

The words smack him in the face. "What did you just say?"

Just as I'm about to apologize, the police rush through the doors, guns aimed in front of them. Alexander grabs me around the back and we hit the floor. I'm pinned beneath him on my knees, bent over, pain pulsing through me. "I'm sorry, Sara Jane."

But the apology sounds like it's for more than just taking me down to shield me. "What's happening?"

"Fuck." His breath is harsh.

The police tell everyone to freeze while two take the lead and check out the bastard's office. The security guard helps them determine the basic situation and we slowly rise to our feet. Alexander cups my face and leans down to look me in the eyes.

"Alexander?"

"Sorry. I saw guns, and I didn't want you hurt. It's going to be a long night. How are you holding up?"

"Stop worrying about me. For fuck's sake, Alexander. Your father has died. How are you?"

"He killed himself. He made that choice, not me, so I'm fine." The edges of his mouth are straight, trouble seen in his brows. He runs his hands through his hair.

"Maybe you're in shock?"

"Maybe I feel a weight lifted?"

"It's okay to not be okay. You don't have to be strong for me."

Taking me by the upper arms, he's insistent. "I walked in on him about to rape you. He lied about my mother. He took me from the woman who gave me life and then tried to kill her. He never loved me. He tolerated me. Is it okay to be okay right now or do I need to put on a grieving face for you?"

"For me, no. Never. For the police, you might want to."

"I will." His bright smile pops into place. I can see there's a lack of sincerity hidden in it, but that's because it's not a smile I'm accustomed to. "I'm going to talk to them. You'll be fine here?"

"I'll be fine. I always am."

He nods and leaves me with Kimberly, whose shirt is wet from tears, biting her nails, and looking around nervously. "He said he wanted to see me exclusively earlier tonight."

She worked with this man for years. How? Why would she want to be exclusive with him? I look her straight in the eyes so she's very clear on the situation. "He was going to rape me before he was caught."

Her mouth drops open, her hand covering it as tears fill her eyes again. She's crying because the bastard who was her boss is dead. A boss she'd been sleeping with. A boss who'd kicked out a different woman from his home not a week before. *She wanted an exclusive relationship with a monster.* A monster capable of depravity I only thought existed in movies. He threatened me, lured me to that damn party. He tried to rape me . . . *"I just expected to be inside her when you walked in."* He wanted Alexander to see me being defiled . . . Oh God. Oh God. *"I want you to watch."* Alexander had used those words. He'd wanted me to watch the school tramp being fucked by another man.

Am I . . .

Am I in love with a monster? Am I no different than Kimberly? Blind? Ignorant?

I look at Kimberly and I feel numb.

No more.

Not her tears.

Not April's.

Not mine. I can't take anymore. My emotions detach, something Alexander *always* wanted for me, yet something I *never* wanted. Looking down I see remnants of Alexander's father's blood, hair, and something I'm praying to God is not part of his brains caught in the fold of the dress at my chest. A breath is sucked in when the air around me begins to thin.

Then another. Serrated like the knife that's destroyed my fairy tale.

I'm not okay.

I look around—the chaos, the police, Alexander, Cruise, the employees here for a party. *A party.* Where their boss committed suicide.

I'm not okay.

My head is light, my thoughts subdued and fuzzy

around the edges. I take a deep breath and leave Kimberly there, not able to help another soul, not sure if I can even help myself. I walk toward the door and push it open. Police officers and paramedics are filing out of the elevators, and I step aside to let them pass. No one says anything to me, so I step on the elevator and push the button for the lobby, wanting air that's not contaminated by death and surrounded by hate.

The instrumental version of some past pop hit plays through the elevator intercom. Staring into my eyes in the reflection of the silver doors, I've lost the life that once lived there. I've lost who I am.

The door opens and I walk. Just walk.

"Miss?" I look at the officer at the desk. He's not much older than I am. His uniform is crisply ironed and the light from a lamp on the desk reflects off his wedding band. "No one is allowed to leave the scene until we've gotten statements."

I wonder how he decided to fight for others. When did he decide to protect and serve so selflessly? What's his wife like? Does he have kids? Is he living the life I thought I would live? *Predictable* as Alexander calls it?

"Miss? Are you okay?"

No. I'm not okay. "Yes. I'm just going to smoke a cigarette and then I'll be right back."

He nods, seeming to understand the need. I push through the door and walk into the night. The area is blocked off. Police, firemen, and paramedics race around— in and out of the building. Reporters push to get in, and I sneak around a cameraman and walk away from the scene.

Away from this nightmare.

Away from this life.

I'm not okay.

23

ALEXANDER

S taring out the window, I wonder where she is.

My Firefly finally flew away.

Part of me finds an inner joy in the knowledge that she was strong enough to save herself. The larger part of me, definitely my more selfish side, misses my soul mate.

I've watched the videos countless times. The security camera shows Sara Jane walking out of the office and through the lobby. Once she reached the garage, she took her car and disappeared No one has heard from her since, except her parents. *Once.*

It was clear they weren't going to tell me her whereabouts, if they even knew where she was. I didn't ask. I knew I'd go after her, but she left for a reason.

Over a month later I'm still in limbo. I can't seem to let her go. Despite the chaos of working through the mess my father left behind, she consumes my days. My nights are lost to memories of her, and us. So many years spent living for the wrong reason when I had the right reason to live all along.

A knock draws my attention from the view to the door.

Kate, a beautiful blonde assistant hired for the transition to replace Kimberly, stands in the doorway. Her skirt is tight. Her heels sky high. Her lips are red, drawing the bees to the honey. The thin belt that wraps around her emphasizes the curve of her waist. "The movers will be here shortly, Mr. Kingwood. The car is downstairs. It's time for us to go."

With my hands flat on the glass surface of my father's desk, I stay seated in his chair a minute longer. Blood still covers the carpet, the evidence remaining when other signs of that night are gone, like Firefly. I stand. "Thank you, Kate."

"You're welcome, sir."

She thinks I'm *that* guy. The one who likes to play daddy to a pretty sugar baby. She thinks her flirting is subtle when it's not. She thinks she has a shot when she has none.

A month ago that response would have been quicker, that thought immediate. These days I'm not so sure I should be closed off to attractive opportunities. My future with Sara Jane is unknown. Do I hold out hope that she'll return just like the firefly she's named after? Or do I move on?

I walk out of my father's office and through the sea of empty cubicles, the silence of the executive offices, and the stilted air that lives long after his death. The employees have moved on with hefty severance deals and the bulk of the company is locked up in legal battles, everyone coming out of the woodwork wanting their share. One million here. Five million there. The remaining pieces of it sold below market. I don't care. My wealth is beyond Kingwood Enterprises. The dirty dealings of Daddy Dearest will eventually be put to rest. In the elevator, she undoes her top button and runs the tips of her fingers along her collarbone. "What if we grabbed a drink together?"

Blatant.

I lean against the opposite wall, angling my head as her fingers slide farther down until another button comes undone. "What would happen if we did?"

The question confuses her at first, but she catches on quickly. Her smile is as pretty as her gray-green eyes. "I could take your mind off things for a while." She moves closer and touches my shirt, her fingertips slipping between two buttons.

Taking hold of her hand, I still it and lower it away from me. "How?"

Not faltering under my disinterested gaze, she says, "We'd start with a drink, or two." She does demure well, though I see right through her. "I don't live that far from here. I have a stocked bar."

"What if we skipped the foreplay, and I fucked you right here in the elevator? Is that what you want?" Kate stands there staring at me with her red lips parted, but then she licks them slowly, trying to keep my attention. Her desperation for me makes the elevator hotter than it was a few floors up. When she reaches for the emergency stop button, I catch her wrist. "It was a question, not an offer."

Her chest heaves, and she breathes out, "Yes. I'd let you fuck me right now in this elevator."

I hold her gaze, but she'll never replace what I had, what I tasted, what I felt when I was with Sara Jane. I'm fucked. The effect she had on my life still persists, still affecting every aspect, even ones she shouldn't any longer. She left. *She left me.*

Backing across the elevator as if the devil himself knew playing with fire would get him burned, I look at this woman who is willing to give me anything, even her dignity, in exchange for a small piece of my fortune. I know that's what she's after. Sara Jane would have never lowered herself for wealth. Hell, she would barely let me buy her dinner.

Kate's breathing is heard, even with distance, her fingers moving against the buttons of her shirt like she doesn't know whether to take it off or button up. I'm about to tell her what she should do when the door opens, the ding heard loudly above. "Thanks for the offer, but I'm not single." I walk out of this hotbox.

"I heard your girlfriend left you."

My feet stop, the arrow she shoots right on target. Yes, my girlfriend left me. Those are the facts I'm having to face. She took my heart, my love, and my soul with her. I turn around and see hope in her eyes, as if her low blow will change my mind. "I misspoke. I'm not *available*." I turn back and head for the waiting car. Climbing inside, I slam the door closed and nod to the driver to leave.

The sun has set and the lights outside are flashing through the dark-tinted windows that hide me inside. The media has been incessant in getting the story of my father's death. As the head of a billion-dollar company, you don't get to commit suicide without piquing the interest of many people. I hate the attention his death has brought, dragging my mother's death back into the spotlight with him. And the worst thing is he took away my chance at justice for her murder. Even in death, he took away what had driven me for so long.

My life is now lived under a microscope. As much as it hurts that she left, it's times like these that I'm glad Sara Jane got out. Taking my phone from my pocket, I call Cruise to check in.

"King."

I don't have time for conversation, so I get to the point. "Update me."

"There's action in the lower fourth. Chad thinks it's the same guys who lead us to April, but I'm not sure. Could be the other guys."

"The ones who kicked our asses?" I ask, followed by a chuckle that's anything but amused.

"The very ones."

"I wouldn't mind meeting them in a dark alley again."

"This time we'll be prepared."

"Set it up."

"Already done." He breaks character to ask, "How are you holding up?"

"The office is officially closed. I just left for the last time." Looking at my watch, I sigh. "I have dinner with the transition team. As soon as it's over, I'll message you for the location."

"I'll be ready. And King?"

"Yeah."

"No word today."

"Me either."

I hang up just as my car pulls up to the manor. It's too quiet, the employees already gone or retired for the evening. *It's always too quiet now.* I head up to my quarters, aware of the fact that what used to be my haven is now more like a tomb. The rest of the house is haunted with my father's sins, but my bedroom is only haunted by Sara Jane.

My pockets are emptied on the silver tray on the coffee table and I flop down on the couch, exhausted. She would laugh at the tray and probably crack a joke asking where my matching spoon is. I lie back and close my eyes with a smile on my face . . .

Sara Jane smiles and my world is brighter for it. Leaning against my bike, I uncross my arms. I want to be ready for her when she reaches me.

Damn if her cheeks aren't turning a deeper shade of pink as she approaches. My sweet girl. "Did you get it?"

She finally reaches me, her smile even bigger despite the rolling of the eyes. "You're worse than my parents."

"Hand it over." She hands me the envelope. I open it and scan down. All A's. "You're so fucking smart."

"Remember our bet?" she asks, her hand going to her hip.

I remember, but I think I might tease her just like I did by setting the bait that she bit hard. "What bet was that?"

"Oh noooo. You don't get out of it. If I made straight A's, you were taking me to your house."

House . . . "About that—"

She pokes me in the chest. "A deal is a deal, Alexander."

Grabbing her wrist, I stop her relentless poking and pull her closer for a kiss. "I'll follow through." I give her a wink. "I always do."

We've been through a lot. She's seen the side of me I've tried to hide, the side I was forced to share to hold on to her. And she's still here despite how badly a night partying with my old schoolmates went. I vowed to myself to make it up to her. She wouldn't say I needed to, but I do.

I went to talk to Cruise out back that night and came inside to find Lanie Monroe and her posse cornering Sara Jane. They couldn't accept that it wasn't that I didn't want a girlfriend. It was that I didn't want them.

I'm shit though. My father always told me I was, and I pushed her so far that I thought she would run, proving me right. She didn't.

She stayed.

I just wonder if she'll stay after coming to my house. She survived a dinner with my father once. That she stuck with me afterward says a lot, but I also managed to keep her away since. I *get her wanting to find her place in my life. She just doesn't realize the place she already fills. What place do I fill in her life?*

"Do you ever talk to anyone from your high school?"

"Sure. Shelly and Chad."

"Any guys I should be aware of?"

She laughs. "No. Why? Are you jealous?"

"Yes. I'm not going to sugarcoat it. I'm a jealous fucker." I hand her a helmet. "And when it comes to you, I'm not changing. Come on. Time to pay my debt."

Riding back to the manor, I drive slower than usual, take the curves in the road a little more carefully. I always do when she's riding with me. For someone who never liked me riding a bike, she urges me to go faster. I think she gets it now. Risking my life is one thing. Risking hers is a whole other.

I stop at the gate and punch in the code. She asks, "You have a code?"

"It opens the gate."

"You have a gate? How big is this house?"

"It's called Kingwood Manor."

Her chest presses and releases against my back when she sighs. "You live in a manor? Like a mansion isn't big enough?"

"No. Mansions are smaller." I pull to the other side of the gate. You can't see the manor from here, so I take the opportunity to warn her. "It's big. Really fucking big. I hate it."

With her head resting on my back, her arms around my middle, she always reads me so well. "You don't have to hold on to so much anger anymore. I love you, Alexander. I'm here for you. No one else."

Looking at the long drive ahead that leads to Kingwood Manor, I held this part of my life back wanting to hold on to what we have so hard that I failed to recognize that she'd love me even if I lived in rubble. "You know, Firefly, one day I'm going to do right by you. You deserve it. If anyone deserves happiness, it's you."

"What you don't see is you've already made me happy."

I lift her hand and kiss it before saying, "Hold on tight."

The mansion comes into view just over the hill and her hold tightens around me. I pull up out front. She swings her leg over and stands there, looking up with Kingwood Manor looming over us. "It's . . . I've never seen anything like this. Not in real life. It looks right out of a travel guide for Europe."

"It was in my mother's family. My father liked it the moment he saw it. My mother used to say it was haunted."

She looks at me wide-eyed. "Is it?"

Chuckling, I set her helmet on the bike. "Not by the dead."

Walking toward the house, she stays a step behind me. "Sometimes you talk like you're older."

"I call it the curse of being an only child. I was stuck around adults all the time."

"Do you wish you had a sibling?"

Stopping on the steps, I wait for her. "No. I'd not wish this life on anyone."

"When you say things like that it hurts my heart. I'll do anything I can to help you. Just tell me how."

Wrapping her in my arms, I close my eyes. "You're in my life. That's all I need." She's about to say something, but stops herself and relaxes in my arms. When we part, I take her hand. "Come on. Let's get this over with."

We walk inside. It's quiet like always. Though I know there are at least three to five employees working right now, the staff stays hidden for the most part. My father just likes things done. He doesn't want to see it being done. "Are you hungry?"

"Not right now," she says. "It's beautiful in here. Lighter than I expected after seeing the outside."

"My mother liked light and sunshine. After she died, my

father had curtains put up along the back wall. Sometimes they're open, but for the most part they stay closed now." I can see the sadness on her face as she looks at a photo of my mom on the table in the entryway.

"Show me your room."

I lead her into the main room and up the stairs to the second story on the south wing. Down the wood-covered hall that leads to my quarters. She whispers, "Is your dad's room down here too?"

"No. His quarters are in the north wing."

. . . My eyes open to the loud sound of a knock. *Shit.* How long was I out? I ramble up, rubbing my eyes. I open the door and see one of the maids. "Your guests are waiting in the dining room."

"Fuck." Scrubbing my face, I forgot. "Dinner?"

"Yes, sir."

"Thank you. I'll be down in a few minutes. Please let them know and make sure they have drinks."

"They do."

"Thank you."

She curtsies when she backs away, so I add, "Don't do that. I'm not my father."

"Yes, sir."

"Just call me Alexander."

"Yes, Alexander."

The cycle's not going to be broken in one night. I need to make changes, but I have other more pressing business to handle first. Like this dinner. I'm dreading it. But like everything else right now, it needs to be dealt with so I can focus on more important business. Like Sara Jane. *God, I miss her.*

I splash water on my face and change shirts before heading downstairs to the dining room. The transition team is here to close out some final details to sell Kingwood

Enterprises. Nastas O'Hare and Connor Johnson are seated at the far end of the table with half-full highball glasses in front of them. I stop before entering. "My father used to sit at the head of this table—he made many deals here that made Kingwood the billion-dollar corporation it is today."

Nastas's smarmy smile and fake laugh do him no favors. "You're a very rich man, Alex."

"Mr. Kingwood," I correct his disrespect. "I'm not my father, but remove yourself from that seat."

He stands quickly and shuffles around the table. "We, umm, brought the paperwork for you to sign. This will close out two deals tonight. That leaves three other divisions, and we have offers to sort through for those."

Connor tosses paperwork down on the shiny wood surface. "We don't have to take much of your time, *Mr.* Kingwood."

Sarcasm coats my name when it leaves his mouth. I should punch him the fuck out, but this is business of a different sort. I have no intention of following in my father's footsteps; I need this company off my shoulders. I sit at the head of the table and start reading over the contract they're presenting. I only make it to page two before the dots connect. "This says the liaisons will receive a three percent fee. Your money was paid upfront by my father."

Shifty Eyes Johnson starts stuttering some excuse, "We, uh, were t-told. A deal was made. We c-can't change-ge it."

"What do you mean a deal was made? On whose behalf?"

Nastas tells him to shut up and takes the opportunity to state his lies as if they're truths. "Your father owes us a stake in the sale of these two divisions. We deserve it."

"My father would never pay twice. The deal was cleared

and paid months ago. He didn't become wealthy by being a fool with his money."

I notice how tightly fisted Nastas's hand is balled. "Your father owes us. Since he's dead. You take on his debt."

"Are you threatening me?"

"Threatening is an ugly word. We want what's owed. Nothing more."

"What did you do for my father other than try to steal money from him?"

"You have led a very sheltered life, Mr. Kingwood. Your father didn't become wealthy from playing by the rules. So before you take your father's reputation and set it on a pedestal, you should be careful how you choose to move forward. There is a lot of dirt out there that can blow back on you. I suggest you sign the papers and move on with your life."

I lost any semblance of patience when the threats were thrown in. "Or what?"

"Or you'll regret going back on a deal that your daddy made while you were off fucking up your life."

One threat on top of another. *Fucker.* "I don't know what you have on my father, but as you mentioned, he's dead." Keeping my eyes locked on him, I see a bead of sweat track down his forehead. I stand. "You come into *my* house with some shitty deal trying to steal *my* money. Our business is concluded."

I walk around the table to leave but stop when Nastas warns, "You're making a mistake, Alex. Sign the deal."

Alex. Fucker.

In seconds, I have him pinned by the neck against a wood-paneled wall where a painting my mother loved hangs. "Don't you ever fucking threaten me. And if you ever utter my name again, even as you bow at my feet, I will hunt you down and fucking rip you to pieces."

I watch as his face turns red, blood trapped by my hand. From behind me, I hear a quivering Connor, "We-we're sorry, Mr. Kingwood."

Dropping him to the ground, I turn my back and leave. My message has been delivered. Fuck them. No one will threaten me. No one.

24

SARA JANE

Three and a half hours northeast of the city I grew up in lies a sleepy town of four hundred, though I've not seen more than fifty at most. They have a gazebo in the town center where the mayor regularly picnics with the citizens. They have one elementary, a middle school, and have to bus over an hour to the high school. With the combined towns all feeding into it to form a Division 1A football.

Each Friday, they make the trek to follow the players from town to town and support their team. By ten at night, the diner gets busy. By eleven, it's packed and the celebration over their victory or pep talk that they'll *get 'em next time* begins overflowing into the parking lot.

Three and a half hours northeast of where I grew up and one month after the night I constantly relive in my nightmares, I've become a part of this tight-knit community. I spent my twenty-first birthday working a double shift and taking a piece of pie to eat in the solitude of the motel across the street, where I've been staying.

The people here are kind and open, but best of all, they respect my privacy. I think a lot of them are escaping their own pasts. Here, I've been given a new start. Here, I don't have to think about the past. I don't even have to worry about my future. Here, I go to work and return to the motel. I get a free meal each shift and pay the motel through my weekly wages and tips. I don't need much—the uniform was provided—one pair of jeans, a few shirts I picked up at the charity shop, and a floral dress I scored for two dollars recently. I would have never worn it in my old life, but something about it allows me to be who I am now.

Lost in the middle.

I have a roof over my head, steady work, and a few new friends. I don't need much. What I do need, I shouldn't want. *What I want, I shouldn't need.*

Alexander.

I miss him. Half my soul stayed with him when I left. I've thrown my stuff in my car, and sat in the driver's seat ready to return more times than not. I know I shouldn't though.

Space was needed. When I'm around him, he's my priority. His life consumes mine. Time has been necessary. I needed to really look inward, look at the life I was living, the life I was choosing. Time has given me a new perspective. Maybe I can live a simpler life and be happy. Maybe I can live without Alexander, although that seems impossible. An ache is forever present where my heart used to reside. It's only been one month. One month isn't going to wash away a lifetime.

I'm not stupid. I knew what I was giving up to live in his world. I guess I never realized the true consequences of that decision. A Grand Canyon-sized hole existed in my chest. That emptiness was growing the more he pursued his personal mission. His determination to solve a mystery came at the expense of who he was, which ate away at me and who we were together.

He carried the weight of his mother's death when I met him, so I don't blame him for wanting answers or for carrying that darkness with him through the years.

I wasn't strong enough for him.

I couldn't help him.

I couldn't save him, not even from himself.

If I return, I will return knowing what I go back to. This time I'll have no excuses. This time I'll know the person I have to be to be with him.

I'm not that person yet.

———

"THIS IS the first time you've bought anything other than water, soda, or snacks. Going with the hard stuff, huh? Rough day?"

I look up from the money in my hand to the guy behind the counter. He's relaxed, like he's sat there for hours. A soccer game is playing on a tablet behind the counter that he seems interested in by the way he occasionally glances back. "No. Just predicting a rough night."

He laughs awkwardly. "I was giving you a hard time about the wine by calling it hard—*Never mind*. Bad joke. Sorry about the rough night. You should go out."

I don't laugh. Dread fills my veins. I can tell I'm going to have a long night. I've been shaking all day. I'll spend the next few hours reliving every moment I ever had with Alexander. Then the next few I'll spend in and out of the car, debating, torturing myself if I should return home or not. "I don't go out." I stay invisible. "I just work and keep to myself."

"I know. That's why you should go out."

When I look at him this time, he looks different. He

comes into focus for the first time, not just a blur, or a random person helping me survive without knowing it. Now he has a face, and when I glance down, a name. "Larry?"

"Eric," he replies with a light, embarrassed laugh. "The last guy who worked here was named Larry. I never got a nametag so I just took ownership of Larry's."

"What happened to Larry?"

"He died." My expression must say it all because he quickly adds, "He was ninety-eight. He had a good life."

"I'm not sure that justifies things, but it's good to hear that it's possible."

"That he died? We'll all die one day."

"I understand death. It's the good life that seems like the impossibility."

"Maybe some of his good luck will rub off on me."

"Maybe." Pointing to the bottle of wine on the counter, I ask, "How much?"

A section of his wavy brown hair falls over his forehead. I've never seen him like this before, and now I'm noticing a good smile and athletic build. "It's on me."

"I can't let you do that."

"It's already done. We all have rough nights now and again."

Taking the bottle by the neck, I look down at it and set it back on the counter. "I don't want to owe anything to anyone. I pay my debts."

"You won't owe me anything but a *hi* next time."

When I look up, his kind caramel-colored eyes summon a smile from me. "Thank you. I appreciate it." I take the bottle again and turn to the door but pivot back to face him just as fast. "Goodbye, Larry."

"See you tomorrow, Alice."

My smile grows and I walk out feeling a lot better than

when I came into the convenience mart. Kicking a rock as I walk across the dusty lot to the motel, the bell chimes above the door, and I hear, "Hey, Alice?"

I turn back, and he says, "A few of us are going to Growly's tonight. I know you don't go out, but maybe, maybe tonight you can make an exception?"

"Growly's is a bar."

"Yes, I know." He laughs then settles on a smirk that could make him dangerous to be around after a few drinks.

"I can't tonight. Thanks, but maybe another time."

"I'll ask again."

Nodding, I smile to myself and turn around, having a feeling he keeps his promises.

There's another car parked at the motel. There's rarely another car parked at the motel. This isn't a town where people stop, much less stay in, unless they're looking to disappear for a while, like me. I find my steps slowing, my heartbeat picking up.

I look inside the car as I pass. It's empty, and I find myself scanning the area and across the street to the diner. I don't see any signs of the owner. Pulling my key from my purse, I unlock the door and go inside quickly. I toss my purse on the dresser and set the bottle down before closing the curtains.

My paranoia is going haywire. No one can find me, I remind myself. I'm not even using my real name. There's no record of me here or anywhere for that matter. I destroyed my bank cards the day I arrived. I threw my phone off a bridge into a river one hundred feet below. I'm untraceable.

I peek out the curtains. No one in the vicinity. I go for the wine, the good feelings Eric filled me with disappeared the second a threat was poised to expose me. I get a glass from the towel in the bathroom where I left them drying last night. Standing at the dresser, I peel the foil away from the top of the wine bottle and stare at it. Angling my head to the side, disappointment rolls through me when I realize I need a corkscrew.

This would have been my first legal drink and I can't drink it. Damn it.

I look around the room for anything I can use to wedge the cork in or out of that bottle. Pen. Lip gloss. Spoon. Knife.

Knife.

I grab the knife from the bathroom counter and return to the bottle. Stabbing it a few times only pulls apart the cork, dropping pieces onto the dresser. "Fuck." I throw the knife down. As it skids across the cheap laminate surface, I drop down on the bed and cry, letting my bottled-up emotions pour out. It's been a few days since I was overcome and this is my penance . . .

I've never seen Alexander shy like he is now—strong, capable, arrogant—but never shy. He stands in the middle of his bedroom, his head lowered, eyes peeking up at me. "Bedroom?" I ask. "This is bigger than the whole upstairs of my house."

"They call them quarters."

"They?"

"The staff."

Nodding, I repeat, "The staff. Right. And what do you call this place?"

"My quarters."

I burst out laughing in response, which makes him smile. "I never felt poor until I was standing in the middle of your quarters."

"You're not."

"I know." I grab the hem of my plaid, pleated Catholic school uniform skirt. "I go to private school, but man, Alexander, this place is huge." I move to the doors that lead to the balcony and

open them. Stepping out, the fresh air settles my nerves until I look beyond the balcony. "That's the backyard?"

"Thirty acres."

"I live in a neighborhood with the creepy boy, whose bedroom window looks into mine, less than a dozen feet away." *Turning around, I lean against the balcony and look at Alexander who remains where I left him.* "Nobody can hear you scream here."

"Do you plan on screaming?"

"Just noting."

"I shouldn't have brought you here. I knew it was a mistake." *He moves to the end of the bed.* "That's why I never brought you here before."

"Why didn't you? You've never given me a good reason."

"I never wanted you to look at me like you're looking at me now."

I go inside and stand in front of him, nudging his feet with mine. He parts them and I slide between his parted knees. When he looks up at me, I ask, "How am I looking at you?"

"Like you don't know me at all."

"I know you, Alexander. I know who you are deep down. I see the soul of the man. I see you. I know where your heart lies, your goodness lives, and where your thoughts wander. I know because I'm just like you."

"You're not like me. You're better."

"No, I'm not better. I'm just better at hiding it." *I lean down and kiss him. His lips taste of the cinnamon gum he was chewing, the gum he tossed when he saw me after school.*

His hands cover my hips, rocking them just enough to tempt me for more. Reaching down, I touch his erection over his jeans, and whisper, "Make love to me."

I'm flung onto my back on the bed and he's over me, kissing my neck. One of his hands slides under my skirt. "You're sin wrapped in a good-girl package." *Goosebumps cover the skin of my inner thigh. When the tips of his fingers reach under my panties, he says, "I want you."*

"I've wanted you for so long," I say on a wanton breath.

"I love you, Sara Jane."

"I love—ah, God." One finger enters, another teasing my clit.

"What do you love, baby?"

"You. I love you," I reply, my moans louder than my words. The other finger is added and my hips respond. "Please, Alexander. Please."

"As much as I love watching you squirm, I fucking love hearing you beg for my cock." My cheeks heat from his dirty words. "You want my cock in your wet, silky pussy?"

"Alexander," I say, not used to that kind of talk.

"Baby, say it for me." He watches my face while fucking me with his fingers. "Tell me what you want and I'll give you anything."

Struggling to keep my eyes open, much less focused on him, I squirm. "Why do you want me to say those words?"

His hand stops and disappears from my body. I want to scream no, but he adjusts so I can feel his steel against me, making me ache even more. "If you want me to take your virginity, I'm going to devour every last fucking ounce of it." He slips his fingers into his mouth and drags them slowly out, savoring me like the most delectable dish he's ever tasted.

He starts to sit up, but I grab at him to keep him here. "I want you."

"You want me to what, Firefly. Tell me."

"I want you to make love to me." When he starts to turn, I add, "I want you to fuck me, Alexander. I want to feel your cock deep inside my pussy, so much that you're still a part of me long after we're done."

A smirk slides into place. Leaning down and kissing me on the cheek and then my lips, he whispers, "Don't you know, baby, we'll never be done. You're it for me."

"You're it for me. I love you."

Slowly, he undresses me, my schoolgirl uniform replaced by raw, bare skin that radiates to life. Just like when I met him, he brought my soul to life. I've never been touched like this. He treats me like I'm the most beautiful treasure. He treats me like I'm his. And though I've said it before, now I know what it feels like to be his.

Our connection runs more than skin deep. He fucks my body and makes love to my soul. We lie in the aftermath of our love, my purity destroyed in a blissful annihilation.

"Promise me, Firefly, you'll never leave me."

"I'll never leave you."

"No, that was too fast. Don't answer yet. I want you to think about it, and then answer when you know. When you feel it inside," he says, rubbing my chest over my heart.

I kiss him and lie back down. Rolling to my side, he covers me from behind, and I close my eyes, knowing the answer already. But I wait, because when I say it aloud, I want him to believe it.

. . . Lifting my head, I feel groggy after sleeping and turn to see the time. Three hours. It's almost ten. I see the bottle of wine and feel the frustration instantly return. I get up and use the restroom, my head still full of the memories of losing not just my virginity, but my soul to Alexander.

I could break the top of the wine bottle. I dismiss the idea since it might put small glass shards in the wine. When I come back out, I see the floral dress hanging from the top of the bathroom door. I decide to change into it with no real reason other than I need a change in my routine. I put on a little makeup, keeping it light, and pull on a pair of wool socks. Grabbing the old hiking boots I bought on closeout from the shop, I put them on. I pull my hair down from the rubber band and fluff it. I won't spend too much time getting ready or guilt will settle in and keep me here.

Walking out the door, I lock the bolt and tuck the key in my jean jacket. Growly's sign is glowing red in the distance, the "r" flashing as it threatens to burn out. It only takes a few minutes to walk down the street, but each step feels heavy. It's these moments when I miss Shelly and Chad. Even before I met Alexander, we hung around mostly just with each other. Cutting myself off from Alexander has also cut me off from my friends. And I wonder how they are. If they ever wonder where I am or worry if I'm okay. I've never gone out on my own. I've never even been to a bar. I've never started my life over before either, so I go anyway, needing something to numb these memories crowding my mind and suffocating my heart.

The music is heard from outside, so when I open the door, it seems the whole town has come out tonight. I hesitantly walk in and head to an empty barstool at the far end. I slide on top and when the bartender, a diner regular, spies me, he comes over. "Hey, Alice. Good to see you. What are you drinking?"

Before I can answer, a deep, friendly, and familiar voice, says, "Get the lady whatever she wants and put it on my tab."

25

SARA JANE

Three beers in and I'm feeling the effects. Country music is something I would have never listened to at home, but here in this town, in this bar with the laughter, the dancing, and the drinking, I kind of like it. Eric leans on the bar next to me, a smug grin on his face. "Dance with me."

"I don't dance." My voice doesn't sound like my own. It's more relaxed and drawn out, kind of like the people in this town. Maybe I fit in more than I thought.

"Go on," Della says over my shoulder. I can hear the laughter in her voice. My boss at the diner is having her first night out since she filed her divorce papers almost a year ago. Like me, Eric sweet-talked her into stopping by for a drink. Leaning against my back, she whispers, "He sure is cute."

"Listen to the lady. I sure am cute." He nudges me with his elbow. "Anyway, you're not the first city girl I've taught to two-step."

"How do you know I'm from the city, country boy?" I lean on the bar, angling in his direction.

"Well, I know you're not from around these parts. I would have heard about you."

"I think I believe you. This town keeps tabs on everyone."

Della laughs. "Boy, do I know that." Patting me on the back, she says, "I'm going home. One drink is enough for me."

Turning to hug her, I say, "You have a good night."

She whispers, "Dance with him. You're young. Have fun."

"Yeah. Yeah. Be safe."

"Will do."

Eric tells her good night, and then squints at me with a wonky, pursed smirk. I raise my shoulders and ask, "What?"

"You."

"What about me?"

"Your eyes are like Pandora's box. Full of intrigue and secrets."

"I'm not that exciting. I work and I go home."

"Home. The motel isn't temporary?"

Turning the bottle of beer around by the neck, I think about my slip. "The motel is not my home, but something that's become a habit."

Leaning over just a little bit, he whispers, "Sometimes we're lucky enough to have habits grow into more. You think I could ever become one of your habits?"

"That's very forward considering you don't know me at all."

He takes a long swig of his beer, and then says, "I know enough to want to know more."

His niceness is tempting in ways that shouldn't be for a girl caught in a whirlwind of unresolved affections for another. "You're a nice guy—"

"Nope. Let's not go there. The kiss-off hurts my ego more than my feelings." He pushes off the bar when a new song starts playing. "I like this one. Come on. Dance with me," he says, his hand out for me.

"If you know I don't dance, why do you insist on wasting a perfectly good song on me?"

The smile I've grown accustomed to fades. "'Cause I think you could use something to take your mind off your troubles." The grin returns, and he moves closer, his middle against my knees. When his hands rest on my legs, I look down.

Alexander.

Coming here, to this town and to Growly's, I thought I was escaping a life that consumed me. I left the chaos of that world behind.

I thought. Feelings don't let you forget. Memories are there to remind, to bring back the emotions you felt, still feel.

"Give me a chance, Alice."

Take a chance, Sara Jane.

"I'm gonna go." I land on my feet and start walking backward. "Thanks for the beer."

Reaching forward, he grabs my hand. "Don't go yet."

Slipping out of his reach, I smile. "I'll see you around, Larry."

He laughs and tips his cap to me. "See you around, Alice."

I'm glad I came out. It beat sitting in that motel room another night watching bad TV. I push the door open and step into the cool night. It's quiet out here, the gravel under my feet the only sound in the air. I shove my hands in my jacket pockets and look up at the stars as I walk. I've never seen so many. Stars like this don't shine where I'm from. I wonder if they ran away to this town too. A smile creases my cheeks as my breath comes out in white puffs.

I chalk up my good mood to the beer and company and continue walking and smiling like this is real life, like it's natural to feel this good. I'm starting to feel like myself, the good parts finally starting to heal the bad.

Looking down the highway at the motel, my breath shortens, my feet stop, and I stare ahead. I don't need light to recognize the silhouette and that motorcycle parked out front. The stars provide enough light, and my body is instinctively drawn to him. Without waiting for an internal nod of permission, I start walking again.

Alexander stands, his arms uncrossing when he sees me. I want to run into his arms and pretend none of the past year happened, but we both know that's not possible. So my pace stays steadier than the beating inside my chest. When I reach the motel, his face comes into view. Those blue eyes I love so much trained on me as if I had the strength to run away twice.

"Alice?"

I turn back, and Eric is jogging toward me. *No. No. No. No.*

"Sara Jane?"

Closing my eyes, I don't know what to do. When I open them, I head back to Eric. I've got to make him leave. Alexander won't understand, just as Eric doesn't now. He looks over my shoulder at Alexander when he approaches. "I wanted to make sure you made it back safely." Nodding in Alexander's direction, he asks, "Everything okay?"

"Everything's fine. Thanks. I'll see you tomorrow?"

"Yeah, sure. I'm working all day." His eyes narrow, not satisfied, my nonchalance not believable. "You sure you're okay?"

I plaster on a fake smile I've mastered and am about to placate him when we both hear, "She's fine."

Shit. Pleading with my eyes, my tone reflects my panic as the words rush out, "I'm good. I promise."

I hear the crunch of the rocks under Alexander's boots. "Go back to the bar and mind your own business."

Eric's eyes dart from me to Alexander and back again. Time ticks like the rush of blood with each heartbeat. When he steps closer, panic rises inside and is reflected back in his eyes. "My name's not Eric. It's Jason, and I'm not from anywhere near here."

"Why are you telling me this?"

"Because if you're not here tomorrow, if I never see you again, I want you to know my real name." When he speaks, my breath halts in my throat. I can feel Alexander within a few feet of me, but I don't look back. Not yet. Jason continues, "We've all come here to escape something. You can stay. We can go somewhere else. You don't have to go back. I can help you."

Good. He's so good. Looking into the comfort of his eyes, maybe I should have taken that offer for the dance. But standing between the two of them, I will always choose Alexander. "I may have been escaping but it wasn't from him. He won't hurt me."

Jason stares into my eyes, and when he finds what he's looking for, he glances back at Alexander. I see the relief in his forehead as the lines smooth. The war was over long before this battle ever began. He's knows which side I'm on without having to ask. "Okay." He acknowledges Alexander with a nod, then says, "Take care of her."

Taking a deep breath, I look back over my shoulder at Alexander. He's staring at Jason, but there's no animosity. An understanding passes between two men who appear to be on the same side. The name feels foreign, and makes him vulnerable, but he trusted me with it, so I give him the same respect. I exhale, and say, "Take care of yourself, Jason."

"I always do." He shrugs, gives me a wink, and heads back to Growly's.

When I face Alexander, his arms—the arms I've missed each night as I've gone to bed—go out wide, and I embrace him fully. *Home.* The tears come easily and I break down under the stars I was too blind to see before tonight. Letting my love pour out, I say, "I love you."

Whispering into my hair, he kisses my head, and says, "I know, but do you know how much I love you?"

Leaning back, I nod. "I'm sorry for leaving."

"Don't be. I was proud of you."

"You were?"

"It was a long time coming."

The wind picks up along the deserted highway, and I shiver. "Want to come in?"

"If you want me to."

"I do." I take his hand and we go in together. He looks around the small room, a disapproving expression coating his handsome face. He's nice enough to not voice his real feelings on the matter.

I shut the door and lock it. "It's not the manor."

That makes him laugh. "You got out."

Tossing the keys on the dresser, I sit on the edge of the bed. "I took a break. That's all, Alexander."

"You could have taken me with you." He leans against the dresser and looks right at me. "Or was I what you were taking the break from?"

"It wasn't because of you. You were the only thing keeping me there anymore."

"What about school?"

Swallowing my disappointment and the credits I'll lose, I reply, "It's just a break."

"What about that guy outside? You can tell me, Sara Jane." *Not Firefly.* "I'll still love you. Is he just a break too?"

"He's nothing."

"He seemed to really care about you for someone who's nothing."

I stand and walk to the dresser, leaning against it with space between us. "I've been here a month, and I just learned his name today. So when I say he's nothing, I mean it. He's just a nice guy caught up in my mess." I step closer. "I expected you sooner." *I hoped deep down.*

His eyes focus on mine, trying to read my thoughts. "I didn't know if you wanted to be found."

"I'm still not sure."

"You don't have to be. I just needed to know you were okay."

His heart was always bigger than the both of us. I close the distance and lean my head against his chest, our arms remaining by our sides. Raising my hands, I rest my palms on the front of his shirt, inside his leather jacket. "Are you okay?"

"No." His response comes quickly, then he holds me, and kisses the top of my head. "Not without you, so you need to tell me how long this break is going to last, or if I need to come to terms with losing you forever."

I lean back, the passion I always felt for him in full effect. "Can you? Can you come to those terms? Because I can't. Not when it comes to losing you."

"I told you once that there is no one else. You're it for me. So if this break turns into forever, I'm not moving on like you didn't change my life."

Lifting up on my toes, I kiss the lips I've missed so much,

the lips that speak words of love and forever so naturally with me. Those soft kissable lips that embrace mine, showing me that I'm his whole world. And he kisses me back telling me I am his. Forever.

I take hold of the opening of his jacket and work it down over his shoulders. He does the same with mine. Our lips separate, but we remain silent, not using words to express our love, but our bodies. I take my boots and socks off, then start on the buttons of my dress. He pulls his shirt and undershirt off.

It's only been a month, but my memories of his perfection weren't doing me justice. I follow the lines that carve into his stomach, highlighting his ab muscles and the top of a V that trails down to ecstasy. His biceps are cut, all his muscles more defined. Standing with my dress open in the front, I release the buttons to run my fingers over him. Valley to peak, each muscle is distinct and hard. He says, "I've been working out in my free time." His voice is huskier, the air between us thickening,

"You sure have," I reply with a grateful grin. His skin is firm and smooth, beautiful like him. I move to kiss his chest, but when his scent—soap, leather, and the open road—infiltrates my senses, I press my tongue against him and taste him instead. My dress slides from my shoulders and puddles around my ankles, the rough pads of his fingertips scraping against my skin. I welcome the damage. I welcome him back—the beautiful torture to my soul, the miniscule demarcation between pain and hope, the desire that only comes from him and for him.

With his palm flat to my belly, his fingers dip below the lace of my panties and takes what he knows is his. He's not gentle or rough but somewhere in between, a lot like us.

Moisture coats his fingers, and he smirks. "So wet. So wet for me, baby."

"I've missed you touching me."

"I've missed being inside you." His thumb finds my clit and teases.

Watching my chest rise and fall, his hand abandons me and his belt is undone. I pull the leather loose and drop it to the floor. Together, we strip the rest of our bodies till we're naked, standing in front of each other, bodies exposed, souls bared.

I move to the bed, not shy or embarrassed to be followed by his watchful gaze. Folding down the blanket, I lie on top of the sheets while he waits for me to settle. When my eyebrows cinch together, he comes over and sits on the bed next to me. "You've changed, Firefly."

My heart soothes from hearing my name from his lips once more, taking immense pleasure in its comfort. But then the statement creeps into my insecurities, revealing my anxiety. "I've lost weight. Do I look bad?" I ask, bringing my knees up to my chest, and hiding myself. What if he doesn't find *me* attractive anymore?

"No," he says with such confidence while loosening my arms and spreading me open again slowly. "You're beautiful, although you didn't need to lose weight."

"I didn't on purpose."

"That's what worries me." Leaning down, he kisses my chest, and then sits back up. "I was going to say you're softer around the edges. Your eyes, your reactions, the way you carry yourself. Is that what I did to you? Did I make you hard?"

"You made me come alive." Taking his hand, I bring it to my breast. "Make me feel that way again, Alexander."

He stands, goes to the bathroom, flips on the light, returns to my side, and turns the lamp off. The room is now dim, but we're left with enough light to see each other's intentions. I move away from the headboard, and he levels himself next to me.

I admit, "I'm nervous."

"Don't be, baby. It's me, just me and you." Alexander caresses my cheek and kisses me lightly. My body reacts as my mind welcomes him back. Our kiss deepens, and I wrap my hands over his shoulders. His hand slides to my chest. Lightly pinching my nipple, a moan follows before I even realize it came from me, so easily from his touch. With a roguish smile turning me into putty, he moves lower and takes my nipple into his mouth while I run my fingers through his hair. "You're so beautiful." Moving on top of me, he aligns until the tip of his cock is touching my entrance. He kisses my jaw and my lips again and whispers, "I love you so much," and presses into me.

My mouth opens for air as my body takes him in, reveling in the stretch and burn I haven't felt in too long. When he moves, he's agile and strong, muscles flexing in his arms and jaw. I watch him, feeling him deep inside, reaching parts of my soul that have only ever been touched by him. Our connection overwhelms me, and I feel a tear slip from the corner of my eye.

Alexander stops and looks into my eyes. "Don't cry, Firefly."

"I left you when you needed me most. Will you ever forgive me?"

A soft, understanding smile highlights his handsome features. "There's nothing to forgive. You did what you needed to do. It doesn't make it hurt less, but you needed the time."

Rubbing his cheek, I say, "You waited for me."

"I'd wait three lifetimes for you." He smiles, reassuring me. "You feel amazing, baby."

He starts slowly moving inside me, and my tears dry. "You feel so good. I needed this, more than you know."

"I'm happy to oblige." When his gentle strokes inside turn into thrusts, he looks up and says, "Hold on to the headboard."

I take hold of the wood above my head and stop thinking, wanting to lose myself to feelings and this man that is all consuming. Alexander thrusts harder, chasing the pleasure only I can give, and he takes it full bodied. My orgasm hits hard, my nails digging into the wood while his name rolls off my tongue.

My name comes fast with his orgasm seconds later, paired with two swear words and whispers of love. An hour later, he's asleep on his back. The smell of our bond lingers in the air, sweet sweat and dirty sex. Alexander's scent is stuck to my skin, and I'm tempted to never shower again. I lightly run my fingers over the stubble on his chin, the same stubble that made the skin of my inner thighs feel raw and equally heavenly.

Careful not to wake him, I move closer and lick the wounds that I emblazoned on his skin the second time he took me to the edge and let me fall under his spell. He reaches over and wraps his arm around me. Kissing my temple, he whispers, "If you come back, it's for good."

It's not a question or a threat but lies somewhere within the love our souls share. He's right so there's no need for a discussion. I kiss his neck, close my eyes, and find sleep soon after.

Light slips through the small opening in the curtains, and I open my eyes—rested and relaxed.

"You have nightmares."

I look at Alexander who's sitting up with his back against the headboard, and reply, "Every night since . . ." I don't need to finish. He knows which night I'm talking about.

"I don't. Does that make me a bad person?"

"You've found peace with him gone, but I don't know if I'll ever get that night out of my head." *The smell of whiskey from his father's breath as he hovered over me. The dark and evil glint in his eyes as he groped me. The loud blast and the thump of his body as it hit the ground. That is what I hear the most. The thump. Over and over again. Then the blood. The mess . . .*

"I'm sorry you have to live with that."

"You don't need to apologize." *In time I will heal.* I lift up, sidling up to him. I weave my fingers with his and our hands rest on top of his leg. I like the size difference. I've always loved how much bigger he is than me. His strength in the way he leads his life is an aphrodisiac. I'm tempted to start another round with him, but I don't, feeling time is slipping away from us. "You saved me."

"I think you were doing a fine job of saving yourself."

"I wouldn't have done it. I wouldn't have been able to use that pen."

"You would have if you needed to. You were holding it against his neck, not wavering, just doing what had to be done."

I put my head on his shoulder. "He touched me . . . he was going to . . ." I stop speaking, my emotions a lump in my chest.

"I'm sorry." Remorse wraps around his tongue when he speaks, and I hate it. I hate the sound of it in his voice. I hate the way the corners of his eyes tilt down as if he has any reason to apologize.

He's not a monster. I hadn't fallen in love with a monster like I feared.

"You're not your father, Alexander. You're better than he ever was." When he doesn't say anything, I do. "You're King for a reason."

"I don't mind being Alexander with you, even if just for a little while." The sentiment makes me smile until I realize it's only in sentiment. We can't be Alexander and Sara Jane. Not anymore. Like our innocence, the people we once were are long gone. He sighs, and pulls his hand from mine before leaving the bed. He disappears into the bathroom, and I watch when he returns to get dressed.

"Do you need me to carry your stuff to the bike?"

Stuff? I don't have enough to fill a grocery sack, much less take with me. I look up, our eyes meeting in an impossible world as if a day never passed when we were apart. "No," I reply, holding on to the awful coverlet that never saw better days or happy travelers. Studying the room and how my few acquired belongings fit so neatly into it, I know this is it. This is where I decide how I lead the rest of my life. I pull the dress with little flowers back on and put on a pair of sneakers. Sitting at the end of the bed, I look at the life I created. It's not much, but it is mine.

"It's almost eleven," he says as if time matters anymore. The door opens, the sun floods in, and Alexander walks out.

I follow but stop in the doorway, my feet refusing to cross the threshold. His body moves with precision and certainty. Taking hold of the motorcycle, he uses his boot to move the kickstand out of the way. He knows the moment he sees me. His breath is almost audible I'm so in tune with his reactions. Closing his eyes, he lowers his head. When he looks back up, I see the hopeful yet guarded, confident yet burdened, expression. It reminds me so much of the day I first saw him. The day I heard him tell Cruise who I was, or rather, who I would be. *"She's not some girl. She's* my *girl.*" But now, he looks unsure. "Is this forever, Firefly?"

"No."

"Don't take too long."

I can't give him an answer to the silent question he's asking, so I tell him the only thing I'm sure of, "I love you, Alexander."

One nod and no words. That's what he gives me in return. His leg swings over and with his back to me, he sits with the engine idling. I hold on to the doorframe, knowing if I let go I'll get sucked back into his world. I'm not ready for that, so my grip tightens.

Alexander never looks back, but my eyes never leave him as I watch him ride away until I'm staring down an empty highway.

26

SARA JANE

I take a sip of coffee just as the diner door opens, letting in a cool wind. Eric/Jason walks in and sits at the counter in front of me. "You stayed?"

"I wasn't ready to go."

"I'm glad."

"Okay, okay, settle down," I joke. "I haven't even had my coffee yet." My audience is captive and entertained, making me smile. "Coffee?"

"Yes, please. I'm nursing a hangover."

"That's what you get for partying so much." I reach for a mug and the coffeepot and fill the cup in front of him.

"What can I say, the ladies love my company."

Laughing, I offer a menu, glad that this, whatever it is—friendship, I question—is easy between us. "Having break-fast today?"

He points to the menu in front of him. "A number one, eggs over easy."

I place the order. With the coffeepot back in hand, I walk around the diner filling cups and delivering checks. When I return, his plate is up and I set it in front of him. "Bon appétit."

He's about to dig in, his fork hovering over his plate, but he stops and asks, "Alice?"

"Yep?"

"That guy last night . . ."

No need to hide behind lies anymore. "That's my boyfriend."

The short answer seems to be enough. He knows where we stand and where I stand with Alexander. "He's a lucky guy."

"I'm a lucky girl." I don't mean to sound so wistful, but after last night, Alexander has made all those romantic feelings resurface. I didn't intend for my heart to be stuck in the clouds of hope again, but here we are, going round in this circle again. Maybe I'll never be free from loving him. His love is so ingrained in me I'm not sure where Alexander ends and I begin. Even after all this time, I'm still a mess of unsettled emotions. One thing I know for sure is I have a lot to think about.

Jason goes back to his breakfast, letting the subject die down just as Della rushes in the front door and behind the counter. "My damn ex-husband has decided to fight for custody of my kid again." This is nothing new. She's always dealing with that asshole over something. "I have a court date. In case it takes longer than expected, can you stay a little late, if needed?"

She's a good woman—nice boss, great mother, town saint for feeding so many who can't pay their checks. I've been thinking about going home since Alexander showed up, but I can't leave her in a lurch like that. What's another week at this point anyway. "Sure. I'll cover."

"You're a godsend, Alice. Thank you."

Although he says I've softened, my heart has hardened since Alexander left. I spend the next few days in my regular routine. I haven't had any alcohol since that night, not liking how freely my mind wanders under the influence. I threw the bottle of wine out the next day too, the thought of wine turning my stomach. I've stuck with water and juice. I've been craving Cheetos and ice cream though. After another ten-hour shift, I stop by the convenience store to grab some goodies. Jason isn't working, so I head to the motel and settle in. I end up staring at the TV until I fall asleep.

Per usual, my sleep is restless, the nightmares more vivid, but instead of seeing him kill himself, I feel that monster's breath against my neck and his hands touching my body. I wake up in a sweat and run to vomit the memories away. So many questions remain. What if Alexander wouldn't have come in when he did? Would I have been able to stab him to stop him from raping me? *What if? What if? What if?*

These questions haunt my day, the torture now around the clock. I vomit often, my body rejecting *his* presence inside my mind.

Weeks go by and I've successfully avoided facing reality . . . continued to successfully avoid making long-term plans or any decisions regarding life. Three weeks have felt like a cycle of nightmares that have become so vivid I'm running more on caffeine these days than sleep. I can't live my life like this anymore. I need to face the demons of my past to help clear the air for my future. That means going home. It's time.

Ever since Della won her custody case, she's been in a great mood. I hate to dampen her mood, but I need to tell her what I've been thinking. I'd rather tell her when she's in a good mood than bad. So when I return from my break, I rinse my mouth so the horrific memories from *that* night don't leave such an acrid taste behind. "Do you have a minute, Della?"

"Sure, honey, what do you need?"

I wrap my arm across my stomach, afraid I'll be sick again if I start crying. "I'm leaving. I hate to do it like this, but it's time I go home."

Sympathy settles on her face. "Aw, I hate to hear that, but I understand. I can tell the pregnancy has taken a toll on you. You should be with your family."

My rebuttal comes fast and punctuated with a laugh, "I'm not pregnant."

"You're not?"

"No," I reply self-assuredly.

"Are you sure?" Her gaze analyzes mine.

My arms wrap tighter around my middle. "I can't be pregnant."

"I just thought with you throwing up so much . . . I heard your boyfriend was in town visiting . . . Maybe you should take a test."

I was on birth control before I started having sex, but since I left the pills behind, and I wasn't planning on having sex with anyone other than Alexander, I let it slide. My mouth drops open when I realize how natural it is for us to fall into each other like we always have—bare, skin to skin —that I didn't even think of birth control when he was here. "Oh my God." My hand covers my mouth in shock.

"Why don't you take the afternoon off and take a test, Alice. You need to know."

Grabbing my purse from under the counter, I mumble, "Yes, I need to know. Thanks." I hurry out the door and across the street to the convenience mart. I'll have to face

Jason, but I need to know, so I'll deal with the embarrassment.

He greets me with a smile when I enter the store. "Hey, Alice."

"Hi." I rush down the first aisle, which has pharmacy needs, and grab two pregnancy test boxes from the bottom shelf. I also grab a large bottle of water and some pork cracklins to distract him. Who am I kidding? There's no hiding the tests, but I still keep the pork rinds. I dump my stuff on the counter and talk too fast to hide my nerves. "I'll need a bag today, please."

The silence that follows slays me, my face heating as he stares at the boxes. Without a word, he grabs a paper bag from under the register and keeps his eyes down. "Sure thing." He punches a few buttons on the register then looks up. "You doing okay?"

"Yeah, fine." Please just let this torture end and let me leave.

He gives me my total, and when I pay him, he says, "If you ever need a friend to talk to or help, you can come to me. I won't make judgments."

I try to interject some humor into the conversation, hoping to sidetrack him as well. "Well, what's the fun in that? Isn't that what friends are for? To judge us?" I laugh but it's shallow.

When I reach for the bag, he reaches out and touches my hand. "I mean it, Alice. I'm here if you need anything."

Looking at his hand covering mine, his genuine sincerity, I feel ill. Everything about his touch is wrong. My body rejects it altogether, and I pull back. "I'm fine. Thank you though."

"No problem. I'll be here all night if you need to talk."

"Thanks." My response is clipped, but I have no doubt he understands why.

Not five minutes later, I enter my room and empty the contents of the bag onto the bed, grabbing one of the boxes. I pull the stick from the package and read the directions. One line—*not pregnant*. Two lines—*pregnant*. Got it.

As soon as I finish peeing on the stick, I replace the cap and set it flat on the bathroom counter and start the three-minute countdown. My hands start to shake as I stare at the white window box waiting for anything to happen, but praying that whatever the outcome, life will be better because of it.

I am strong.

I am— My old mantra enters my head for the first time since that night at Kingwood Enterprises. I cut it short, not ready to pretend I'm stronger than I am. Yes, *I have survived on my own. That is something I have proven. But I can also see I'm stronger with Alexander.*

Thirty seconds. *Shit.* Adrenaline is coursing through me, so I get up and pace to the motel door and back again. Five times. Each time, checking the window. Nothing detectable yet.

One minute and twenty seconds. I take a deep breath as I approach the stick. When I look there's pink. Success! Oh wait, what does it mean? I bend over for a closer look. Pink. I grab the box and look at the photos again, then skim the included pamphlet once more to confirm. If any part of two pink lines appear—*pregnant*. I look down at my watch. Three minutes.

Taking the stick in hand, I stare at two very defined pink lines. My head feels light, and I grab hold of the towel bar to keep myself upright. *Pregnant.*

I don't know how long I stand there, time escaping me like sand running through my fingers. *I'm pregnant.*

Setting the stick on the dresser, I lie on the bed and curl onto my side. My arm protectively covers my stomach, and I close my eyes. I see Alexander, the boy who swooped me up into his dark world and let me shine my light in. He's the man who would do anything for me, but save himself. The image of that photo that hangs in his closet comes to mind, but the memory vanishes before I have a chance to hold on to it. His father's eyes pierce my happiness and a sharp pain shoots through my side.

A severe gasp cuts through my throat, the terror of that night wreaking havoc on my body. I run to the bathroom to throw up. Landing hard on my knees, I hover over the bowl, hoping to expel the violent memories along with my lunch.

When I'm done, I lean against the opposite wall, exhausted with nothing left to give, just like when I walked away from my previous life. The gravity of the situation hits me hard. I'm pregnant with Alexander's baby. Something I don't think he wants as his words come hissing back. *I'd not wish this life on anyone.*

The tears come hard and fast, my body wracked with fear—fear of the unknown, fear of disappointing my family, fear of what my life will become if I don't finish school, fear of Alexander's reaction, and the worst of fears—fear of failing this child.

I refuse to fail this baby. Pushing up off the floor, I brush my teeth, splash cool water against face, and look at myself in the mirror. Really look at myself. This is it. This is who I am, in ugly and beautiful times, but throughout it all I'm the woman Alexander Kingwood IV loves and cherishes. I'm Sara Jane Grayson. I hold my chin up. I'm the mother of

Alexander V, and this child will be raised in a house built on love. I'll make sure of it.

I know what I need to do. I know what I *want* to do. I've never felt surer about anything in my life. I'm going to end the nightmare I've been living and create the happily ever after I deserve.

If you come back, it's for good.

It's time I return home. For good. It's time I return to Alexander. *Forever.*

My stuff doesn't take more than ten minutes to pack up. As predicted, I fit most of it in a sack. I load it into the trunk and do one last walk-through before leaving. After locking the room, I drop the key off at the vacant front desk, and then walk to the store. I push the door open and walk straight for the register. Jason's feet are up on the counter, but he quickly stands. I don't give him a chance to say hi or make a funny quip like he usually does. I just say what I need him to know, "I'm happy. Despite the puffy eyes and dried tears, I'm happy."

"That's good. I'm glad," he replies with his hands in his pockets. "But why are you telling me this?"

"Because if anything ever happens to me, I don't want you wondering if I made the right choice. There are no other choices. There's only him for me, and now this baby." I release a breath. "I'm leaving."

"I figured." He looks out the dust-covered windows. "A motel's no place to raise a kid."

"Neither is a manor."

"Huh?"

"Nothing."

When he looks back to me, a small grin shows up. There's also a sense of relief found in his expression. "I'm happy you're happy. I wish we could all be so sure of ourselves."

"What are you going to do?"

"I think I'll stick around a while longer. There's this new waitress down at Growly's."

I laugh, albeit lightly. "Good luck, Jason."

"Have a great life, Alice."

Turning to leave, I pause to soak in his words. When I look at him again, the words come so readily and with ease, "I will." I push open the door, the chime I've become so familiar with rings one last time, and I turn back. "I hope you find your own happiness one day."

He chuckles. "You and me both."

Nothing more is needed, so I walk away and cross over to the diner for one last goodbye and maybe something to eat on the road. Della meets me at the door with a big hug and congratulatory greetings. "How did you know?" I ask while we walk to the end of the counter.

"Eh, I'm an old hand at this. Did you come to say goodbye?"

"I did. I'm sorry I'm leaving you one waitress down."

"Don't be. You've got more important things on your mind than the pie of the day. I'll miss you, but I can see by the look in your eyes that this is right."

"I feel it in my bones."

"Well, let's not drag this out. I'm sure you want to get to wherever you're going before dark." She grabs a sandwich from a plate ready to go out to a customer and wraps it in foil. On the way to the back, she calls out for the order to be replaced by the cook. I laugh, knowing I'll miss her spunkiness. When she returns, she hands me a bag. "I've stuck a piece of your favorite pie in there too. Put on some weight for that baby."

I don't take the bag. I hug her first, hard. "Thank you for giving me a job and for everything else."

"You're welcome, honey. Now go get that man I keep hearing caused quite the commotion when he was here." *Uproar. Yep, that would be Alexander all right.*

"Take care, Della."

"You too, Alice." She winks and hands me the bag. They all know it's not my name, but not one of them ever said any different. While walking to the car, I look both ways across the empty highway and breathe deeply, my lungs and mind finding peace at last. I've never regretted being here. I needed this place. I needed these people. The angry waters that raged inside me are calmer because of it, because of them. The good in these people will stay with me long after I've gone.

A smile full of pride. *I did it.* I stood on my own two feet for the first time. I put myself first and found out what I'm really made of. I am strong. It's not a mantra. It's the truth. My smile grows when I realize what I can do once I'm home and have everything I already need and more at my disposal.

I'm ready to go home.

I'm ready to take my throne.

I'm ready to be queen to Alexander's king.

27

SARA JANE

The drive is dragging. Two hours in, and I'm too anxious to be patient. A million emotions have played through my head. No matter how the reunion with Alexander plays out, I always come back to the fact that he wants me. He has made himself clear for what feels like my whole life. And I know he'll want this baby. Our love made something bigger than us, bigger than any of our problems or bad dreams. This baby is a brand new beginning for us, one that will come with a life full of love, laughter, and happiness.

Thirty minutes until I see him. I try to decide if I should go to the penthouse or the manor. With no phone, I can't call to find out where Alexander is. My body shivers with giddiness I'm so excited to see him, to tell him everything.

Releasing the fears that have been dragging me down, I take the exit that leads to the manor. New beginnings. Checking my appearance in the rearview mirror, I'm briefly distracted by a blue sedan tailgating me. I pull to the side, straddling the line to allow the car to overtake me on this two-lane road. When the car passes, I look over. Hate-filled eyes stare back, and I slam on my brakes in response, alarms ringing in my ears. Red flags are raised along with the hairs on my arm. I slowly pull back into the lane and keep my distance as the other car speeds ahead.

Kingwood Manor isn't much farther, and I take a deep breath to pull myself together again. My excitement builds easily just thinking about seeing Alexander again. When I round a bend, I smile. Then I'm slamming on my brakes to avoid hitting the blue car, the road becoming a blur as I swerve off the road into a clearing. I jolt to a stop in shock as my belt tightens against my chest. I gasp and shift the car into park before tugging at the seatbelt to loosen it from hurting the baby. When it won't, I unbuckle it and start to pull at it again to reset the lock mechanism, but freeze with my hand in the air.

On the other side of my window stands the man with vengeance set in his eyes, holding a gun aimed straight at me. Reflexively, I duck down, frantically searching for anything I can use as a weapon. I have nothing. Nothing. *Shit.* I find an umbrella under my seat, but that won't save me. Keys. I take the keys and tuck them into my pocket.

My door is opened, and he's grabbing me by the shirt and yelling at me, "Get out! Get out, bitch!"

I'm yanked from the car, not able to stop my eyes from filling with tears. "Okay. Okay." I put my hands in front of me, hoping it calms him enough to lower his gun. "Please don't hurt me. You can take the car. I don't have much cash." He uses the gun to signal where he wants me. I move quickly to the back of the car, holding my head up. My ribs ache from trying to cage my raging heart. Panic takes over and I begin to cry, pleading, "Please don't hurt me. Please. My cash is in the glove compartment."

"I don't want your money."

"What do you want?"

"I didn't want to hurt you."

I look up, hoping the hate is gone from his dark eyes. "You can take the car—" Wait . . . *didn't*. Past tense. The words stuck to the back of my throat. He didn't want to hurt me.

He's going to hurt me.

He growls, his lips rising into a snarl. "This is payback. I got fucked, so you get fucked."

"What? No. Please. I think there's been a mistake."

His eyes are crazed, glassy and hollow, and I wonder if he even has a soul. "No mistake. We had a deal. Your boyfriend apparently finds it good business to destroy people's lives, so I'm going to destroy his world." My thoughts are racing, trying to grab hold of something that makes any sense. Getting right up in my face, he adds, "Kingwood is going to burn in the pits of hell for fucking me over. No one fucks me over and lives to tell the story."

Kingwood.

A sinking feeling starts spinning in my stomach, picking up speed. "Please. Please. I don't know what you're talking about. Surely it was a misunderstanding. He killed himself. I was never his girlfriend. He shot himself."

"Shut up! I'm talking about your boyfriend, not his father. We had a deal with the old man. He was good to us, knew when to pay up. His son needs to learn a hard lesson."

So close. I'm so close to returning to my heart and soul. *Oh God, if you can hear me, please help me make it home. Please.* "We can clear this up. We . . . we can clear this up. One phone call. That's all I need. Please. Please. Please."

"You fuck scum, which makes you scum. Why should I trust you? You're just another spoiled rich bitch."

"No. No. I'm not rich, but I can help you. I promise. Please. One phone call."

The handle of his gun slams against my cheek. I drop to the ground, landing on my hands and knees. Pain scorches through me as I watch blood drip from my nose and bleed into the dirt.

From above me, he kicks my foot. "Make the call, and you better be convincing. I want him or the money or you won't see the sun set." He drags me to my feet by my elbow. My legs shake under the pain, my hand shaking from terror.

I am strong.

I swallow the blood that coats my lip and glance up long enough to memorize his face. I've seen him—at Kingwood Manor—at the party, watching Alexander and me when we went upstairs. I remember him. Sweating, nervous, staring.

He will pay for this. Alexander will make sure of it. The phone appears in front of me and I look down at the screen. On the screen, there's a photo of a woman—mid-forties, maybe slightly older. Pretty. Too pretty for him. This is my chance, my only chance to save myself. Blowing out a breath, I take the phone and dial Alexander's number.

One ring.

Two rings.

I swallow. Closing my eyes, I will him to answer.

Three rings.

"He's not answering."

"You're a dead bitch if he doesn't." He starts pacing, keeping the gun locked on me—his target.

Four rings.

Answer. Please answer, Alexander, I pray.

Five rings.

All my hopes of survival vanish as soon as my call is sent to voicemail. My grip loosens, the phone almost falling.

When I look up, I can barely swallow, my throat too dry. Then it occurs to me, and I try one last tactic. "He won't answer your call. You said yourself that he won't do business with you."

"And?"

Hope lives on when he shows interest in my line of thinking. Dropping another breadcrumb down for him, I say, "I need to make another call."

"Fuck that. No. Get to your knees."

"No. Please. I can call a friend. He'll get Alexander for me. He'll take my call."

He stares at me, his own twisted hope coming out to play when his pocked cheek rises in a happy sneer. Sweat beads on his forehead, and he wipes it away with his hand. "Fine. One more call. You better pray to whatever god you believe in that you get hold of him."

Without the number handy, I struggle to remember Shelly's number, but I dial, taking the chance.

One ring.

The call is answered. *Thank God!* "Hello?"

One chance. "Shelly," I reply. "I need Alexander."

"Sara Jane?"

"It's me. It's me," comes rushing out of my mouth.

"What's wrong? Where are you?"

"I need Alexander. Please." I break down and start crying again.

"He's not here, Sara Jane. Hold on. I'll ask Chad."

While staring into my death, I hear muffled voices and then Chad takes the phone. "Sara Jane? Where are you?"

"A few miles from the manor—" I'm backhanded, coughing into the phone.

"What the hell is happening?"

"I need Alexander."

"Hang tight. I'll find him and have him call you back."

"I don't have time for that—"

"Get off the phone," my captor shouts at me, spittle hitting my face.

"What's wrong? Tell me."

"I need to go," I say, realizing I'm out of chances. "Tell him I love him."

"Don't hang up. I can help. How can I help?"

The man disconnects the call, tucking his phone into his pocket. He grabs my arm, his fingers squeezing hard enough to leave a mark. Pulling me forward, he knees me in the stomach. "Say a prayer, bitch! You're gonna fucking die for his sins."

I fall to the ground when he kicks me in the back.

I am strong.

I am strong.

I am—

My world goes black . . .

A hard hit to my face jumbles my mind awake. My vision is blurry, and my ears are ringing. I wipe drool from my mouth, but when my hand pulls back my vision clears, and I see the blood and dirt dredged across my skin. Looking up at the man with hate-filled eyes, he spits on me and scowls. "I should fuck you, take everything from him and send him the leftovers. He thinks he's a king, but I'll make him a pauper."

A noise that sounds unlike myself comes screaming out. The man who stalks my nightmares comes to mind, his body pressed to my backside, the feel so real it's as if it's happening all over again. My fear is visceral and deep. *Fight.* "No. Please. I'll get you the money. I'll talk to Alexander."

"Shut the fuck up. Too late for negotiating." He reaches to touch my cheek, but I bat his hand away. Standing up, offended, his lip twitches. "Yeah, I'll fuck you, which will fuck your boyfriend up." He walks to the back of the car and opens the trunk. "He'll never look at you the same. Oh wait, he won't anyway since you'll be dead."

The screeching of a car rounds the bend and skids to a stop. Chad jumps out, leaving the car running. Before he sees what's happening, he yells, "Oh shit, Sara Jane," and rushes to my side.

Using every ounce of energy I have left, I shout, "Run!"

The sound is loud and instant.

No compassion is found in gunfire.

For the moment, Chad looks confused. But then reality dawns, and his expression morphs as his hands cover his chest. I scream, moving to reach him as fast as I can as he drops to the ground. Blood spreads through the threads of his striped shirt. "Sara Jane?"

"*Nooo.* No, Chad. Oh God!"

Tension leaves his features, his eyes focusing through me. "I'm sorry."

Sobs take over, my breath coming short, and my lungs close as panic sets in again. Chad's head hits the ground. His eyes are wide open. I touch his face, to beg him to stay. "Please, Chad. Fight." It's then that I see the life leave his eyes. This man. My friend for so many years. He can't leave. He just can't. Scrambling closer, I drop my head down on his shoulder. "I'm sorry. I'm so sorry." *Oh, Shelly. Oh God. What have I caused?*

"You're going to be. I'm going to fucking kill every last person who ever mattered to the young heir." The voice that will haunt me to my dying breath, hangs over me singing, "One down. You to go."

Looking up through watering eyes, I know I'm not going to make it out of this alive. It's clear he's going to kill me, his hate infused into his view of me long before we ever met. I only have one option left.

To fight.

I pull myself up, walking my hands up the side of the car. My body hurts. Something broken or bruised in my chest making it hard to breathe. But I do. I breathe because I must. For me. For this baby. For Alexander. "You are going to die before I take my last breath."

"Small threats from such a little bitch."

"It's not a threat." My glare hits him hard. "It's a promise."

"I'm going to shove my dick so far down your throat you're gonna feel it in that fucking cunt of yours."

Every second slows, the wind settling. My eyes take one long blink, and then I fight for my baby's life. Whipping the car keys from my pocket, I flick it open from the fob and swing solid, nothing stopping me.

The skin of his cheek rips open and blood pours out. Like all tragic love stories, Alexander's and mine is no different. Death comes too easily when faced with evil. Struck, a slicing pain rips through me, the bang quieter than my scream. Maybe death doesn't storm in. Maybe it tiptoes in when you're not expecting it.

Alexander.

From the moment we met, we were always meant to go down in a blaze of glory. Our love flamed hot, burning us from the insides and scorching our souls, marking them for long after this life.

It was easy to believe in love and fairy tales with Alexander. He, the hero of my story, of my life, and I, his heroine.

It's too bright. I open my eyes, and considering the pain I'm feeling, the sun shouldn't be shining. The bright blue sky reminds me of the only blue I want to see. Brilliant blue eyes, not found in the heavens, but here on earth.

The world dims momentarily. "Where's your boyfriend?" the man asks.

How did I end up here? *Like this?*

I know. I just don't want to admit the truth. *Even now.*

Closing my eyes to block him out, I search my mind for the answer. "He'll come for us," I whisper.

I'm too broken to feel another kick, but I see when he pulls his foot back and lands it against my middle.

A car. Blue. Swerve. Della. Jason. Kingwood. Alexander. "He'll come for us," I whisper, unsure if he hears me.

Us.

Another sharp slap to my face sends my head to the right. *He heard me.* I'm too stubborn to scream again, to give him the satisfaction, even as the taste of copper coats my mouth. I'm going to die. I will die silently before I give him anything more. Curling to the side, I hold my stomach protecting the only thing that matters. I haven't told Alexander. I haven't had the chance. I was going to, but this unforeseen detour has brought me here, a mere two miles from the manor.

What if I survive? I can. Maybe. I think. If I hold on, just a little longer. Reaching out, I touch the red pooled in front of me, wondering if that's someone else's blood. It can't be mine. There's too much to be mine. I'm alive, but now I'm wondering for how long.

"Where's King?" is shouted. Again. I assume, still at me, but I refuse to say more. *How did this man find me?*

I don't know the answer anyway. I haven't seen him since he left me. The memory of his face when I let him ride away causes my breath to stutter in my throat and I cough. I wish

I could change the past. I wish I could go back to the beginning and relive our love from the start.

His life is full of lies—the kind he tells and the ones he lives. Lies that have become mine and will haunt me as I learn to live without him. Those lies still haunt me as if they are mine to survive.

He once told me he would give me the life I dreamed about—the ending I deserved—a happy ending—but with rocks cutting into my skin and a stranger kicking the life from me, I start to wonder if all hope is lost.

Until I hear that familiar sound—the distinctive sound of a custom Harley exhaust foreshadowing my knight in shining armor. Peace settles over me when I see Alexander.

It doesn't matter how long it's been since I've seen him.

It doesn't matter what bad has happened between us.

Our love will never die, even if I do.

"I told you he'd come for us."

Knowing he'll be here soon, I close my eyes, and dream of the fairy tale we almost had . . .

Tires screeching to a stop follow shortly after. I'm too weak to lift my head, but the scuffle of shoes from people rushing around me rings clear. Cruise rushes to Alexander's side. Someone else comes into view. Jason. *Why is Jason here?*

My gaze falls to Alexander as shock overwhelms him. His hands go to his hair. "What the fuck?"

"Don't," I whisper, not wanting to see his tears, but I don't think he hears me. *Did I even say that out loud?*

With tears streaming through the lines of anger on his face, he stands firm with his gun held straight out. Only bad will come of this. The flash of light and the loud gunfire should startle me, but my heart is too weak to react.

Dropping to his knees in front of me, he lifts me into his arms. Contentment. *I'm home.*

"Firefly. Sara Jane. Stay with me. Stay with me."

In his arms I'm home.

"Don't cry, not over me."

"Help me, Cruise," he yells, looking up. The abrupt action causes one of his tears to fall between my lips. "Fuck. Help her. Help her."

I swallow, wanting anything that is my Alexander. He rocks back on his feet and carries me to the car. "You're gonna be okay, baby. I promise you."

I hate seeing him broken again, broken like when I met him. I'm curled on his lap when the door is closed and the tires squeal. "You lied."

"I'm sorry. I'm sorry."

My cheeks feel lighter when I look at him. "No, you lied . . . first time we ever met."

"What'd I lie about, baby?"

"You whispered . . . right in my ear. '*I don't need anything.*' You lied, Alexander. Because . . . you needed me."

"I need you. Stay with me, and I'll never lie to you again." His voice is muffled as if distance has settled in when he yells, "Is he dead? Jesus fucking Christ, don't let Chad be dead."

"Alexander?"

"What baby?"

"Tell me something happy."

His body is wracked with the sobs he's fighting to hold in and the tears he can't control any longer. I wait patiently as if I have time to spare. My world begins to spin, like my thoughts, when he says, "You gave me a reason to live when all I wanted to do was die."

No, you can't die. "Live for me."

"There is no life without you, Firefly."

Using all my efforts, I smile. "I love you."

"I love you," he says, stroking my cheek. A slash of blood colors his forehead but I know it's not his. I start to shiver.

Cold.

So cold.

"I love you. I'll save you. I promise I'll save you."

"Let me go, Alexander." I close my eyes. "I'm tired."

"Don't go to sleep. Stay with me. Drive fucking faster, Cruise."

He didn't shave. There's just enough stubble to make me smile as my fingertips graze over and fall away, my arm not feeling my own anymore. "Alexander," I mouth, his name a breath across my lips. "Let me go."

"I promise. I'll get help. I'm never letting you go, Firefly."

"I'm already gone." The sun's too bright, so I close my eyes and listen to his heartbeat, considering how great my life was.

His palm comforts my cheek, and he strains to hold back his devastation. "Listen to me. Focus on me, baby." I look into his eyes as he holds my complete attention like he always held my heart. "You once asked me why you. Why I picked you. It was always you for me. I was just lucky enough that you chose me. Do you hear me? I'm the lucky one."

"It's been good. So good living this life with you." My throat feels dry, but I try to speak, for him. I try because the boy I watched become a man needs to hear it. "You were always destined for greatness. Live up to your name. Be the king I know you can be."

"Only if you'll be there with me. You were born to be queen. *My* queen, baby. Stay with me."

"I can't make that promise . . . but the ride was good. We were good. So good."

So cold. So tired.

"Don't you leave me. Don't you fucking leave me, Sara Jane."

"You promised me a ride. I got the ride of a lifetime."

"No. No, Sara Jane. Please stay with me." Kisses cover my forehead, the rest of my body already numb to touch and feelings. His body shakes, his hand brushing the hair away from my face as he kisses me with his tears and anguish. "You're going to make it. Damn you. Don't give up on me."

I could never. "I always believed in you." How I love him. "You were always meant to reign, my sweet King."

"Don't call me that. I'm Alexander for you. Alexander."

I smile but wonder if it touches my lips. My body is cocooned in his arms when realization dawns on me as my world begins to blur. "I'm going to die, Alexander."

"No. Stay awake, baby. Fight. Stay with me." Sobs wrack his body as he holds me to him. "Don't leave me here without you."

Beyond what savage light he brings, to me, he was everything. With the last ounce of my energy, I force my eyes open and look at my tarnished angel. I would give up a sky full of stars for one more night in his darkness. Maybe I already did. Maybe this is me holding up my end of the bargain. Reaching up, I try to touch his face once more, once more to feel his skin beneath mine, but my body's already given up. "Our baby would have been handsome, just like you."

His body stills and he stares down at me, his eyes a brighter blue through the tears. "Our babies will be beautiful like their mother. So strong. You're the strongest, bravest person I know, Firefly."

"I don't think we're going to make it."

"We're so close, Sara Jane. I need you to hang on a few more minutes. We're almost there."

I can't tell if it's his or my tears streaking down my cheek anymore, the numbness spreading everywhere but where I want. I hate how empty I feel, my baby gone before he was given a chance. "The baby. I'm sorry for losing our baby."

"What? What are you talking about?"

"I need rest." I'm shaken awake, the world quieter when I open my eyes this time. "I'm so tired. Please."

"Baby. *No. No. No.* Don't leave me. You're my queen. Always my queen." His lips move, but the words are barely heard. When I can't seem to summon my words, his lips press to mine, and I savor the sweet pressure. "I love you."

There comes an acceptance when you're given the chance to let go on your own terms. I wouldn't have chosen this ending, but now that I'm here, I find peace wrapped in love that will last long after this life. My body disconnects, my worries for him are finally released, my chest feeling lighter. Sunlight streams in through the window, trying to distract me from what I want to see. As I look at Alexander, I can't take away his pain. If I were stronger I'd make it go away, keep his soul the lighter of the two. But I'm not.

Acceptance.

My heart refuses to leave its confines. A slow, steady beat still knocks against my chest. He always had a way of making me feel so much more of everything—life, happiness, sadness, anger, joy. Love. So much love.

He was my savior and my death, but love in its purest form. He kisses my face. Gentle and rough, determined, and full of passion, fitting of the man giving them. I smile, content with this life.

We're jolted forward, but the chaos is calm to my sleepy mind. His voice the only thing I hear. "Don't leave me."

When his lips touch mine, I whisper, "I will always . . . always be with you." I take my last breath and then slowly exhale. "I love—"

The End.

To be continued in SAVIOR

SAVIOR

Grab your copy of SAVIOR, Book 2 of the captivating Kingwood Duet, and continue this all consuming epic story.

ON A PERSONAL NOTE

Thank you for taking this publishing roller coaster ride with me. Your support has truly made a difference in my life. Thank you!

Thank you to my amazing husband and kids for always being there for me, for supporting the LONG hours, and for loving me endlessly. You are dream supporters, encouragers, and truly the loves of my life.

I have an awesome family that I am grateful for every day even when we're miles away. Thank you for loving me across the miles. You're presence is always in my heart. XOX

My team of awesome. Thank you is not enough, but I'm giving it with a huge helping of love as well. Adriana, Amy, Andrea J., Annette, Heather M., Irene, Jennifer S., Jessica H., Karen, Kerri, Kirsten, Kristen, Liv, Lynsey, Marion, Marla, Melissa K., Ruth, and Serena.

Sweet Scotties and Spoiler Group Girls - I adore you. You are amazing and make me smile all the time. Thank you for being active in there and so awesome!

Thank you to Sarah for the INCREDIBLE covers!

ALSO BY S.L. SCOTT

Dylan

Austin

From the Inside Out Compilation

Stand Alone Books

Missing Grace

Until I Met You

Naturally, Charlie

A Prior Engagement

Lost in Translation

Sleeping with Mr. Sexy

Morning Glory

To keep up to date with her writing and more, her website is www.slscottauthor.com or to receive her newsletter with all of her publishing adventures and giveaways, sign up for her newsletter: http://bit.ly/1pF049r

Join S.L.'s Facebook group here: http://bit.ly/2bq2Tfa

65436099R00179

Made in the USA
Lexington, KY
12 July 2017